W. H. G. Kingston

Tales of the Sea

W. H. G. Kingston

Tales of the Sea

ISBN/EAN: 9783337073466

Printed in Europe, USA, Canada, Australia, Japan

Cover: Foto ©Andreas Hilbeck / pixelio.de

More available books at **www.hansebooks.com**

TALES OF THE SEA

AND OF

Our Jack Tars.

BY

W. H. G. KINGSTON

AUTHOR OF " THE CRUISE OF THE FROLIC," " THE FIRE SHIPS,"
" UNCLE BOZ," ETC.

———— ❖ ————

London:
GALL AND INGLIS, 25 PATERNOSTER SQUARE;
AND EDINBURGH.

CONTENTS.

" And so you don't seem to be sea-sick, like other fellows," said Clem.— p. 15.

" Climbing on to the spar, to which I managed to lash the basket, I then got into the latter."— p. 31.

" It seemed as if the whole vessel was lifted out of the water, while up into the air shot her mainmast and spars."— *p.* 68

" ' It's Jack come back,' answered my sisters and Grace in chorus."— *p* 90

" Katty, in her eagerness, upset the basin as she sprang forward to throw herself into Uncle Boz's arms."—*p. 119.*

" As we leaped down on board over the bulwarks, we found only one man on deck." — p. 189.

TALES OF THE SEA.

Happy Jack.

CHAPTER I.

HAVE any of you made a passage on board a steamer between London and Leith? If you have, you will have seen no small number of brigs and brigantines, with sails of all tints, from doubtful white to decided black—some deeply laden, making their way to the southward, others with their sides high out of the water, heeling over to the slightest breeze, steering north.

On board one of those delectable craft, a brig called the *Naiad*, I found myself when about fourteen summers had passed over my head. She must have been named after a negress naiad, for black was the prevailing colour on board, from the dark, dingy forecastle to the captain's state cabin, which was but a degree less dirty than the portion of the vessel in which I was destined to live. The bulwarks, companion-hatch, and other parts had, to be sure, once upon a time been painted green, but the dust from the coal, which formed her usual cargo, had reduced every portion to one sombre hue, which

7

even the salt seas not unfrequently breaking over her deck had failed to wash clean.

Captain Grimes, her commander, notwithstanding this, was proud of the old craft; and he especially delighted to tell how she had once carried a pennant when conveying troops to Corunna, or some other port in Spain.

I pitied the poor fellows confined to the narrow limits of her dark hold, redolent of bilge water and other foul odours. We, however, had not to complain on that score, for the fresh water which came in through her old sides by many a leak, and had to be pumped out every watch, kept her hold sweet.

How I came to be on board the *Naiad* I'll tell you—

I had made up my mind to go to sea—why, it's hard to say, except that I thought I should like to knock about the world and see strange countries. I was happy enough at home, though I did not always make others happy. Nothing came amiss to me; I was always either laughing or singing, and do not recollect having an hour's illness in my life. Now and then, by the elders of the family, and by Aunt Martha especially, I was voted a nuisance; and it was with no small satisfaction, at the end of the holidays, that they packed me off again to school. I was fond of my brothers and sisters, and they were fond of me, though I showed my affection for them in a somewhat rough fashion. I thought my sisters somewhat demure, and I was always teasing them and playing them tricks. Somehow or other I got the name among them and my brothers of "Happy Jack," and certainly I was the merriest of the family. If I happened, which was not unfrequently the case, to get into a scrape, I generally managed to scramble out of it with flying colours; and if I did not, I laughed at the punishment to which I was doomed. I was a broad-shouldered, strongly-built boy, and could beat my elder brothers at running, leaping, or any other athletic exercise, while, without boasting, I was not behind any of them in the school-room. My father was somewhat proud of me, and had set his mind on my becoming a member of one of the learned professions, and rising to the top of the tree. Why should I not? I had a great-uncle a judge, and another relative a bishop, and there had been admirals and generals by the score among our ancestors. My father was a leading solicitor in a large town, and having somewhat ambitious aspirations for his children, his intention was to send all his sons to the university, in the hopes that they would make a good figure in life. He was therefore the more vexed when I declared that my firm determination was to go to sea. " Very well, Jack," he said, " if such is your resolve, go you shall; but as I have no interest in the navy, you must take your chance in the merchant service." " It's all the same to me, sir," I replied ; " I shall be just as happy in the one as in the other service ;" and so I considered the matter settled.

When the day of parting came, I was as merry and full of fun as ever, though I own there was a strange sensation about the heart which bothered me ; however, I was not going to show what I felt—not I.

I slyly pinched my sisters when we were exchanging parting kisses, till they were compelled to shriek out and box my ears—an operation to which I was well accustomed—and I made my brothers roar with the sturdy grip I gave their fingers when we shook hands ; and so, instead of tears, there were shouts of laughter and screeches and screams, creating a regular hullabuloo which put all sentimental grief to flight. "No, no, Jack, I will have none of your tricks," cried Aunt Martha, when I approached with a demure look to bid her farewell, so I took her hand and pressed it to my lips with all the mock courtesy of a Sir Charles Grandison. My mother! I had no heart to do otherwise than to throw my arms round her neck and receive the fond embrace she bestowed upon me, and if a tear did come into my eye, it was then. But there was another person to whom I had to say good-bye, and that was dear little Grace Goldie, my father's ward, a fair, blue-eyed girl, three or four years younger than myself. I did not play her any trick, but kissed her smooth young brow, and promised that I would bring her back no end of pearls and ivory, and treasures of all sorts, from across the seas. She smiled sweetly through her tears. "Thank you, Jack, thank you! I shall so long to see you back," she whispered; and I had to bolt, or I believe that I should have begun to pipe my eye in a way I had no fancy for. My father's voice summoned me. "Now, Jack," he said, "as you have chosen your bed, you must lie on it. But remember—after a year's trial—if you change your mind, let me know." "No fear of that, sir," I answered.

"We shall see, Jack," he replied. He wrung my hand, and gave me his blessing. "I have directed Mr. Junk to provide your outfit, and you will find it all right." Who Mr. Junk was I had no conception; but as my father said it was all right, I troubled my head no more about the matter.

My father's old clerk, Simon Munch, was waiting for me at the door, and hurried me off to catch the Newcastle coach. On our arrival there he took me to the office of Junk, Tarbox, & Company, ship-brokers.

"Here is the young gentleman, Mr. Junk," he said, addressing a one-eyed, burly, broad-shouldered personage, with a rubicund countenance, in a semi-nautical costume. "You know what to do with him, and so I leave him in your hands. Good-bye, Jack, I hope you may like it."

"No fear of that, Mr. Munch," I answered; "and tell them at home that you left me as jolly and happy as ever."

"So, Master Brooke, you want to go to sea?" said Mr. Junk, squirting a stream of tobacco-juice across his office, and eyeing me with his sole blood-shot blinker; "and you expect to like it?"

"Of course I do; I expect to be happy wherever I am," I answered in a confident tone.

"We shall see," he replied. "I have sent your chest aboard of the *Naiad*. Captain Grimes will be here anon, and I'll hand you over to him."

The person he spoke of just then made his appearance. I did not particularly like my future commander's outside. He was a tall, gaunt man, with a long weather-beaten visage and huge black or rather grizzled whiskers; and his voice, when he spoke, was gruff and harsh in the extreme. I need not further describe him; only I will observe that he looked considerably cleaner then than he usually did, as I afterwards found on board the brig. He took but little notice of me beyond a slight nod, as he was busy with the ship's papers. Having pocketed them, he grasped me by the hand with a "Come along, my lad; I am to make a seaman on ye." He spoke in a broad Northumbrian accent, and in a harsh guttural tone. I was not prepossessed in his favour, but I determined to show no signs of unwillingness to accompany him.

We were soon seated in the stern of an excessively

dirty boat, with coal-dust-begrimed rowers, who pulled away with somewhat lazy strokes towards a deeply-laden brig lying out in mid-stream. "Get on board, leddie, with you," said the captain, who had not since my first introduction addressed a single word to me. I clambered up on deck. The boat was hoisted in, the topsails let fall, and the crew, with doleful "Yeo-yo-o's," began working round the windlass, and the *Naiad* in due time was gliding down the Tyne.

She was a very different craft to what I had expected to find myself on board of. I had read about the white decks and snowy canvas, the bright polish and the active, obedient crew of a man-of-war; and such I had pictured the vessel I had hoped to sail in. The *Naiad* was certainly a contrast to this; but I kept to my resolve not to flinch from whatever turned up. When I was told to pull and haul away at the ropes, I did so with might and main; and, as everything on board was thickly coated with coal-dust, I very soon became as begrimed as the rest of the crew.

I was rather astonished, on asking Captain Grimes when tea would be ready—for I was very hungry—to be told that I might get what I could with the men forward. I went down accordingly into the forecastle, tumbling over a chest, and running my head against the stomach of one of my new shipmates as I groped my way amid the darkness which shrouded it. A cuff which sent me sprawling on the deck was the consequence. "Where are your eyes, leddie?" exclaimed a gruff voice. "Ye'll see where ye are ganging the next time."

I picked myself up, bursting into a fit of laughter, as if the affair had been a good joke. "I beg your pardon, old fellow," I said; "but if you had had a chandelier burning in this place of yours it would not have happened. How do you all manage to see down here?"

" As cats do—we're accustomed to it," said another voice; and I now began to distinguish objects around me. The watch below were seated round a sea-chest, with three or four mugs, a huge loaf of bread, and a piece of cheese and part of a flitch of fat cold bacon. It was rough fare, but I was too hungry not to be glad to partake of it.

A boy whom I had seen busy in the caboose soon came down with a kettle of hot tea. My inquiry for milk produced a general laugh, but I was told I might take as much sugar as I liked from a jar, which contained a dark-brown substance unlike any sugar I had before seen.

" Ye'll soon be asking for your bed, leddie," said Bob Tubbs, the old man whose acquaintance I had so unceremoniously formed. " Ye'll find it there, for'ard, if ye'll grope your way. It's not over airy, but it's all the warmer in winter."

After supper, I succeeded in finding the berth Bob had pointed out. It was the lowest berth, directly in the very bows of the vessel—a shelf-like space, about five feet in length, with height scarcely sufficient to allow me to sit upright,—Dirty Dick, the ship's boy I have mentioned, having the berth above me. Mine contained a mattress and a couple of blankets. My inquiry for sheets produced as much laughter as when I asked for milk. " Well, to be sure, as I suppose you have not a washer-woman on board, they would not be of much use," I sang out ; " and so, unless the captain wants me to steer the ship, I will turn in and go to sleep. Good night, mates."

" The leddie has got some spirit in him," I heard

Bob Tubbs observe. "What do you call yourself, boy?"

"Happy Jack!" I sang out; "and it's not this sort of thing that's going to change me."

"You'll prove a tough one, if something else doesn't," observed Bob from his berth. "But gang to sleep, boy. Ye'll be put into a watch to-morrow, and it's the last time, may be, that ye'll have to rest through the night till ye set foot on shore again." I little then thought how long a time that would prove; but, rolling myself up in my blanket, I soon forgot where I was.

Next morning I scrambled on deck, and found the brig plunging away into a heavy sea, with a strong southerly wind, the coast just distinguishable over our starboard quarter. The captain gave me a grim smile as I made my way aft.

"Well, leddie, how do you like it?" he inquired.

"Thank you, pretty well," I answered; "but I hope we sha'n't have to wait long for breakfast."

He smiled again. "And you don't feel queer?"

"No, not a bit of it," I replied. "But I say, captain, I thought I was to come as a midshipman, and mess with the other young gentlemen on board."

He now fairly laughed outright; and looking at me for some time, answered, "We have no young gentlemen on board here. You'll get your breakfast in good time; but you are of the right sort, leddie, and little Clem shall show you what you have got to do," pointing as he spoke to a boy who just then came on deck, and whom I took to be his son.

"Thank you, captain," I observed; "I shall be glad of Clem's instruction, as I suppose he knows more about the matter than I do."

"Clem can hand, reef, and steer as well as any

one, as far as his strength goes," said the captain, looking approvingly at him.

"I'll set to work as soon as he likes, then," I observed. "But I wish those fellows would be sharp about breakfast, for I am desperately hungry."

"Well, go into the cabin, and Clem will give you a hunch of bread to stay your appetite."

I followed Clem below. "Here, Brooke, some butter will improve it," he said, spreading a thick slice of bread. "And so you don't seem to be sea-sick, like most fellows. Well, I am glad of that. My father will like you all the better for it, and soon make a sailor of you, if you wish to learn."

I told Clem that was just what I wanted, and that I should look to him to teach me my duties.

"I'll do my best," he said. "Take my advice and dip your hands in the tar bucket without delay, and don't shirk anything the mate puts you to. My father is pretty gruff now and then, but old Growl is a regular rough one. He does not say much to me, but you will have to look out for squalls. Come, we had better go on deck, or old Growl will think that I have been putting you up to mischief. He will soon pick a quarrel with you, to see how you bear it."

"I'll take good care to keep out of his way, then," I said, bolting the last piece of bread and butter. "Thank you, Clem, you and I shall be good friends, I see that."

"I hope so," answered my young companion with a sigh. "I have not many on board, and till you came I had no one to speak to except father, and he is not always in the mood to talk."

Clem's slice of bread and butter enabled me to hold out till the forecastle breakfast was ready. I did ample justice to it. Directly I made my re-appearance on deck, old Growl set me to work, and I soon had not only my hands but my arms up to the elbows in tar. Though the vessel was pitching her head into the seas, with thick sheets of foam flying over her, he quickly sent me aloft to black down the main rigging. Clem showed me how to secure the bucket to the shrouds while I was at work, and in spite of the violent jerks I received as the vessel plunged her bluff bows into the sea, I got on very well. Before the evening was over I had been out on the yards with little Clem to assist in reefing the topsails, and he had shown me how to steer and box the compass.

Nothing particular occurred on the voyage, though we were ten days in reaching the mouth of the Thames. Clem and I became great friends. The more I saw of him the more I liked him, and wondered how so well-mannered a lad could be the son of such a man as Captain Grimes.

I saw nothing of London. I should, indeed, have been ashamed to go on shore in my now thoroughly begrimed condition. We were but a short time in the Thames, for as soon as we had discharged our cargo we again made sail for the Tyne.

Before this time old Growl, the mate, had taught me what starting meant. He had generally a rope's end in his fist, and if not, one was always near at hand. If I happened not to do a thing well enough or fast enough to please him, he was immediately after me, laying the rope across my shoulders, or anywhere he could most conveniently reach. I generally managed to spring out of his way, and turn round and laugh at him. If he followed me, I ran aloft, and, as I climbed much faster than he could, I invariably led him a long chase.

"I'll catch you, youngster, the next time. Mark

me, that I will," he shouted out to me one day, when more than usually angry.

"Wait till the next time comes, mate," I sang out, and laughed more heartily than before.

The men sympathised with me, especially Dirty Dick. His shoulders, till I came on board, had been accustomed to suffer most from the mate's ill temper. Now and then old Growl, greatly to his delight, caught me unawares ; but, suffering as I did from his blows, I never let him see that I cared for them, and used to laugh just as heartily as when I had escaped from him. On this, however, he would grin sardonically, and observe, "You may laugh as you like, young master, I know what a rope's end tastes like ; it's a precious deal bitterer than you would have me fancy. I got enough of it when I was a youngster, and haven't forgotten yet."

One day when old Growl had treated me as I have described, and had gone below, Clement came up to me. "I am so sorry the mate has struck you, Brooke," he said. "It's a great shame. He dare not hit me ; and when I told father how he treats you, he told me to mind my own business, and that it was all for your good."

"I don't know how that can be," I answered ; "but I don't care for it, I can assure you. It hurts a little at the time, I'll allow, but I have got used to it, and I don't intend to let him break my spirit or make me unhappy."

Clement all the time was doing his best to teach me what he knew, and I soon learned to steer in smooth water, and could hand and reef the topsails and knot and splice as well almost as he could. Some things I did better, as I was much stronger and more active. I was put to do all sorts of unpleasant work, such as blacking down the rigging, greasing the masts, and helping Dirty Dick to clean the caboose and sweep out the forecastle. Though I didn't like it, I went about the duty, however, as if it was the pleasantest in the world. Pleasant or not, I was thus rapidly becoming a seaman.

———•◆•———

CHAPTER II.

I HAD as before, on reaching the Tyne, to remain and keep ship, though little Clem went on shore and did not return till we had a fresh cargo on board, and were just about sailing.

Scarcely were we clear of the river than a heavy gale sprang up and severely tried the old collier. The seas came washing over her deck, and none of us for'ard had a dry rag on our backs. When my watch below came, I was glad to turn in between my now darkly-tinted blankets; but they soon became as wet as everything else, and when I went on deck to keep my watch, I had again to put on my damp clothes. The forecastle was fearfully hot and steamy. We had to keep the fore hatch closed to prevent the seas which, washing over our decks, would otherwise have poured down upon us. In a short time, as the ship strained more and more while she struggled amid the waves, the water made its way through the deck and sides till there was not a dry space to lie on in our berths. Then I began really to understand the miseries of forecastle life on board a collier, and many other craft too, in which British seamen have to sail; with bad food, bad water, and worse treatment. Ay, I speak the truth, which I know from experience, they have to live like dogs, and, too often, die like dogs, with no one to care for them.

Day after day this sort of work continued. I wondered that the captain did not run back, till I heard him say that the price of coals was up in the London market, and he wanted to be there before other vessels arrived to lower it; so, tough seaman as he was, he kept thrashing the old brig along against the south-westerly gale, which seemed to increase rather than show any signs of moderating. We had always, during each watch, to take a spell at the pumps, and now we had to keep them going without intermission. I took my turn with the rest, and my shoulders ached before I had done; still I sang and laughed away as usual.

"It's no laughing matter, youngster," said old Growl, as he passed me. "You will be laughing the wrong side of your mouth before long."

"Never fear, mate," I replied; "both sides are the same to me."

The captain and mate at last took their turns with the rest of us, for the crew were getting worn out. I did not know the danger we were in, but I was beginning to get tired of that dreadful "clank, clank, clank."

At last, by dint of keeping at it, we had got a good way to the southward, when one night, just as we had gone about hoping to lay our course for the Thames, the wind shifted and came again right in our teeth. I had turned into my wet bunk all standing, when, having dropped off to sleep, I was awoke by a tremendous crash, and on springing up on deck I found that the mainmast had gone by the board. The gale had increased, and we were driving before it. As I made my way aft, the flashes of lightning revealed the pale faces of the

crew, some endeavouring to clear away the wreck of
the mast, others working with frantic energy at the
pumps.   The leaks had increased.   As may be supposed, the deeply-laden collier had but a poor chance
under such circumstances.   Presently the vessel
gave a heavy lurch.   A sea rolled up.   The next
instant I found myself struggling in the midst of
the foaming surges.   All around was dark ; I felt
for the deck of the vessel, it was not beneath me ; I
had been washed overboard.   I struck out for life,
and in another minute I was clinging to the main-
mast, which had been cut clear.   I clambered up on
it, and looked out for the brig.   She was nowhere
to be seen ; she must have gone down beneath the
surge which washed me from her deck.   What had
become of my shipmates ?   I shouted again and
again at the top of my voice.   There was a faint
cry, " Help me ; help me."   I knew the voice ; it
was Clement's.   Leaving the mast, I swam towards
him ; he was lashed to a spar.   The old captain's
last act had been to try and save the young boy's
life ere he himself sank beneath the waves.   I
caught hold of the spar, bidding Clement keep his
head above the water while I towed it to the mast.
I succeeded, and then clambering on it, and casting
off the lashings, dragged him up and placed him
beside me.   We hailed again and again, but no
voice replied.   It may seem strange that we, the
two youngest on board, should have survived, while
all the men were drowned, but then, not one of them
could swim.   We could, and, under Providence,
were able to struggle for our lives.

I did my best to cheer up little Clem, telling him
that if we could manage to hold on till daylight, as
a number of vessels were certain to pass, we should
be picked up.   "I am very, very sorry, Clem, for

your father," I said; "for though he was somewhat gruff to me, he was a kind-hearted man, I am sure."

"That indeed he was," answered Clement, in a tone of sorrow. "He was always good to me; but he was not my father, as you fancy—the more reason I have to be grateful to him."

"Not your father, Clem!" I exclaimed. "I never suspected that."

"No, he was not; though he truly acted the part of one to me. Do you know, Brooke, this is not the first time that I have been left alone floating on the ocean? I was picked up by him just as you hope that we shall be picked up. I was a very little fellow, so little that I could give no account of myself. He found a black woman and me floating all alone on a raft out in the Atlantic. She died almost immediately we were rescued, without his being able to learn anything from her. He had to bury her at sea, and when he got home he in vain tried to find out my friends, though he preserved, I believe, the clothes I had on, and most of her clothes. He sent me to an excellent school, where I was well taught; and Mrs. Grimes, who was a dear, kind lady, far more refined than you would suppose his wife to have been, acted truly like a mother to me. He was very fond of her, and when she died, nearly a year ago, he took me to sea with him. I did not, however, give up my studies, but used to sit in the cabin, and every day read as much as I could. Captain Grimes used to say that he was sure I was a gentleman born, and a gentleman he wished me to be, and so I have always felt myself."

I had been struck by little Clem's refined manners, and this was now accounted for. "I am sure you are a gentleman, Clem," I observed; "and if we ever get home, my father, who is a lawyer, shall try

to find out your friends. He may be able to succeed though Captain Grimes could not. I wonder
he did not apply to my father, as, from my having
been sent on board his ship, the captain must have
known him. I suspect that they wanted to sicken
me of a sea life, and so sent me on board the *Naiad;*
but they were mistaken; and now when they hear
that she has gone down—if we are not picked up—
how sorry they will be !"

The conversation I have described was frequently
interrupted—sometimes by a heavier sea than usual
rolling by, and compelling us to hold tight for our
lives; at others we were silent for several minutes
together. We were seated on the after-part of the
maintop, the rigging which hung down on either
side acting as ballast, and contributing to keep the
wreck of the mast tolerably steady in one position.
We were thus completely out of the water, though
the spray from the crest of the seas which was blown
over us kept us thoroughly wet and cold. Fortunately, we both had on thick clothing. Clement
was always nicely dressed, for the captain, though
not particular about himself, liked to see him look
neat, while I, on the contrary, had on my oldest
working suit, and was as rough-looking a sea-dog as
could be imagined. My old tarry coat and trousers,
and sou'-wester tied under my chin, contributed,
however, to keep out the wind, and enable me the
better to endure the cold to which we were exposed.
I sheltered Clem as well as I could, and held
him tight whenever I saw a sea coming towards
him, fearing lest he might be washed away. I had
made up my mind to perish with him rather than
let him go. Hour after hour passed by, till at length,
the clouds breaking, the moon came forth and shone
down upon us. I looked at Clem's face: it was

very pale, and I was afraid he would give way altogether. "Hold on, hold on, Clem," I exclaimed.
"The wind is falling, and the sea will soon go down;
we shall have daylight before long, and in the meantime we have the moon to cheer us up. Perhaps we
shall be on shore this time to-morrow, and comfortably in bed; and then we will go back to my father,
and he will find out all about your friends. He is
a wonderfully clever man, though a bit strict, to be
sure."

"Thank you, Jack, thank you," he answered.
"Don't be afraid; I feel pretty strong, only somewhat cold and hungry."

Just then I recollected that I had put the best
part of a biscuit into my pocket at tea-time, having
been summoned on deck as I was eating it. It was
wet, to be sure; but such biscuits as we had take a
good deal of soaking to soften thoroughly. I felt
for it. There it was. So I put a small piece into
Clem's mouth. He was able to swallow it. Then I
put in another, and another; and so I fed him, till
he declared he felt much better. I had reserved a
small portion for myself, but as I knew that I could
go on without it, I determined to keep it, lest he
should require more.

I continued to do my best to cheer him up by
talking to him of my home, and how he might find
his relations and friends, and then I bethought me
that I would sing a song. I don't suppose that
many people have sung under such circumstances,
but I managed to strike up a stave, one of those
with which I had been accustomed to amuse my
messmates in the *Naiad's* forecastle. It was not,
perhaps, one of the merriest, but it served to divert
Clem's thoughts, as well as mine, from our perilous
position.

"I wish that I could sing too," said Clem; "but I know I could not, if I was to try. I wonder you can, Jack."

"Why? because I am sure that we shall be picked up before long, and so I see no reason why I should not try to be happy," I answered thoughtlessly.

"Ah, but I am thinking of those who are gone," said Clem. "My kind father, as I called him, and old Growl, and the rest of the poor fellows; it is like singing over their graves."

"You are right, Clem," I said; "I will sing no more, though I only did it to keep up your spirits. But what is that?" I exclaimed, suddenly, as we rose to the crest of a sea. "A large ship standing directly for us."

"Yes; she is close-hauled, beating down Channel," observed Clement. "She will be right upon us, too, if she keeps her present course."

"We must take care to let her know where we are, by shouting together at the top of our voices when we are near enough to be heard," I said.

"She appears to me to be a man-of-war, and probably a sharp look-out is kept forward," Clement remarked. We had not observed the ship before, as our faces had been turned away from her. The sea had, however, been gradually working the mast round, as I knew to be the case by the different position in which the moon appeared to us.

"We must get ready for a shout, Clem, and then cry out together as we have never cried before. I'll say when we are to begin."

As the ship drew nearer Clem had no doubt that she was a man-of-war, a large frigate apparently, under her three topsails and courses.

"She is passing to windward of us," I exclaimed.

"Not so sure of that," cried Clem. "She will be right over us if we do not cry out in time."

"Let us begin, then," I said. "Now, shout away, Hip! Hip!"

"No, no!" cried Clem, "that will not do. Shout 'Ship ahoy!'"

I had forgotten for the moment what to say, so together we began shouting as shrilly as we could, at the very top of our voices. Again and again we shouted. I began to fear that the ship would be right over us, when presently we saw her luff up. The moon was shining down upon us, and we were seen. So close, even then, did the frigate pass, that the end of the mast we were clinging to almost grazed her side. Ropes were hove to us, but the ship had too much way on her, and it was fortunate we could not seize them. "Thank you," I cried out. "Will you take us aboard?" There was no answer, and I thought that we were to be left floating on our mast till some other vessel might sight us. We were mistaken, though. We could hear loud orders issued on board, but what was said we could not make out, and presently the ship came up to the wind, the head yards were braced round, and she lay hove to. Then we saw a boat lowered. How eagerly we watched what was being done. She came towards us. The people in her shouted to us in a strange language. They were afraid, evidently, of having their boat stove in by the wreck of the mast. At last they approached us cautiously.

"Come, Clem, we will swim to her," I said. "Catch tight hold of my jacket; I have got strength enough left in me for that."

We had not far to go, but I found it a tougher job than I expected. It would have been wiser to have remained till we could have leaped from the mast to the boat. I was almost exhausted by the time we reached her, and thankful when I felt Clem lifted off my back, I myself, when nearly sinking, being next hauled on board. We were handed into the stern sheets, where we lay almost helpless. I tried to speak, but could not, nor could I understand a word that was said. The men at once pulled back to the ship, and a big seaman, taking Clem under one of his arms, clambered up with him on deck. Another carried me on board in the same fashion. The boat was then hoisted up, and the head yards being braced round, the ship continued her course. Lanterns being brought, we were surrounded by a group of foreign-looking seamen, who stared curiously at us, asking, I judged from the tones of their voices, all sorts of questions, but as their language was as strange to us as ours was to them, we couldn't understand a word they said, or make them comprehend what we said.

"If you would give us some hot grog, and let us turn into dry hammocks, we should be much obliged to you," I cried out at last, despairing of any good coming of all their talking.

Just as I spoke, an officer with a cloak on came from below, having apparently turned out of his berth. "Ah, you are English," I heard him say. " Speak to me. How came you floating out here?"

I told him that our vessel had gone down, and that we, as far as I knew, were the only survivors of the crew.

"And who is that other boy?"

"The captain's son," I answered.

"Ah, I thought so, by his appearance," said the officer. "He shall be taken into the cabin. You, my boy, will have a hammock on the lower deck, and the hot grog you asked for. I'll visit you soon. I am the doctor of the ship."

He then spoke to the men, and while Clement was carried aft, I was lifted up and conveyed below by a couple of somewhat rough but not ill-natured-looking seamen. I was more exhausted than I had supposed, for on the way I fainted, and many hours passed by before I returned to a state of half consciousness.

CHAPTER III.

IN three days I was quite well, and the doctor sending me a suit of seaman's clothes, I dressed and found my way up on deck. I looked about eagerly for Clem, but not seeing him, I became anxious to learn how he was. I could make none of the men understand me. Most of them were Finns—big broad-shouldered, ruddy, light haired, bearded fellows; very good-natured and merry, notwithstanding the harsh treatment they often received. Big as they were, they were knocked about like so many boys by the petty officers, and I began to feel rather uncomfortable lest I should come in for share of the same treatment, of which I had had enough from the hands of old Growl. I determined, however, to grin and bear it, and do, as well as I could, whatever I was told.

I soon found that I was not to be allowed to eat the bread of idleness, for a burly officer, whom I took to be the boatswain, ordered me aloft with several other boys, to hand the fore royal, a stiff breeze just then coming on. Up I went; and

though I had never been so high above the deck
before, that made but little difference, and I showed
that I could beat my companions in activity. When
I came down the boatswain nodded his approval.
I kept looking out for Clem.   At last I saw my
friend the doctor, with several other officers, on the
quarter-deck.   I hurried aft to him, and, touching
my cap, asked him how Clem was.   The others
stared at me as if surprised at my audacity in thus
venturing among them.   "The boy is doing well,"
he answered ; "but, lad, I must advise you not
to infringe the rules of discipline.   You were, I
understand, one of the ship's boys, and must remain
for'ard.   He is a young gentleman, and such his
dress and appearance prove him to be, will be
allowed to live with the midshipmen."   " I am very
glad to hear that," I answered ; "but I am a gentleman's son also, and I should like to live with the
midshipmen, that I may be with Clem."   "Your
companion has said something to the same effect,"
observed the doctor ; " but the captain remarks that
there are many wild, idle boys sent to sea who may
claim to be the sons of gentlemen ; and as your
appearance shows, as you acknowledge was the case,
that you were before the mast, there you must continue till your conduct proves that you are deserving
of a higher rank.   And now go for'ard.   I'll recollect what you have said."   I took the hint.   The
seamen grinned as I returned among them, as if
they had understood what I had been saying.

I kept to my resolution of doing smartly whatever I was told, and laughed and joked with the
men, trying to understand their lingo, and to make
myself understood by them.   I managed to pick up
some of their words, though they almost cracked
my jaws to pronounce them ; but I laughed at my

own mistakes, and they seemed to think it very good fun to hear me talk.

Several days passed away, when at length I saw Clement come on deck. I ran aft to him, and he came somewhat timidly to meet me. We shook hands, and I told him how glad I was to see him better, though he still looked very pale. "I am very glad also to see you, Jack," he said, "and I wish we were to be together. I told the doctor I would rather go and live for'ard than be separated from you; but he replied that that could not be, and I have hopes, Jack, that by-and-by you will be placed on the quarter-deck if you will enter the Russian service." "What! and give up being an Englishman?" I exclaimed. "I would do a great deal to be with you, but I won't abandon my country and be transmogrified into a Russian." "You are right, Jack," said Clem, with a sigh; "however, the officers will not object to my talking with you, and we must hope for the best." After this I was constantly thinking how I should act should I have the option of being placed on the quarter-deck and becoming an officer in the Russian service, for we were on board a Russian frigate.

Clem got rapidly better, and we every day met and had a talk together. Altogether, as the boatswain's lash did not often reach me, though he used it pretty freely among my companions, I was as happy as usual. I should have been glad to have had less train-oil and fat in the food served out to us, and should have preferred wheaten flour to the black rye and beans which I had to eat. Still that was a trifle, and I soon got accustomed to the greasy fare. Clem was now doing duty as a midshipman, and I was in the same watch with him.

The weather had hitherto been generally fine;

but one night as the sun went down, I thought I
saw indications of a gale.   Still the wind didn't
come, and the ship went gliding smoothly over the
ocean.   I was in the middle watch, and had just
come on deck.   I had made my way aft, where I
found Clem, and, leaning against a gun, we were
talking together of dear old England, wondering
when we should get back there, when a sudden
squall struck the ship, and the hands were ordered
aloft to reef topsails.   I sprang aloft with the rest,
and lay out on the lee fore yard-arm.   I was so
much more active than most of my shipmates, that
I had become somewhat careless.   As I was leaning
over to catch hold of a reef point, I lost my balance,
and felt, as I fell head foremost, that I was about to
have my brains dashed out on the deck below me.
The instant before the wind had suddenly ceased,
and the sail giving a flap, hung down almost against
the mast.   Just at that moment, filled with the
breeze, it bulged out again, and striking me, sent
me flying overboard.   Instinctively I put my hands
together, and, plunging down, struck the now foaming water head first.   I sank several feet, though I
scarcely for a moment lost consciousness, and when
I came to the surface I found myself striking out
away from the ship, which was gliding rapidly by
me.   I heard a voice sing out, "A man overboard."
I knew that it must have been Clem's, and I saw a
spar and several other things thrown into the water.
I do not know whether the life-buoy was let go.   I
did not see it.   Turning round I struck out in
the wake of the ship, but the gale just then coming
with tremendous fury, drove her on fast away from
me, and she speedily disappeared in the thick
gloom.   I should have lost all hope had I not at
that moment come against a spar, and a large

basket with a rope attached to it, which was driven almost into my hands. Climbing on to the spar, to which I managed to lash the basket, I then got into the latter, where I could sit without much risk of being washed out. It served, indeed, as a tolerably efficient life-preserver; for although the water washed in and washed out, and the seas frequently broke over my head, I was able to hold myself in without much trouble. I still had some hopes that the ship would come back and look for me.

At length I thought I saw her approaching through the darkness. It raised my spirits, and I felt a curious satisfaction, in addition to the expectation of being saved, at the thought that I was not to be carelessly abandoned to my fate. I anxiously gazed in the direction where I fancied the ship to be, but she drew no nearer, and the dark void filled the space before me. Still I did not give way to despair, though I found it a hard matter to keep up. I had been rescued before, and I hoped to be saved another time. Then, however, I had been in a comparatively narrow sea, with numerous vessels passing over it. Now I was in the middle of the Atlantic, which, although rightly called a highway, was a very broad one. I could not also help recollecting that I was in the latitude where sharks abound, and I thought it possible that one might make a grab at my basket, and try to swallow it and me together, although I smiled at the thought of the inconvenience the fish would feel when it stuck its teeth into the yard, and got it fixed across its mouth. Happily no shark espied me.

Day at last dawned. As I looked around when I rose to the summit of a sea, my eyes fell alone on the dark, tumbling, foaming waters, and the thick clouds going down to meet them. I began to feel very hungry and thirsty, for though I had water enough around me, I dare not drink it. I now found it harder than ever to keep up my spirits, and gloomy thoughts began to take possession of my mind. No one, I confess, would have called me Happy Jack just then. I was sinking off into a state of stupor, during which I might easily have been washed out of my cradle, when, happening to open my eyes, they fell on the sails of a large brig standing directly for me. I could scarcely fail to be seen by those on board. On she came before the breeze; but as she drew nearer I began to fear that she might still pass at some distance. I tried to stand up and shout out, but I was nearly toppling overboard in making the attempt. I managed, however, to kneel upon the spar and wave my handkerchief, shouting as I did so with all my might. The brig altered her course, and now came directly down for me. I made out two or three people in the forechains standing ready to heave me a rope. I prepared to seize it. The brig was up to me and nearly running me down, but I caught the first rope hove to me, and grasped it tightly. I could scarcely have expected to find myself capable of so much exertion. Friendly hands were stretched out to help me up, but scarcely was I safe than I sank down almost senseless on deck. I soon, however, recovered, and being taken below, and dry clothes and food being given me, I quickly felt as well as usual. "Where am I, and where are you bound to?" were the first questions I asked, hoping to hear that I was on board a homeward-bound vessel. "You are on board the American brig *Fox* bound out round the Horn to the Sandwich Islands and the west coast of North America," was the answer. "But I

want to go home to England," I exclaimed. "Well,
then, I guess you had better get into your basket,
and wait till another vessel picks you up," replied
the captain, to whom I had addressed myself.
"Thank you, I would rather stay here with dry
clothes on my back and something to eat," I said.
"Perhaps, however, captain, you will speak any
homeward-bound vessel we meet, and get her to take
me?" "Not likely to fall in with one," he observed.
"You had better make the best of things where you
are." "That's what I always try to do," I replied.
"You are the right sort of youngster for me, then,"
he said. "Only don't go boasting of your proud
little venomous island among my people. We are
true Americans, fore and aft, except some of the
passengers, and they would be better off if they
would sink their notions and pay more respect to
the stars and stripes. However, you will have
nothing to do with them, for you will do your duty
for'ard I guess." I thought it wiser to make no
reply to these remarks, and as the crew were just
going to dinner, I gladly accompanied them into
their berth under the top-gallant forecastle. The
crew, I found, though American citizens, were of all
nationalities—Danes, and Swedes, and Frenchmen,
with too or three mulattoes and a black cook. They
described Captain Pyke, for that was the master's
name, as a regular Tartar, and seemed to have no
great love for him, though they held him in especial
awe. I was thankful at being so soon picked up,
but I would rather have found myself on board a
different style of craft. The cabin passengers were
going out to join one of the establishments of the
great Fur Trading Company on the Columbia river.
They were pleasant, gentlemanly-looking men, and
I longed to introduce myself to them, as I was

beginning to get somewhat weary of the rough characters with whom I was doomed to associate. But from what the men told me, I felt sure that if I did so I should make the captain my enemy. He and they were evidently not on good terms. I got on, however, pretty well with the crew, and as I could speak a little French, I used to talk to the Frenchmen in their own language, my mistakes affording them considerable amusement, though, as they corrected me, I gradually improved.

Among the crew were two other persons whom I will particularly mention. One went by the name of "Old Tom." He was relatively old with regard to the rest of our shipmates, rather than old in years—a wiry, active, somewhat wizen-faced man, with broad shoulders, and possessing great muscular strength. I suspected from the first, from the way he spoke, that he was not a Yankee born. His language, when talking to me, was always correct, without any nasal twang; and that he was a man of some education I was convinced, when I heard him once quote, as if speaking to himself, a line of Horace. He never smiled, and there was a melancholy expression on his countenance, which made me fancy that something weighed on his mind. He did not touch spirits, but his short pipe was seldom out of his mouth. When, however, he sat with the rest in the forecastle berth, his manner completely changed, and he talked, and argued, and wrangled, and guessed, and calculated, with as much vehemence as any one, entering with apparent zest into their ribald conversation, though even then the most humorous remark or jest failed to draw forth a laugh from his lips.

CHAPTER IV.

THE other person was a lad a couple of years my senior, called always "Young Sam," apparently one of those unhappy waifs cast on the bleak world without relations or friends to care for him. He was a fine young fellow, with a blue laughing eye, dauntless and active, and promised to become a good seaman. In spite of the rough treatment he often received from his shipmates, he kept up his spirits, and as our natures in that respect assimilated, I felt drawn towards him. The only person who seemed to take any interest in him, however, was old Tom, who saved him from many a blow; still, no two characters could apparently have more completely differed. Young Sam seemed a thoughtless, care-for-nothing fellow, always laughing and jibing those who attacked him, and ready for any fun or frolic which turned up. He appreciated, however, old Tom's kindness; and the only times I saw him look serious were when he received a gentle rebuke from his friend for any folly he had committed which had brought him into trouble. I believe, indeed, that young Sam would have gone through fire and water to show his gratitude to old Tom, while I suspect that the latter, in spite of his harsh exterior, had a heart not altogether seared by the world, which required some one on whom to fix its kindlier feelings.

I had been some time on board when we put into a port at the Falkland Islands, then uninhabited, to obtain a supply of water. While the crew of the boats were engaged in filling the casks, Mr. Duncan, one of the gentlemen, taking young Sam with him, went into the interior to shoot wild-fowl.

The casks were filled; and the boats, after wait-

ing for some time the return of Mr. Duncan and
Sam, came back. Mr. Symonds, the second mate,
proposed to return for our shipmates after the casks
had been hoisted on board. The captain seemed
very angry at this; and when Mr. Symonds was
shoving off from the brig's side, ordered him back.
He was hesitating, when another gentleman jumped
into the boat, declaring that he would not allow his
companion to be left behind, and promised the men
a reward if they would shove off. Two of the men
agreed to go in the boat, and the mate, with the rest,
coming up the side, they pulled away for the shore.

The captain walked the deck, fuming and raging,
every now and then turning an angry glance at the
land and pulling out his watch. "He means mischief," muttered old Tom in my hearing; "but if he
thinks to leave young Sam ashore to die of starva-
tion, he is mistaken."

The night drew on, and the boat had not returned.
My watch being over, I turned in, supposing that
the brig would remain at anchor till the morning.
I was, however, awakened in the middle watch by
old Tom's voice. "Come on deck, Jack," he said;
"there's mischief brewing; the captain had a quarrel
with Mr. Duncan the other day, and he hates young
Sam for his impudence, as he calls it, and so I
believe he intends to leave them behind if he can do
so; but he is mistaken. We will not lift anchor
till they are safe on board, or a party has been sent
to look for them. They probably lost their way,
and could not get back to the harbour before dark.
There are no wild beasts or savages on shore, and so
they could not come to harm; you slip into the
cabin, and call the other gentlemen, and I'll manage
the crew, who have just loosed topsails, and are
already at the windlass with the cable hove short."

I was on deck in an instant, and, keeping on one
side, while the captain was on the other, managed to
slip into the cabin. I told the gentlemen of old
Tom's suspicions, and observed that the captain probably thought those in the boat would return
without Mr. Duncan and Sam, when they saw the
vessel making sail.

They instantly began to dress; and one of them,
a spirited young Highlander, Mr. M'Ivor, put a
brace of pistols into his belt and followed me on
deck. I tried to escape being seen by the captain,
but he caught sight of me, I was sure, though I
stooped down and kept close to the bulwarks as I
crept for'ard.

By this time the men were heaving at the windlass, which they continued to do, in spite of what
old Tom said to them. The captain had overheard
him, and threatened to knock the first man down
with a handspike who ceased to work. Old Tom,
however, had got one in his hand, and the captain
did not dare to touch him. In another instant I
heard Mr. M'Ivor's voice exclaiming, "What is this
all about, Captain Pyke? What! are you going to
leave our friends on shore?" "If your friends don't
come off at the proper time they must take the
consequences," answered the captain. "Then, what
I have got to say, Captain Pyke, is, that I'll not
allow them to be deserted, and that I intend to carry
out my resolution with a pretty strong argument—
the instant the anchor leaves the ground I'll shoot
you through the head." "Mutiny! mutiny!"
shouted the captain, starting back, "seize this man
and heave him overboard." As he spoke the other
two gentlemen made their appearance, and old Tom
and I, with two or three others, stepped up close to
them, showing the captain the side we intended to

take. Neither of the mates moved, while the men folded their arms and looked on, showing that they did not intend to interfere.

"Very well, gentlemen," cried the captain, "I see how matters stand—you have been bribing the crew. I'll agree to wait for the boat, and if she does not come with the missing people we must give them up for lost." "That depends upon circumstances," said Mr. M'Ivor, returning his pistol to his belt. He and the rest continued to walk the deck, while the captain went, muttering threats of vengeance, into his cabin.

None of us after this turned in. In a short time the splash of oars was heard, and the boat came alongside. "We have come for food," said Mr. Fraser, one of the gentlemen who had gone in her. "I intend going back at daylight, and must get two or three others to accompany me. We will then have a thorough search for Duncan and the boy— there is no doubt that they have lost their way, and if we fire a few muskets, they will, with the help of daylight, easily find the harbour. Mr. M'Ivor promised to accompany his friend, and I volunteered to go also." "No, Jack," said old Tom, "you remain with me. If we all go, the captain may be playing us some trick." I don't know what side old Tom would have taken if it had not been for young Sam. Judging by his usual conduct, I suspect that he would have stood with his arms folded, and let the rest, as he would have said, fight it out by themselves.

At daylight the boat pulled away with Mr. M'Ivor and another additional hand, taking a couple of muskets with them. Shortly afterwards the captain appeared on deck—though he cast frequent angry glances towards the shore, he said nothing—probably he could not afford to lose so many hands, as

there were now four away, besides the two gentlemen, while the aspect of old Tom, with the rest of
the crew, kept him from attempting to carry out his
evil intentions. Two or three times, notwithstanding this, I thought he was about to order the anchor
to be hove up ; but again he seemed to hesitate,
and at length, towards noon, the boat was seen
coming off, with Mr. Duncan and Sam in her. The
captain said nothing to the gentlemen, but, as soon
as the boat was hoisted up, he began to belabour
poor Sam with a rope's end. He was still striking
the lad, when old Tom stepped between them,
grasping a handspike. " What has the lad done,
sir ?" he exclaimed. " Why not attack Mr. Duncan ?
If anyone is to blame for the delay, he is the person,
not young Sam." The gentlemen were advancing
while old Tom was speaking, and several of the crew
cried out shame. The captain again found himself
in the minority, and, without replying to old Tom,
walked aft, muttering between his teeth.

These incidents will give some idea of the state of
matters on board the ship.

We now made sail, with a gentle breeze right aft,
but scarcely had we lost sight of the islands when a
heavy gale sprang up. The lighter canvas was instantly handed—young Sam and one of the men
who had gone in the boat were ordered out on the
jibboom to furl the flying jib. As they were about
this work, a tremendous sea struck the bows, the
gaskets got loose, the jibboom was carried away, and
with it the two poor fellows who were endeavouring
to secure the sail. The captain, who had seen the
accident, took no notice of it, but the first mate, not
wishing to have their death on his conscience,
sprang aft and ordered the ship to be brought to,
while others hove overboard every loose piece of

timber, empty casks, or hencoops, which they could lay hands on, to give our shipmates a chance of escape. Old Tom and I instantly ran to the jolly-boat, and were easing off the falls, when I felt myself felled to the deck by a blow on the head, the captain's voice exclaiming, "What, you fools, do you wish to go after them and be drowned too?" When I came to myself I saw the boat made fast, and could just distinguish the articles thrown overboard floating astern, while old Tom was standing gazing at them with sorrowful looks, the eyes of all on board, indeed, being turned in the same direction.

"It would have been no use, Jack," he said, heaving a deep sigh; "the captain was right, the boat couldn't have lived two minutes in this sea, but I would have risked my life to try and save young Sam, though, for your sake, my boy, it's better as it is."

After this the ship was put on her course, and we stood on, plunging away into the heavy seas which rose around us, and threatened every instant to break on board the brig. The passengers looked, and, I daresay, felt very melancholy at the accident, for young Sam especially, was liked by them, and on that account Mr. Duncan had taken him on his expedition. Old Tom could scarcely lift up his head, and even the rest of the crew refrained from their usual gibes and jokes. The captain said nothing, but I saw by the way he treated the first mate that he was very savage with him for the part he had taken in attempting to save the poor fellows.

After this old Tom was kinder than ever to me, and evidently felt towards me as he had towards young Sam, whose duties as everybody's servant I had now to take, being the youngest on board, and least able to hold my own against the captain's tyranny, and the careless and often rough treatment of the crew.

I had some time before told poor young Sam how I used to be called "Happy Jack," and he went and let out what I had said among the men. When one of them started me with a rope's end, he would sing out, "That's for you, 'Happy Jack.'" Another would exclaim, "Go and swab the deck down, 'Happy Jack ;'" or, "'Happy Jack,' go and help Mungo to clean out the caboose, I hope you are happy now—pleasant work for a young gentleman, isn't it ?" "Look you," I replied one day, when this remark was made to me, "I am alive and well, and hope some day to see my home and friends, so, compared to the lot of poor young Sam and Dick Noland, who are fathoms deep down in the ocean, I think I have a right to say I am happy—your kicks and cuffs only hurt for a time, and I manage soon to forget them. If it's any pleasure to you to give them, all I can say is, that it's a very rum sort of pleasure ; and now you have got my opinion about the matter."

"That's the spirit I like to see," exclaimed old Tom, slapping me on the back soon afterwards, "You'll soon put a stop to that sort of thing." I found he was right ; and, though I had plenty of dirty work to do, still, after that, not one of the men ever lifted his hand against me. The captain, however, was not to be so easily conquered, and so I took good care to stand clear of him whenever I could.

The rough weather continued till we had made Cape Horn, which rose dark and frowning out of the wild heaving ocean. We were some time doubling it, and were several days in sight of Terra del Fuego, but we did not see anything like a burning mountain—indeed, no volcanoes exist at that end of the Andes.

The weather moderated soon after we were round the Horn, but in a short time another gale sprung up, during which our bulwarks were battered in, one of our boats carried away, our bowsprit sprung, and the foretop-sail, the only canvas we had set, blown to ribbons. Besides this, we received other damages, which contributed still further to sour our captain's temper. We were at one time so near the iron-bound coast that there seemed every probability that we should finish off by being dashed to pieces on the rocks. Happily, the wind moderated, and a fine breeze springing up, we ran on merrily into the Pacific.

Shortly after, we made the island of Juan Fernandez, and, as I saw its wood-covered heights rising out of the blue ocean, I could not help longing to go on shore and visit the scenes I had read about in Robinson Crusoe. I told old Tom about my wish. Something more like a smile than I had ever yet seen, rose on his countenance. "I doubt, Jack, that you would find any traces of the hero you are so fond of," he observed; "I believe once upon a time an Englishman did live there, left by one of the ships of Commodore Anson's squadron, but that was long ago, and the Spaniards have turned it into a prison, something like our Norfolk Island."

CHAPTER V.

WE, however, did call off another island in the neighbourhood, called Massafuera, to obtain a supply of wood and water. The ship was hove-to, and the pinnace and jolly-boat were sent on shore with casks. I was anxious to go, but old Tom kept me back. "You stay where you are, Jack," he said, "or the skipper may play you some trick. It's a dangerous place to land at, you are sure of a wetting, and may lose your life in going through the surf."

In the evening, when the party returned, I found this to be the case. Still, I might have been tempted, I think, to run off and let the ship sail away without me, as I heard that there were plenty of goats on the island, abundance of water, and that the vegetation was very rich.

It is also an exceedingly picturesque spot, the mountains rising abruptly from the sea, surrounded by a narrow strip of beach. Those who went on shore had also caught a large quantity of fish, of various sorts, as well as lobsters and crabs, which supplied all hands for several days.

Perhaps old Tom had a suspicion of what I might have been tempted to do, and I fancied that was his chief reason for keeping me on board.

The idea having once taken possession of my mind, I resolved to make my escape at the next tempting-looking island we might touch at, should I find any civilized men living there, or should it be uninhabited. I had no wish to live among savages, as I had read enough of their doings to make me anxious to keep out of their way, and I was not influenced by motives which induce seamen to run from their ships for the sake of living an idle, profligate life, free from the restraints of civilization.

A few days after leaving Massafuera, we got into the trade winds, which carried us swiftly along to the northward. Again we crossed the equator; and about three weeks afterwards made the island of Owhyee, the largest of the Sandwich

Islands.   As we coasted along, we enjoyed the most
magnificent view I had ever beheld.   Along the
picturesque shore were numerous beautiful plantations, while beyond it rose the rocky and dreary
sides of the gigantic Mouna Roa, its snow-clad
summit towering to the clouds.   It was on this
island that Captain Cook was murdered by the now
friendly and almost civilized natives, who have, indeed, since become in many respects completely so,
and taken their place among the nations of the
world.

We sailed on, passing several islands, when we
brought up in the beautiful bay of Whytetee.   Near
the shore was a village situated in an open grove of
cocoa-nut trees, with the hills rising gently in the
rear, presenting a charming prospect.   The more I
gazed at it, the more I longed to leave the brig, and go
and dwell there, especially as I heard that there were
several respectable Englishmen and Americans already
settled on the island, and that they were held in
high favour by the king and his chiefs.   Still old Tom
had been so kind to me, and I entertained so sincere
a regard for him, that I could not bear the thoughts
of going away without bidding him farewell.   I was
afraid, however, of letting him know my intentions.
Often I thought that I would try and persuade him
to go too.   I began by speaking of the beautiful
country, and the delicious climate, and the kind
manners of the people, and how pleasantly our
countrymen, residing there, must pass their lives.
" I know what you are driving at, Jack," he said,
" You want to run from the ship; isn't it so?"
I confessed that such was the case, and asked him to
go with me.   " No, Jack," he replied, " I am not one
of those fellows who act thus; I have done many a
thing I am sorry for, but I engaged for the voyage,

and swore to stick by the brig; and while she holds
together, unless the captain sets me free, I intend to
do so. And Jack, though you are at liberty to do
what you like, you wouldn't leave me, would you?"
He spoke with much feeling in his tone. "Since
young Sam went, you are the only person I have
cared to speak to on board, and if you were to go,
I should feel as if I were left alone in the world.
I should have liked to have made friends with those
fine young men, Duncan and M'Ivor. Once (you
may be surprised to hear it) I was their equal in
position, but they don't trouble themselves about
such a man as I now am, and they will soon be
leaving the brig for the shore. If I thought it was
for your advantage, I would say, notwithstanding
this, go; but it isn't. You will get into bad ways if
you go and live among those savages—for savages
they are, whatever you may say about them. And
you will probably be able to return home by sticking
to the brig sooner than any other way."

These arguments weighed greatly with me, and
I finally abandoned my intention, greatly to old
Tom's satisfaction. He redoubled his kindness to
me after this. Towards every one else he grew more
silent and reserved.

I may just say, that the next day we anchored off
Honoluloo, the chief town, where the king and his
court resided; and that we carried on some trading
with the people, his majesty in particular, and taking
some half-a-dozen Sandwich islanders on board to
replace the men we had lost, and, as old Tom
observed, any others we might lose, we sailed for
the American coast.

From that day I could not help observing a more
than usually sad expression on my friend's countenance; indeed, every day he seemed to become

more and more gloomy, and I determined to ask him what there was on his mind to make him so. I took the opportunity I was looking for one night when he was at the helm, and the second mate, who was officer of the watch, had gone forward to have a chat, as he sometimes did, with the men. The night was fine and clear, and we were not likely to have eaves-droppers. "Tell me, Tom," I said, "what is the matter with you? I wish that I could be of as much use to you as you have been to me." "Thank you, Jack," he answered; "the fact is, I have got something on my mind, and as you have given me an opportunity, I'll tell you what it is. I think I shall be the better afterwards, and you may be able to do for me what I shall never have an opportunity of doing myself, for, Jack, I cannot help feeling sure that my days are numbered. If that captain of ours wishes to get rid of me, he will find means without staining his hands in my blood, he will not do that, there are plenty of other ways by which I may be expended, as they say of old stores in the navy. For myself I care but little, but I should wish to remain to look after you, and lend you a helping hand should you need it." "Thank you, Tom," I said, "I value the kind feelings you entertain for me, and I hope that we shall be together till we reach England again. But I was going to ask why you think that the captain wishes to get rid of you? He can have no motive that I can discover to desire your death."

"He hates me, that's enough; he's a man who will go any lengths to gratify his hate," answered old Tom. "But I promised to tell you about the matter which weighs on my mind. Jack, I did many things when I was a young man, which I am sorry for, but I was then chiefly my own enemy. A time came, however, when I was tempted to commit a crime against others, and it's only since I began this voyage that I have had a wish to try and undo it as far as I have the power. You must know, Jack, I am the son of a gentleman, and I went to college. I had got into bad ways there, and spent all my property. When my last shilling was gone, I shipped on board a merchant vessel, and for years never again set foot on the shores of old England. I knocked about all that time in different climes and vessels, herding with the roughest and most abandoned class of seamen, till I became almost as abandoned and rough as they were. Still, during all my wanderings, I had a hankering for the associates and the refinements of society I had so long quitted. Thoughts of home would come back to me even in my wildest moments, although I tried hard to keep them out. At length I returned to England with more money in my pocket than I had ever again expected to possess. Throwing aside my seafaring clothes as soon as I got on shore, I dressed myself as a gentleman, and repairing to a fashionable watering-place, where I found several old friends, managed to get into respectable society. I forgot that unless I could obtain some employment my money must soon come to an end. It did so, but the taste for good society had been revived in me. It was now impossible to indulge in it, and I was compelled once more to seek for a berth on board ship. Thoughtlessly, I had never studied navigation while I was at sea, and consequently had again to go before the mast. I got on board an Indiaman, and reached Calcutta. On the return voyage we had a number of passengers. I of course knew but little about them, as I seldom went aft except to take my trick at the helm. I observed, however, among them a gentleman of refined appearance, with his wife and their little boy. They had a native nurse to take care of him. No one could be more affectionate than the gentleman was to his wife and child, but he seemed of a retiring disposition, and I seldom saw him speaking to any one else. We had had particularly fine weather during the greater part of the passage, when the ship was caught in a tremendous gale. During it the masts were carried away, several of the hands—Lascars and Englishmen—were lost overboard, while she sprung a leak, which kept all the crew hard at work at the pumps.

"It became evident, indeed, before long, that unless the weather moderated the ship would go down. We had four boats remaining, but as they would not carry a third of the people on board, the captain ordered all hands to turn to and build rafts. We were thus employed when night came on; such a night I never before had seen. The thunder roared and the lightning flashed around us, as if it would set the ship on fire. Some hours passed away; we could get on but slowly with our work. I was on the after-part of the deck, when I remember seeing the gentleman I have spoken of come up and make an offer to the captain to lend a hand at whatever might be required to be done. I observed at the time that he had a small case hanging to his side. He did not seem to think that there was any danger of the ship going down for many hours to come; nor indeed did any one; for the leaks were gaining but little on the pumps, although they were gaining. He seemed so well to understand what he was about that I suspected he was a naval officer. We worked away hard, and it was nearly morning, when a dreadful peal of thunder, such as I had never heard before, broke over our heads, and it's my belief that a bolt passed right through the ship. Be that as it may, a fearful cry arose that she was going down. The people rushed to the boats. Discipline was at an end. The gentleman I spoke of shouted to the men, trying to bring them back to their duty. Then I saw him, when all hope of doing so had gone, hurry into the cuddy. Directly afterwards he came out with his wife and child, together with the nurse. Supposing, I fancy, that the boats were already full, or would be swamped alongside, he secured the nurse to the raft we had been building, and had given her the child to hold, calling on me and others to assist in launching it overboard, intending to take his place with his wife upon it. He was in the act of securing her—so it seemed to me—when the ship gave a fearful plunge forward, and a roaring sea swept over her. I at once saw that she would never rise again. On came the foaming waters, carrying all before them. Whether or not the gentleman and his wife succeeded in getting to the raft, I could not tell; there was no room, I knew, for me on it. Just before I had caught sight of one of the boats, which had shoved off with comparatively few people in her, dropping close under the ship's quarter. I sprang aft, and, leaping overboard, struck out towards her, managing to get hold of her bow as it dipped into the sea. I hauled myself on board. By the time I had got in, and could look about me, I saw the stern of the ship sinking beneath a wave, and for a moment I thought the boat would have been drawn down with her. Such fearful shrieks and cries as I never wish to hear again rose from amid the foaming sea, followed by a perfect and scarcely less terrible silence. We had but three oars in the boat, which we could with difficulty, therefore, manage in that heavy sea. Most

of the men in her were Lascars, and they were but
little disposed to go to the assistance of our drowning shipmates. There were three Englishmen in
the after-part of the boat, and I made my way
among the Lascars to join them. Even the Englishmen belonged to the least respectable part of the
crew. They, however, sided with me, and, seizing a
stretcher, I swore that I would brain the fellows if
they would not try to pick up some of the drowning
people. Two or three on this drew their knives,
flourishing them with threatening gestures. Knowing them pretty well, I felt sure that if we did not
gain the day, they would take the first opportunity
of heaving us overboard; and with all my might I
dealt a blow at the head of the man nearest me, who
held his weapon ready to strike. The stretcher
caught him as he was in the act of springing up,
and he fell overboard, sinking immediately. "Any
more of you like to be treated in the same way?"
I exclaimed. The wretches sank down in their
seats, thoroughly cowed; but in the scuffle one of
the oars was lost overboard, and was swept away
before we could recover it. Some time was thus
lost, and the boat had drifted a considerable distance
from the spot where the Indiaman had gone down.
We could hear, however, cries for help rising above
the hissing and dashing sounds of the tumbling
waters. Every instant I expected that the boat
would be swamped; when at length the Lascars,
who had the oars, were induced by my threats to
pull away and keep her head to sea. I had taken
the helm, and though we made no progress, the rafts
and various articles which had floated up from the
wreck came drifting down towards us, scattering far
and wide over the tossing ocean. I caught sight of
a boat and two or three other rafts, but they were

too far off to enable me, through the gloom, to distinguish the people on them. The shrieks had gradually ceased; now and then the cry of some strong swimmer, who had hitherto bravely buffeted the sea, was heard ere he sank for the last time. Daylight was just breaking when, as I was standing up in the stern-sheets, I saw a person clinging to a piece of timber, and I determined, if possible, to save him. I pointed him out to the English seamen; and two of them, springing up, seized the oars from the hands of the Lascars, and by pulling away lustily we got up close to the spot. The man saw us coming. It was not without difficulty that we managed to haul him on board so as to avoid striking him or staving in the boat against the piece of wreck which had kept him up. To my surprise I found that he was the very gentleman who had assisted in forming the raft before the ship went down. I knew him by the case, which he still had secured to his side. He was so exhausted that for some minutes he could not speak, though he was evidently making an effort to do so. At length, beckoning me to put my ear down to his mouth, he asked in a low voice whether we had seen his wife and child, with the nurse. The only comfort I could afford him was by telling him that I had caught sight of several small rafts, and possibly they might be upon one of them. He had been washed away before he could secure himself when the ship foundered; and though he was carried down with her, on rising to the surface he had caught hold of the piece of wreck to which we had found him clinging.

"There we were, fourteen human beings in a small boat out in the middle of the Atlantic, the dark foaming seas surrounding us, without a particle of food or a drop of fresh water, while our two oars scarcely enabled us to keep her head to the sea, and save her from being capsized or swamped.

"I do not like to talk or even to think of the horrors which followed. Daylight had now come on, but all around was gloom, the dark clouds appearing like a pall just above our heads, and hanging round on either side, so as to circumscribe the horizon to the narrowest limits. Here and there I occasionally thought that I saw a few dark spots, which might have been the boats and rafts, or pieces of the wreck.

" The day passed by and there was no abatement of the gale. The Lascars had again taken the oars, but as night again approached, worn out with hunger and fatigue, they refused to pull any longer, and the gentleman offering to steer, the three other men and I took it by turns to labour at the oars.

" Thus the second night passed by. I had begun to feel faint and hungry, and to experience the pangs of thirst ; and, judging by my own sensations, I felt sure that, should we not fall in with a ship during the coming day, some of my companions would give way. Another morning dawned, but no sail was in sight. One of the Lascars lay dead in the bows, the rest were stretched out under the thwarts, unable even to continue baling, and apparently no longer caring what might become of them. The gentleman, though the most delicate-looking of us all, held out the best. His eye was constantly ranging over the ocean in search of the raft or boat which might contain those he loved best on earth. I had great difficulty in persuading him to let me take the helm again while he got a little sleep.

"As the day drew on the gale moderated, and the sea went down. So weak were the three other

Englishmen by this time, that I believe we should
not otherwise have been able to prevent the boat
being swamped. The Lascars were in a worse state.
Two more died, and as their countrymen would not
heave them overboard, we were obliged to do so.
Eagerly we looked out for a sail, but none appeared.
Before the next morning broke all the Lascars were
dead, and I saw that one of my messmates was
likely soon to follow them. Another, however, died
before him, but ere the sun rose high in the heavens,
he was gone.

"Besides the gentleman, only I and one man remained, the latter indeed was near his last gasp. I
will not tell you what dreadful thoughts passed
through my mind. Just then, as I was stooping
down, I put my hand under the after seat. There,
stowed away, was a large lump of grease. I felt
round farther, and drew forth two bones with a
considerable amount of meat on them. One of the
dogs, I have no doubt, had made it his hiding place.
The selfish thought came across me, that had the
Lascars and the other two men been alive, this food
would have gone very little way, but now it might
support the existence of my two companions and
me for another day or two. Eagerly I seized the
putrid meat in my mouth, offering a piece to my
companions. My messmate attempted to eat it, his
jaws moved for a few seconds, then his head fell
back. He had died in the effort. The gentleman
could with difficulty swallow a few morsels. 'Water!
water!' he muttered, 'without water it is too late.'
I tried some of the grease, and felt revived.

"Not without difficulty we hove the last who had
succumbed into the sea, and then the gentleman
and I were alone. His spirits, which had hitherto
kept up, were now, I saw, sinking. He beckoned

me to sit close to him, and I saw that he was engaged in trying to loosen the strap which held the case to his side. 'You are strong, my friend,' he whispered, 'and may possibly survive till you are picked up, I feel that I can trust you. Take charge of this case—it contains an important document, and jewels and money of considerable value. Here, too, is a purse of gold, to that you are welcome,' and he handed me a purse from his pocket. 'The case I as a dying man commit to your charge, and solemnly entreat you to take care of it for the benefit of my widow and orphan child, for the belief is still strong within me that they survive. You will find within this metal case full directions as to the person to whom it is to be delivered.' He said this with the greatest difficulty, and it seemed as if he had exhausted all his strength in the effort. I promised to fulfil his wishes, and fully intended doing so. He took my hand, and fixed his eyes on me, as if he was endeavouring to read my thoughts. I tried to make him take some more food, but he had no strength to swallow it. Before the evening closed in he too was gone.

"I had not the heart at once to throw him overboard. As I stood looking at him, prompted I believe by the spirit of evil, an idea came into my head. Should I reach shore the purse of gold would enable me to enjoy myself for some time, and perhaps I might obtain permanent employment in a respectable position, instead of knocking about at sea. I took off the dead man's clothes, and dressed myself in them, though I was so weak that the task was a difficult one. I then lifted the body overboard. Having secured the box round my waist, I placed the metal case and purse in my pocket.

"I was alone, and though suffering greatly from thirst, I still felt that there was some life in me. I gazed around, but no sail was in sight. A light breeze only was blowing, and the sea had become tolerably calm, so eating a little more of the grease and meat, I lay down in the stern-sheets to sleep. I was awoke by feeling the water splashing over me. It was raining hard. There were two hats and a bucket in the boat. I quickly collected enough water to quench my thirst, and at once felt greatly revived. The rain continued long enough to enable me to fill the bucket. Had it not been for that shower I must have died.

"Two days longer I continued in the boat, when, just as the sun rose, my eyes fell on a sail in the horizon. How eagerly I watched her; she was standing towards me. Securing a shirt to the end of an oar, I waved it as high as I could reach. I was seen—the ship drew nearer. Being too weak to pull alongside I made no attempt to do so, and this being observed, the ship hove-to and lowered a boat, which soon had mine in tow. I was carefully lifted up the side, and on my dress being observed, I was at once treated as a gentleman. A cabin was given up to me, and every attention paid to my wants. I found that the ship was an emigrant vessel, outward bound, for Australia.

"I was some time in recovering my strength, and when I appeared among the passengers I took care to evade any questions put to me. I found the life on board very pleasant, and having purchased some clothes and other articles I was able to appear on an equality with the rest.

"We fell in with no other ship till Sydney was reached. I went on shore, purposing to amuse myself for a short time, and then return home and fulfil

the dying request of my unfortunate companion in
the boat. Would that I had gone on board a vessel
sailing the very day of our arrival. Jack, never put
off doing your duty, under the idea that it may be
done a little time hence, lest that roaring lion we
read of may catch hold of you and tempt you to put
it off altogether. I remained on day after day,
mixing in society, and rapidly spending my money.
It was all gone, and then, Jack," and old Tom lowered
his voice, " I did that vile deed—I broke open the
box and took possession of the money I found within
—the widow's and orphan's gold. I tried to persuade myself that they had certainly been lost. At
first I only took the gold, intending to go home
with the other articles; then I got to the notes. I
had some difficulty in getting them changed, and
was afraid of being discovered. At last I began to
dispose of the jewels.

" At length I got a hint that I was suspected, and
securing the case I once more dressed myself as a
seaman, bought a chest, and got a berth on board a
homeward-bound ship. I was miserable—conscience
stung me—I could get no rest.

" The ship was cast away on the west coast of
Ireland, and nearly all on board perished. I had
secured about me the case, which still contained the
parchment, the title-deeds of a large property, and a
few jewels.

" I, with a few survivors, reached the shore. I
was afraid to go back to England to deliver the
case to the person to whom it was addressed, and so,
making my way to Cork, where I found a ship bound
for America, I went on board her.

" Jack, I have been knocking about ever since,
my conscience never at rest, and yet not having the
courage to face any danger I might incur, and make

the only reparation in my power to those who, if still alive, I have deprived of their property. Now, notwithstanding what you say, there's something tells me that I have not long to live. I never had such a notion in my head before, but there it is now, and I cannot get rid of it. You are young and strong, and I want you to promise me, if you get home, to do what I ought to have done long ago. I will give you the case when we go below. Take it to the lawyer to whom it is addressed, and tell him all I have told you, and how it came into your possession, he'll believe you, I am sure, and though the money and most of the jewels are gone, the remainder will, I hope, be of value to the rightful owners."

I of course promised old Tom that I would do as he wished, at the same time I tried to persuade him to banish the forebodings which haunted him, from his mind. "That's more than I can do, Jack," he said, "I shouldn't mind the thoughts of death so much, if I could find the means of undoing all the ill I have done in the world—that's what tries me now." Unhappily neither I nor any one on board could tell the poor fellow that there is but one way by which sins can be washed away. I did indeed suggest that he should try and borrow a Bible from one of the gentlemen in the cabin, if they had one among them, for there was not one for'ard nor in the captain's or officers' berths.

When our watch was over, old Tom sat down on his chest, waiting till the rest of the watch had turned in and gone to sleep. He then cautiously opened his chest, and exhibited within, under his clothes, a small box, strongly bound with silver, and the metal case he had spoken of. "Here, Jack," he said, "I make you my heir, and give you the key of my chest : I'll tell the men to-morrow that I have done so, and let the captain and mates know it also, that there may be no dispute about the matter." I thanked old Tom, assuring him, at the same time, that I hoped not to benefit by his kindness.

In about three weeks we reached the mouth of the Columbia river. A strong gale from the westward had been blowing for several days, and as we came off the river a tremendous surf was seen breaking across the bar at its mouth. " I hope the captain won't attempt to take the vessel in," observed old Tom to me. " I have been in once while the sea was not so heavy by half as it is now, and our ship was nearly castaway." Still we stood on. Presently, however, the captain seemed to think better of it, and indifferent as he was to the lives of others, he apparently did not wish to lose his own, and the brig into the bargain. She was accordingly hauled to the wind, and we again stood off. It was only, however, to heave-to, when he ordered a boat to be lowered. He then directed the first mate to take four hands to go in her and sound the bar. The mate expostulated, and declared that the lives of all would be sacrificed in the attempt. " You are a coward, and are afraid," exclaimed the captain, stamping with rage. " Take old Tom and 'Happy Jack,' and two others," he called out their names. " No man shall justly say I am a coward," answered the mate ; " I'll go, but I'll take none but volunteers. My death and theirs will rest on your head, Captain Pyke." " I'll not go if the boy is sent," exclaimed old Tom ; "but I am ready to go if another man takes his place." " Let me go, Tom," I said ; "if you and the mate go I am ready to accompany you." " No, Jack, I'll do no such thing," answered my friend. " You stay on board. Unless others step forward the boat won't go at all. The bar is not in a fit state for the vessel to cross, much less an open boat." The captain, however, seemed determined to go into the river, and now ordered another man to go instead of me. "I'll make you pay for this another day," he cried out, looking at me. I saw the mate shaking hands with several on board before he stepped into the boat. "Remember the case, Jack," said old Tom as he passed me, giving me a gripe by the hand. "You have got the key, lad."

The boat shoved off and pulled towards the bar. I watched her very anxiously; now she rose to the top of a roller, now she was hidden by the following one. Every instant I expected her to disappear altogether. I couldn't help thinking of what old Tom had said to me. Some time passed, when the captain ordered the helm to be put up, and the brig was headed towards the bar. He had been looking with his glass, and declared he had seen the mate's signal to stand in. The wind by this time had moderated. The brig was only under her topsails and mainsail, and I began to wonder at the mate's apprehensions. We had not stood on long when I saw the boat to the northward of us, much nearer the breakers than we were. She seemed to be carried by beyond the control of those in her. A strong current had caught hold of her. Presently she passed, not a pistol shot from us. The three men were shouting and shrieking for aid; old Tom was in the bows, sitting perfectly still; I could even distinguish the countenance of the mate, as he turned it with a reproachful glance, so it seemed to me, towards the captain. Beyond her appeared a high wall of hissing, foaming breakers, towards which she was driving. The captain seemed scarcely to notice the unfortunate men ; indeed his attention was occupied with attending to the brig, our position being extremely critical. I couldn't take my eyes off the boat. Would she be able even yet to stem the current and get back into smooth water ? Suddenly, however, it seemed as if the wall of foaming breakers came right down upon her, and she disappeared amidst them. A cry of horror escaped me. "We may be no better off ere long," I heard one of the men exclaim. He had scarcely spoken when the brig struck, and the foaming waters leaped up on either side, as if about to break on board. Another sea came roaring on, and she again moved forward. Again and again the brig struck, and at last seemed fixed.

Darkness was coming on, the foaming waters roared around us, frequently breaking on board, and we had to hold on to escape being washed away. The hatches had been battened down, or the vessel would have filled. She must have been a strong craft, or she could not have held together. The passengers behaved like brave men, though they evidently thought that it was the captain's obstinacy which had brought them into their present perilous position.

Hour after hour passed by, with no object discernible beyond the foaming waters surging round us. The men declared that they could hear the shrieks and cries of our shipmates. The captain swore at them as fools for saying so, declaring that their voices must long since have been silenced by the breakers. Every instant it seemed that the brig must go to pieces, and that we should be carried away to share their fate. Suddenly, however, I felt the brig move. The topsails were let fall and sheeted home, and we once more glided forward. In another hour we were safely at anchor in a sheltered bay within the mouth of the river.

The next morning several natives came off to us in their canoes. They were red-skinned painted savages, but appeared inclined to be friendly. By means of Mr. Duncan, who understood something of their language, they were told of the accident which had happened to the boat, and they undertook to search along the shore, in the possibility of any of the crew having escaped, and been washed on to the beach. On hearing of this my hopes of seeing old Tom again somewhat revived, though I scarcely believed it possible that any boat getting into those fearful breakers could have survived. Mr. Duncan and two of the other gentlemen agreed to accompany the savages.

In the evening the boat which had taken them on shore was seen coming off. I anxiously watched her. Besides those who had gone away, I distinguished one other person, he turned his face towards the vessel as the boat approached, and, to my delight, I saw that he was old Tom. "And so you have escaped, have you?" said the captain, as he stepped on board. "Yes, sir, but the others have gone where some others among us will be before long," answered Tom, gloomily, "and those who sent them there will have to render an account of their deeds." "What do you mean?" exclaimed the captain. "I leave that to others to answer," said Tom, walking forward.

He told me that the boat, on entering the surf, was immediately capsized, and that all hands were washed out of her. That he had managed to cling on with one man, and that when they got through the surf they had righted the boat, and picking up two of the oars, after bailing her out, had succeeded in paddling, aided by the current, some distance to the northward. On attempting to land the boat was again capsized. He had swam on shore, but the other poor fellow was drowned, and he himself was almost exhausted when met by the party who brought him back. "You see, Tom," I observed, " your prognostications have not come true, and you may still live to get back to old England again." "Oh no, Jack, though I have escaped this once, I am very sure my days are numbered," he answered ; do all I could, I was unable to drive this idea out of his head.

The crew were so indignant at the boat having been sent away, declaring that the captain wished to get rid of the mate and old Tom, that I felt sure another slight act of tyranny would produce a mutiny. While the gentlemen remained on board this was less likely to happen, but they were about to leave us, and take up their residence on shore.

Some time was occupied in landing their goods and stores, and then we found that we were to proceed to the northward, on a trading voyage with the Indians, and that Mr. Duncan was to accompany us. We had also received on board an Indian, who had long resided with the whites, and who was to act as our interpreter.

A fair wind carried us over the bar, and, steering to the northward, we continued on for several days, till we brought up in a deep bay, on the shore of which was situated a large native village. Large numbers of the Indians came off in their canoes, with furs to exchange for cutlery, cotton goods, looking-glasses, beads, and other ornaments. Many of them were fine looking, independent fellows, but veritable savages, dressed in skins, their heads adorned, after their fashion, with feathers, shells,

and the teeth of different animals. The captain
treated them with great contempt, shouting at them,
and ordering them here and there, as if they were
beings infinitely inferior to himself. I saw them
frequently turn angry glances at him, but they did
not otherwise exhibit any annoyance. One day,
however, he had a dispute with one of their chiefs
about a matter of barter, when, losing his temper,
he struck the savage and knocked him over on the
deck. The Indian, recovering himself, cast a fierce
glance at him, then, folding his arms, walked away,
uttering some words to his companions, which we
did not understand.

The next day, Mr. Duncan, who had gone on
shore, returned on board hurriedly, with the interpreter, and warned the captain that the Indians intended to take vengeance for the insult their chief
had received. The captain laughed, declaring that
he did not fear what ten times the number of
savages who as yet had come on board, would venture to do. "They are daring fellows, though,
Captain Pyke, and treacherous, and cunning in the
extreme," observed Mr. Duncan. "Take my advice
and keep them out of the ship. We have already
done a fair trade here, and the natives have not
many more skins to dispose of." "I am not to be
frightened as other people are," answered the captain, scornfully. "If they have no skins they will
not bring them, and if they have, I am not the man
to be forgetful of the interests of the Company, by
refusing to trade."

This was said on deck in the hearing of the crew.
"I'll tell you what, Jack," observed old Tom to me,
"the captain will repent not following Mr. Duncan's
advice. If the Indians come on board, keep by me
—we shall have to fight for our lives. I know these

people. When they appear most friendly, they are often meditating mischief."

That very evening several canoes came off, and in them was the chief whom the captain had knocked down. He seemed perfectly friendly, smiling and shaking hands with the captain as if he had entirely forgotten the insult he had received.

When the savages took their departure, they were apparently on the best of terms with us all.

CHAPTER VI.

THE next morning we were preparing to put to sea, when two large canoes came off, each carrying about twenty men. As they exhibited a considerable number of furs, the captain allowed them to come on board, and trade commenced as usual. In the meantime, three other canoes came off with a similar number of men, and a larger quantity of furs of the most valuable descriptions. They also were allowed to come up the side like the rest.

" Jack, I don't like the look of things," said old Tom.

" Do you observe that the savages are wearing cloaks such as they have not appeared in before. Just come down for'ard with me."

I followed Tom below. " Here," he said, " fasten this case under your jacket. If the savages attack us, we will jump into the boat astern ; they will be too much intent on plunder to follow us, and we will make our escape out to sea. I propose to do this for your sake. As for me, I would as lief remain and fight it out. I have mentioned my sus-

picions to several of the men, and advised them to
have an eye on the handspikes ; with them we may
keep the savages at bay till we can make good our
retreat."

I asked him why he did not warn the captain.
" Because he is mad, and would only laugh at me,"
he answered. " Mr. Duncan and the interpreter
have already done so, and they are as well aware as
I am that mischief is brewing."

On going on deck, we saw the captain speaking to
the Indians, and ordering them to return to their
canoes. They appeared as if they were going to
obey him, when suddenly, each man drawing a
weapon from beneath his cloak uttered a fearful
yell, and leaped at the officers and us. The captain,
with only a jack-knife in his hand, defended himself
bravely, killing four of his savage assailants.

Led by old Tom, I, with three or four other men,
fought our way aft to join the officers, intending,
should we be overpowered, to leap, as we had proposed, into the boat. I saw poor Mr. Duncan
struck down and hove into a canoe alongside. The
captain was apparently trying to reach the cabin,
probably to get his fire-arms, when he fell, struck by
a hatchet on the head.

" Follow me," cried Tom. " We may reach the
boat through the cabin windows." As he said this,
he sprang down the companion-hatch, I and two
others following him. The remainder of our number were overtaken by the savages before they could
reach it. The last, Andrew Pearson, our boatswain,
contrived to secure the hatch. This gave us time to
get hold of the fire-arms fastened against the bulkheads, and to load and place them ready for use on
the table. There were at least a dozen muskets,
and as many brace of pistols. Had these been in

our hands on deck, we should probably have driven the savages overboard, or they would have been deterred from making the attack. With them, we might now defend our lives against vastly superior numbers.

The scuffle on deck was still going on, the yells of the savages rising above the stifled groans and cries of our unfortunate shipmates. They soon ceased, and then arose a shout of triumph from our enemies, and we knew that we were the only survivors. But we too were in a desperate plight. Tom was severely wounded, and the boatswain and the other man had received several gashes. I, indeed, thanks to the way in which Tom had defended me, was the only person unhurt.

"Green, do you look after the hatchway," said Pearson to the other man who had escaped. "Tom, do you and Jack show your muskets through the stern windows, I have some work to do. The savages think they have us in a trap, but they are mistaken." He opened, as he spoke, a hatch which led to the magazine, and I saw him uncoiling a long line of match, one end of which he placed in the magazine, while he led the other along the cabin to the stern-port. Meantime, the savages had all clambered on board, and were shrieking and shouting in the most fearful manner, crowding down into the hold, as we could judge by the sounds which reached us, and handing up the rich treasures they found there.

"No time to be lost," said Pearson, hauling up the boat. He went to the locker, and collected all the provisions he could find. "Jump in, Tom and Jack," he said. "Now for the fire-arms." He handed them in, and told us to place them along the thwarts, ready for use. "Now, Green," he said in a low voice, "jump in." We three were now in the boat, which was hidden under the counter from those on deck. He struck a light, and placed it to the slow match, and, having ascertained that it was burning, slipped after us into the boat, in which the mast was fortunately stepped.

"Jack, do you take the helm, and steer directly for the mouth of the harbour," he said, cutting the painter and seizing an oar. Tom and Green did the same, and pulled away lustily. We had already got several fathoms from the vessel before we were perceived. The sail had been placed ready for hoisting. It was run up and sheeted home. The savages were about to jump into one of the canoes, and chase us, but three muskets pointed towards them made them hesitate. We were rapidly slipping away from the doomed brig. We could see the savages dancing and leaping on deck, their shouts and yells coming over the water towards us.

"They will dance to another tune soon," muttered Pearson between his teeth.

He and the other two had again taken to the oars. Even now a flight of arrows might have reached us, but fortunately the savages had not brought their bows with them, and probably that was the chief reason why they had not ventured to pursue us. They well knew that several of their number would have been shot down with our bullets had they made the attempt. Still we could see some of the chiefs apparently trying to persuade their warriors to follow us, and we knew that though we might fight till all our ammunition was expended, we should at last be overwhelmed by numbers.

Our chance of ultimate escape seemed small indeed. "They will not come," said Pearson. "See!" We had got half-a-mile or more from the brig, when a deep thundering sound reached our ears. It seemed as if the whole vessel was lifted out of the water, while up into the air shot her main-mast and spars, and fragments of her deck and bul-warks, and other pieces of timber, mingled with countless human bodies, with limbs torn off and mangled in a fearful manner. At the same time the canoes with those who had escaped were paddling with frantic energy towards the shore, probably be-lieving that the Great Spirit had sent forth one of his emissaries to punish them for their treachery to the white people. We concluded that some such idea as this was entertained by them, as we saw no canoes coming off in pursuit of us.

Rowing and sailing, we continued to make our way out to the open ocean. It was blowing fresh but, the wind coming off shore, the sea was tolerably calm, and we agreed that at all events it was better to undergo the dangers of a long voyage in an open boat than trust ourselves in the power of the revengeful savages. We had reached the mouth of the harbour, and could still see the village far off on its shore, when, to our dismay, we found the sea breeze setting in. We had accordingly to haul our wind, though we still hoped to weather the headland which formed its southern point, and get an offing.

Tom all this time had uttered no complaint, though I saw the blood flowing down his side. The boatswain and Green had, with my help, bound up their wounds. I wanted Tom to let me assist him. " No," he said; " it's of no use. If you were to swathe me up, I could not pull. It will be time enough for that when we get round the headland." He was evidently getting weaker, and at last the boatswain persuaded him to lay in his oar, and try to stop the blood. The wounds were in his back and neck, inflicted by the savages as he fought his way onward to the cabin. I bound our handkerchiefs round him as well as I could; but it was evident that he was not fit for rowing, and that the only chance of the blood stopping was for him to remain perfectly quiet.

During the last tack we made I fancied, as I looked up the harbour, that I saw the canoes coming out. I told the boatswain. "We will give them a warm reception, if they come near us," he answered.

I felt greatly relieved when we at last weathered the point, and were now able to stand along shore, though we couldn't get the offing which was desirable.

Night was coming on. The weather looked threatening, and our prospects of ultimately escaping were small.

At last we got so near the surf that the boatswain determined to put the boat about and stand out to sea. Although the other tack might bring us almost in front of the harbour's mouth, it was the safest course to avoid being cast on shore.

The night came on very dark, but the wind was moderate, and there was not much sea. Still the weather was excessively cold, and my companions suffered greatly from their wounds. Tom had been placed in the stern-sheets near me. Though he said less, he suffered more than the rest, and I could every now and then hear low groans escaping from his bosom. At last I heard him calling me. "Jack," he whispered, "what I told you is coming true. I am going; I feel death creeping over me. Remember the case. Do all you know I ought to have done. I have been a great sinner; but you once said there is a way by which all sins can be blotted out. I believe in that way. Jack, give me your hand. It's darker than ever; and I am cold, very cold." He pressed my hand, and I heard him murmuring to himself. It might have been a prayer, but his words were indistinct; I could not understand what he said. I kept steering with one hand, looking up at the sails, and casting a glance now and then at him, while the other two men pulled away to keep the boat to windward. Presently I felt his fingers relax; an icy chill came from his hand. I knew too well that my friend was dead. It was some time before I could bring myself to tell the boatswain what had happened. "Poor fellow ! But it may be the lot of all of us before another day is over," he said; "yet, as men, we will struggle to the last.'

The night passed on, and we still persevered in endeavouring to obtain an offing, though so indistinct was the land that we could not tell whereabouts we were. What was our dismay, when morning broke, to find that we were directly off the mouth of the harbour, and at such a distance that the keen eyes of the savages on the hills around might easily perceive our sail. We at once put the boat about, hoping to get again to the south'ard before we were discovered. "It's too late," cried Green; "I see the canoes coming." "We must fight them, then," said the daring boatswain, calmly. "We don't just expect mercy at their hands after the treat we gave them," and he laughed at the fearful act he had committed. Still I thought what could we three, in a small boat, with our dozen muskets, do against a whole fleet of fierce savages.

We could now see the canoes coming out of the harbour. The sea was smooth, and they would without fail venture after us. Our only chance of escape seemed in a sudden gale springing up, but of that

there was little probability. I was turning my eyes
anxiously towards the offing in hopes of seeing signs
of a stronger breeze coming, when I caught sight of
a sail. I pointed her out to the boatswain. "She
is a large vessel," he exclaimed, "and standing this
way." "Perhaps the savages will be more than ever
anxious to catch us, for fear we should persuade the
people on board yonder ship to punish them for
what they have done," I observed. "They will
catch us if they can," answered Pearson; "but they
will have to pay a good price yet if they make the
attempt," and he cast his eyes at the muskets which
lay ready loaded. The canoes were drawing nearer
and nearer, and we could now distinguish the figures
of the plumed warriors as they stood up in the bows.
The boat at the same time was slipping pretty
quickly through the water. "The breeze is fresh-
ening," I observed; "we may escape them yet." "I
don't much care if we do or do not," said Pearson;
"I should like to knock over a few of these boasting
fellows; we may hit them long before they can get
near enough to hurt us." I for my part did not
wish to see more of the savages killed, for they had
only followed the instinct of their untutored natures,
and we had already inflicted a terrible punishment
on them in return. In a few minutes the breeze
came down even stronger than before, and greatly to
my satisfaction, the canoes appeared to be scarcely
gaining on us, even if they did so at all. I continued
to give a glance every now and then at the ship, for
I was afraid after all she might alter her course, and
stand away from us.

At length, to my joy, I saw the savages in the
canoes cease paddling. They apparently were afraid
of venturing farther out into the ocean, or saw that
it would be hopeless to attempt overtaking us. For

some minutes they waited, as if holding a consulta-
tion, and then round they paddled and made their
way back into the harbour.

"Just like them," exclaimed Pearson. "Those
cowardly red-skins will never fight unless they can
take their enemies at an advantage."

We had to make several tacks towards the ship,
and then when we got near enough for the sound of
our muskets to reach her, we fired several as a signal.
They were at length, we concluded, heard on board.
She kept away towards us. She drew nearer. We
saw that she was a whaler, with the English colours
flying at the peak. She rounded to, and we went
alongside. "What has happened?" exclaimed several
voices, as old Tom's body was seen lying in the stern-
sheets. A few words told our tale. I was able to
climb up the side, but Pearson and Green were so
stiff from their wounds that they had to be helped
up. They were far more hurt indeed than they had
supposed, especially Pearson; but his dauntless spirit
had hitherto kept him up. Our boat was hoisted
on board, and old Tom's body was taken out and
laid on deck. We were treated with great kindness,
and the captain, greatly to my satisfaction, volunteered to give old Tom Christian burial. He had, as
we supposed, intended to go into the harbour to
obtain wood and water, and to trade with the
natives; but when he heard of what had occurred he
resolved to steer for a port farther south, and he
told me that he was very grateful to us for giving
him warning of the danger which he otherwise would
have run.

In the evening I saw my poor friend lashed up in
a hammock, and committed to his ocean grave.

All night long I was dreaming of him and of the
dreadful scenes I had witnessed.

The ship was the *Juno*. Her commander, Captain Knox, was a very different sort of person to my late captain; and from his kind manner, and the way he spoke to the officers and men, he seemed truly to act the part of a father to his crew. The ship had been out a year and a half, and it was expected she would remain another year in the Pacific.

Though I was anxious to get home, yet when the captain asked me to enter on board, I was very glad to do so. Pearson continued to suffer fearfully from his wounds. Whether the deed he had done preyed on his mind, I cannot say; but a high fever coming on, he used to rave about the savages, and the way he had blown them up. At the moment he committed the deed I daresay he had persuaded himself that he was only performing a justifiable act of vengeance. The day before we entered the harbour to which we were bound he died, and poor Green did not long survive him, so that I alone was left of all the crew of the ill-fated *Fox*.

CHAPTER VII.

THE captain of the *Juno* took every precaution to prevent her being surprised by the Indians. Boarding nettings were triced up round the ship every night, and the watch on deck had arms ready at hand. None of the natives were allowed to come on board, and only two or three canoes were permitted alongside at a time. We judged by their manner, though they were willing enough to trade, that they had already heard of what had occurred to the northward.

Having got our wood and water on board, we

again put to sea, cruising in various parts of the
ocean known to be frequented by whales. A bright
look-out was kept for their spouts as the monsters
rose to the surface to breathe. The instant a spout
was seen all was life and animation on board; the
boats were lowered, generally two or three at a time,
and away they pulled to be ready to attack the
whale as it again rose to the surface. I remember,
the first time I saw one of the monsters struck, I
shouted and jumped about the deck as eagerly as if
I myself were engaged in the work. Now I saw
the lines flying out of the boat at a rapid rate, as
the animal sounded; now the men in the boats
hauled it in again, as the whale rose once more to
the surface; now they pulled on, and two more
deadly harpoons were plunged into its sides, with
several spears; now they backed to avoid the lashing strokes of its powerful tail; now the creature
was seen to be in its death-flurry, tumbling about
and turning over and over in its agony. At length
it lay an inert mass on the surface, and the boats
came back, towing it in triumph. Next there was
the work of "cutting in," or taking off the blubber
which surrounded it; the huge body being turned
round and round during the operation, as the men
stood on it cutting off with their sharp spades huge
strips, which were hoisted with tackles on deck.
Last of all came the "trying out," when the blubber,
cut into pieces, was thrown into huge caldrons on
deck, with a fire beneath them; the crisp pieces,
from which the oil had been extracted, serving as
fuel. It was a curious scene when night came on,
and fires blazed up along the deck, surrounded by
the crew, begrimed with oil and smoke, looking like
beings of another world engaged in some fearful in-
cantation.

This scene was repeated over and over again. We visited several islands in the Pacific. At some, where Christian missionaries had been at work, the inhabitants showed by their conduct that they were worthy of confidence; but at others the captain deemed it necessary to be constantly on his guard, lest they might attempt to cut off the crew and take possession of the ship, as we heard had frequently occurred.

At length, to my delight and that of all the crew, the last cask we had on board was filled with oil, and with a deeply-laden ship we commenced our homeward voyage. We encountered a heavy gale going round the Horn, but the old *Juno* weathered it bravely, though, as she strained a good deal, we had afterwards to keep the pumps going for an hour or so during each watch. We, however, made our way at a fair rate northward, and once more crossed the line.

It may seem surprising that I had not hitherto examined the metal case which old Tom had committed to my charge. The box itself I had resolved not to open. I did not suppose that I should be induced to act as he had done, but yet I thought it wiser not to run the risk of temptation. We for several days lay becalmed, and one evening, while the crew were lying about the decks overcome with the heat, I stowed myself away for'ard, at a distance from the rest, and drew the paper out of the case. Great was my surprise to find that it was addressed to my own father. It contained a reference to the parchment in the box, and gave a list both of the jewels, the notes, and gold. The writer spoke of his wife and infant son, and charged my father, should any accident happen to him, to act as their guardian and friend as well as their legal adviser. The letter was signed " Clement Leslie."

" This is strange," I thought. " Then there can

be no doubt that little Clem is the very child old Tom saw placed in his nurse's arms on the raft, and his poor mother must have been washed away when the ship went down. Those Indian nurses, I have often heard, will sacrifice their own lives for the sake of preserving the children committed to their charge, and Clem's nurse must have held him fast in her arms, in spite of the buffeting of the waves and the tossing of the raft during that dreadful night when the Indiaman went down; and if she had any food, I dare say she gave it to him rather than eat it herself. But, poor fellow, what may have happened to him since we parted."

I now felt more anxious than ever to reach home, and longed for the breeze to spring up which might carry us forward through the calm latitudes. It came at last, and the *Juno* again made rapid progress homeward. We were bound up the Irish Channel to Liverpool; when, however, we got within about a week's sail of the chops of the Channel, it came on to blow very hard. The leaks increased, and we were now compelled to keep the pumps going during nearly the whole of each watch. The weather was very thick, too, and no observations could be taken. The crew were almost worn out; yet there was no time for rest. The gale was blowing from the south-west, and the sea running very high, when in the middle watch the look-out shouted the startling cry of "Land! on the starboard bow." The yards were at once braced sharply up, and soon afterwards the captain ordered the ship to be put about. We were carrying almost more canvas than she could bear, but yet it would not then do to shorten sail. Just as the ship was in stays, a tremendous squall struck her, and in an instant the three masts went by the board.

There we lay on a lee shore, without a possibility of getting off it. The order was at once given to range the cables, that immediately the water was sufficiently shallow to allow of it we might anchor.

I will not describe that dreadful night. Onward the ship drove towards the unknown shore. We had too much reason to dread that it was the western coast of Ireland, fringed by reefs and rugged rocks. As we drove on it grew more and more fearfully distinct. We fired guns of distress, in the faint hope that assistance might be sent to us; but no answering signal came. Too soon the roar of the surf reached our ears, and it became fearfully probable that the ship and her rich cargo, with all on board, would become the prey of the waves. I secured the precious box and case as usual, determined, if I could save my own life, to preserve them. The lead was continually hove, and at last the captain ordered the anchors to be let go. They held the ship but for a few minutes; then a tremendous sea struck her, and sweeping over her deck, they parted, and again onward she drove. A few minutes more only elapsed before she struck the rocks, and the crashing and rending sounds of her timbers warned us that before long she would be dashed into a thousand fragments. The sea was breaking furiously over the wreck, and now one, now another of the crew was washed away. I was clinging with others to a part of the bulwarks, when I felt them loosening beneath us. Another sea came, and we were borne forward towards the shore. For an instant I was beneath the boiling surf; when I rose again my companions were gone, and in a few seconds I found myself dashed against a rock. I clung to it for my life, then scrambled on, my only thought being to get away from the raging waters. I succeeded at length in

scrambling out of their reach, and lay down on a dry
ledge to rest. I must have dropped to sleep or
fainted from fatigue. When I came to myself, the
sun was up, and I heard voices below me. The tide
had fallen, and numbers of country people were
scrambling along the rocks, and picking up whatever was thrown on shore. I managed to get on
my feet and wave to them. Several came up to me,
and the tones of their voices showed me at once that
they were Irish.

Out of the whole crew, I was the only person who
had been saved, and I was very doubtful how I
might be treated. However, I wronged them. It
was a matter of dispute among several who should
take charge of me; and at length a young woman,
whose cottage was not far off, carried me up to it.
She and her husband gave me the best of everything they had; that is to say, as many potatoes and
as much buttermilk and bacon as I could swallow.
I was so eager to get home that, after a night's rest,
I told them I wished to start on my journey. I
was, I knew, on the west of Ireland, and I hoped
that, if I could manage to get to Cork, I might
from thence find means of crossing to England.
Though my host had no money to give me, he
agreed to drive me twenty miles on the way, pro-
mising to find a friend who would pass me on; and
his wife pressed on me a change of linen, and a few
other articles in a bundle. With these I started on
my long journey.

I was not disappointed, for when I told my story
I was fully believed, and I often got help where I
least expected it.

At length I reached Cork, where I found a vessel
just sailing for Liverpool. The captain agreed to
give me a free passage, and at last I safely landed

on the shores of old England. I must confess that I had more difficulty after this in making my way homeward, and by the time I reached the neighbourhood of my father's house my outer clothing, at all events, was pretty well worn to rags and tatters.

CHAPTER VIII.

IT was the early summer when one evening I came in sight of my home. The windows and doors were open. Without hesitation I walked up the steps, forgetting the effect which my sudden appearance might produce on my family. One of my youngest sisters was in the passage. I beckoned to her. "What do you want?" she asked; "you must not stop here; go away." "What! don't you know me?" I asked. "No," she answered; "who are you?" "Jack—your brother Jack," I answered. On this she ran off into the drawing-room, and I heard her exclaim, "There's a great big beggar boy, and he says he is Jack—our brother Jack." "Oh no, that cannot be!" I heard one of my other sisters reply. "Poor Jack was drowned long ago in the *Naiad.*" "No, he was not," I couldn't help exclaiming; and without more ado I ran forward. My appearance created no small commotion among three or four young ladies who were seated in the room. "Go away; how dare you venture in here?" exclaimed one or two of them. "Will you not believe me?" I cried. "I am Jack, I assure you, and I hope soon to convince you of the fact." "It is Jack, I know it is!" exclaimed one of them, jumping up and coming forward. I knew her in an

instant to be Grace Goldie, though grown almost
into a young woman. "It is Jack, I am sure it
is," she added, taking my hand and leading me
forward. "Oh, how strange that you do not know
him!" My sisters now came about me, examining
me with surprised looks. "How strange, Grace,"
said one; "surely you must be mistaken?" "No,
I am sure I am not," answered Grace, looking into
my face, and putting back the hair from my fore-
head; "Are you not Jack?" "Yes, I believe I
am," I answered, "though if you did not say so I
should begin to doubt the fact, since Ann, and
Mary, and Jane, do not seem to know me." "Well,
I do believe it is Jack," cried Jane, coming up and
taking my other hand, though I was so dirty that
she did not, I fancy, like to kiss me. "So he is—
he must be!" cried the others; and now, in spite of
my tattered dress, their sisterly affection got the
better of all other considerations, and they threw
their arms about me like kind girls as they really
were, and I returned their salutes, in which Grace
Goldie came in for a share, with long unaccustomed
tears in my eyes. Just then a shriek of astonishment was heard, and there stood Aunt Martha at
the door. "Who have you got there?" she exclaimed. "It's Jack come back," answered my
sisters and Grace in chorus. "Jack come back!
impossible!" cried out Aunt Martha, in what I
thought sounded a tone of dismay. "Yes, I am
Jack, I assure you," I said, going up to her; "and I
hope to be your very dutiful and affectionate nephew,
whatever you may once have thought me;" and I
took her hand and raised it to my lips. "If you
are Jack I am glad to see you," she said, her feelings
softening; "and it will at all events be a comfort
to your poor mother to know that you are not

drowned." "My mother! where is she?" I asked
—"I trust she is not ill." "Yes, she is, I am sorry
to say, and up-stairs in bed," replied my aunt; "but
I'll go and break the news to her, lest the sound of
all this hubbub should reach her ears, and make her
inquire what is the matter."

I had now time to ask about the rest of my family.
My father was out, but was soon expected home,
and in the meantime, while Aunt Martha had gone
to tell my mother, by my sisters' advice I went into
the bedroom of one of my brothers, and washed, and
dressed myself in his clothes. By the time Aunt
Martha came to look for me I was in a more pre-
sentable condition than when I entered the house.

I need not dwell on my interview with my mother.
She had no doubts about my identity, but drawing
me to her, kissed me again and again, as most
mothers would do, I suspect, under similar circumstances. She was unwilling to let me go, but at
length Aunt Martha, suggesting that I might be
hungry, a fact that I could not deny, as I was almost
ravenous, I quickly joined the merry party round
the tea-table, when I astonished them not a little by
the number of slices of ham and bread which I
shortly devoured. My father soon arrived. He was
not much given to sentiment, but he wrung my hand
warmly, and his mind was evidently greatly relieved
on finding that his plan for breaking me of my
desire for a sea life had not ended by consigning me
to a watery grave. He was considerably astonished,
and evidently highly pleased, when I put into his
hands the box and case which old Tom had given
into my care; and I told him how I had fallen in, on
board the *Naiad*, with the boy I fully believed to
be Mr. Clement Leslie's heir.

"This is indeed strange," he muttered, "very

strange, and we must do our best to find him out,
Jack. It's a handsome estate, and it will be a pity
if the young fellow is not alive to enjoy it. I must
set Simon Munch to work at once." "Perhaps if
the Russian frigate has returned home, we may learn
from her officers what has become of him," I suggested. "We will think the matter over. Would
you like a trip to Russia, Jack?" "Above all
things, sir," I answered. "I could start to-morrow
if it were necessary;" though I confess I felt very
unwilling to run away again so soon from home,
especially as my mother was so ill. Perhaps, also,
Grace Goldie entered somewhat into my considerations.

Next morning while we were at breakfast, and
my father was looking over the newspaper, he exclaimed, "We are in luck, Jack! Did you not say
that the name of the Russian frigate which picked
you up was the *Alexander?* I see that she has
just arrived at Spithead, from China and the Western
Pacific. If so, there is not a moment to be lost, for
she will probably be off again in a few days. You
must start at once. Get your sisters to pack up
such of your brother's things as will fit you, and I'll
order a post-chaise to the door immediately." "I
shall be ready, sir, directly I have swallowed another
egg or two, and a few more slices of toast," I
answered. "Munch must go with you, that there
may be no mistake about the matter," said my father.
"He will be of great assistance."

All seemed like a dream. In a quarter of an
hour I was rattling away as fast as a couple of
posters could go, along the road to London. I sat
in a dignified and luxurious manner, feeling myself
a person of no little consequence—remembering
that, at the same hour on the previous day, I had

been trudging along the road ragged and hungry, with some doubt as to the reception I was to meet with at home. My tongue was kept going all the time, for Munch wished to hear all about my adventures. "Well, Master Jack, I am glad to have you back," he said. "To tell the truth, my conscience was a little uncomfortable at the part I had taken in shipping you off on board the collier, though I might have known—" he cast a quizzical look at me—"that those are never drowned who are——"

"Born to end their lives comfortably in bed," I added, interrupting him. "You needn't finish the sentence in the way you were about to do; I was never much of a favourite of yours, Mr. Munch, I know."

"I hope we shall be better friends in future, Master Jack," he remarked. "You used, you know, to try my temper not a little sometimes."

As the old clerk was accustomed to long and sudden journeys, we stopped nowhere, except for a few minutes to get refreshments, till we rattled up to the George Inn at Portsmouth.

Much to our satisfaction, we heard from the waiter that the Russian frigate was still at Spithead, and as the weather was fine, we hurried down the High Street, intending at once to engage a wherry and go off to her. As we reached the point a man-of-war's boat pulled up, and several officers stepped on shore. "That is not the English uniform," observed Munch; "perhaps they have come from the Russian frigate." He was right, I was sure, for I thought that I recognised the countenances of several I had known on board the *Alexander*. Among them was a tall, slight young man, dressed as a sub-lieutenant. I looked at him earnestly, scanning his features. It might be Clement, yet I should not under other circumstances have thought it possible. The young man stopped, observing the way I was regarding him, and I began to doubt that he could be Clement, as he did not appear to know me. I could bear the uncertainty no longer, so, walking up to him, I said, "I am Happy Jack! Don't you know me?" His whole countenance lighted up. With a cry of pleasure he seized both my hands, gazing earnestly in my face. "Jack, my dear fellow, Jack!" he exclaimed. "You alive, and here! Happy you may be, but not so happy as I am to see you. I mourned you as lost, for I could not hope that you had escaped a second time." His surprise was great indeed when I told him I came especially to search for him, and we at once agreed to repair to the "George," that I might give him the important information I had to afford, and settle, with the aid of Mr. Munch, what course it would be advisable for him to pursue.

He was overwhelmed, as may be supposed, with astonishment and thankfulness when I told him of the wonderful way in which I had become possessed of the title-deeds and jewels, which would, I hoped, establish his claims to a fair estate.

This matter occupied some time. "With regard to quitting the ship," he observed, "there will, I trust, be no difficulty. I am but a supernumerary on board, and as I could not regularly enter the service till the frigate returned to Russia, the captain will be able to give me my discharge when I explain the circumstances in which I am placed."

Having settled our plans, Mr. Munch and I went on board with Clement. The captain at once agreed to what Clement wished, though he expressed his regret at losing him. My friend the doctor recognised me, and treated me, as did several of the other officers, with much kindness and politeness. I was, however, too anxious to get Clement home to accept their courtesy, and the next morning we were again on the road northward.

Clement had studied hard while on board the Russian frigate, and had become a polished and gentlemanly young man, in every way qualified for the position he was destined to hold. He was made not a little of by my family, and though at one time I felt a touch of jealousy at the preference I fancied he showed to Grace Goldie, he soon relieved my fears by telling me that he hoped to become the husband of one of my sisters.

My father, after a considerable amount of labour, proved his identity with the son of Mr. Clement Leslie, who perished with his wife at sea, and established his claims to the property.

I had had quite enough of a "life on the ocean wave," and though I had no great fancy for working all day at a desk, I agreed to enter my father's office and tackle to in earnest, my incentive to labour. I confess, being the hope of one day becoming the husband of Grace Goldie. We married, and I have every reason still to call myself "Happy Jack."

Uncle Boz;

OR, HOW WE SPENT OUR CHRISTMAS DAY, LONG, LONG AGO.

CHAPTER I.

THOSE were some of the pleasantest days of my boyhood which my brother Jack and I spent with Uncle Boz in his curious-looking abode on the shore of the loud-roaring, tumultuous German Ocean, or North Sea, as it is more frequently called. On the English shore, I should have said; for Uncle Boz would not willingly have lived out of our snug little, tight little island, had the wealth of the Indies been offered him to do so.

"It's unique, ain't it?" Uncle Boz used to say, as he pointed with a complacent air at his domicile. How Uncle Boz came to pick up that word *unique*, I do not know; had he been aware of its Gallic derivation, he would never have admitted it into his vocabulary—of that I am sure. Singular it certainly was; I doubt if any other edifice could have been found at all like it in the three kingdoms. It had been originally, when Uncle Boz first became its owner, a two-roomed cottage, strongly built of

86

roughly-hewn stone, and a coarse slate roof calculated to defy the raging storms which swept over it. It stood on a level space in a gap between cliffs, the gap opening on the sea, with a descent of some twenty feet or so to the sands.

Uncle Boz having made his purchase, and settled himself and his belongings in his new abode, forthwith began to build and improve; but as he was his own architect and builder, the expense was not so great as some folks find it, while the result was highly satisfactory to himself, whatever the rest of the world might have thought about the matter. First he added a wing; but as the room within it, though suited to his height, was not calculated for that of a tall shipmate who occasionally came to see him, he built another on the opposite side of the mansion, of the proper dimensions, observing that, should honest Dick Porpoise, another old shipmate, come that way, the first would exactly suit him; the said Dick amply making up in width for what he wanted in height.

Uncle Boz then found out that, though he could grill a chop before his dining-room fire, the same style of cooking would not suit a number of people; and so he erected what he called the Caboose, at the rear of his mansion. It certainly would not have been taken for what it was, had it not been for the iron flue which projected from the roof.

The greatest work Uncle Boz ever undertook with respect to his abode, was what he called "putting another deck on the craft." I think he must have summoned assistance, and that, relying on the sagacity of others, he did not, as he was wont, employ his own; for when the walls were up, the roof on, and the floors laid, it was discovered that there was no staircase. He was in no way disconcerted, but he had no fancy for pulling down; and so he built a tower outside, near the back door, to contain the staircase; and having got it flush with the roof, he said that it was a pity not to have a good look-out, and so ran it up a dozen feet or so higher, with a platform and a flagstaff at the summit. Several other rooms of different dimensions were added on after this, and numerous little excrescences wherever by any ingenuity they could be run out,— some to hold a bed, and others only a washhand-stand, a trunk or two, or a chest of drawers. No materials seemed to come amiss. A small craft laden with bricks was cast ashore, just as he was about to begin one of his rooms. This was therefore built with her cargo, as were several of the excrescences run out from the ground-floor, while rough stones, and especially wood cast on shore from wrecks, had been chiefly employed. Then his paint-brush was seldom idle; and, as he remarked, "variety is pleasant," he coloured differently every room, both inside and out, increasing thereby the gay appearance, if not the tasteful elegance, of the structure.

"Isn't it unique?" he asked for the hundredth time, as with paint brush in hand, he stood on the lawn in front, surveying the work he had just completed. There was something, however, much more unique present,—not the garden, nor the rock-work, nor the summer-house, nor the seats, nor the fountain, nor the fish pond, nor the big full-rigged ship in front, nor the weathercocks on the chimneys, but Uncle Boz himself, and his factotum and follower, Tom Bambo.

How can I describe Uncle Boz—that is to say, to do him justice? I'll try. He was short, and he was round, and he had lost a leg and wore a wooden one instead, and his face was full of the most extra-

ordinary krinklums and kranklums, wrinkles and
furrows they might by some have been called, but
all beaming with the most unbounded good nature ;
and his little eyes and his big mouth betokened
kindness itself. As to how they did this I cannot
tell. I know the fact, at all events. His head was
bald, the hair, he used to affirm, having been blown
off in a heavy gale of wind off Cape Horn, excepting
a few stumps, which he managed to keep on by
clapping both hands to the side of his head, to save
the rim of his hat when the crown was carried away.
But his nose—foes, if by possibility he could have
had any, might have called it a snub, or a button ;
supposing it was either one or the other, or both, it
was full of expression,—the best of snubs, the best
of button noses, all that expression betokening fun
and humour, and kindness and benevolence. Yes,
that dear nose of Uncle Boz's was a jewel, though
unadorned by a carbuncle. And Tom Bambo—
whereas Uncle Boz was white (at least, I suppose he
once had been, for he was now red, if not ruddy and
brown, with not a few other weather-stained hues),
Tom Bambo was the colour he had ever been since
he first saw the light on the coast of Africa,—
jet black. In other respects there was a strong
similarity. Uncle Boz had lost his left leg, Tom
his right. In height and figure they were wonderfully alike. Bambo's mouth was probably wider, and
his eyes rounder, and his teeth whiter, and his nose
snubbier, but there was the same good-natured
benevolent expression, the same love of fun and
humour ; and, indeed, it was impossible but to
acknowledge that the same nature of soul dwelt
within, and that the only difference between the
white man and the black was in the colour of their
skin. Yes, there was a difference : Uncle Boz had

G

lost his hair, while Bambo had retained, in its woolly integrity, a fine black fleece, which served to keep his cranium cool in summer and warm in winter. Bambo used to be called the shadow of Uncle Boz. A jolly, fat noonday shadow he might have been. He had followed him, I believe, round and round the world, and when at length Uncle Boz went into port, and was laid up in ordinary, Bambo, as a matter of course, did the same.

I have said what Uncle Boz was like, and the sort of house he lived in; but " Who was this Uncle Boz?" will be asked. Uncle Boz was not our uncle really, nor was he really the uncle of a very considerable number of boys and girls who called him uncle. I am not certain, indeed, that he was anybody's uncle: at least, I am very confident that dear old Aunt Deborah, who occasionally came to stay with him, and was his counterpart, barring the wooden leg, had no family, seeing that she was always addressed with the greatest respect as Miss Deborah. The real state of the case is this. Uncle Boz was beloved by all his shipmates, and his kind heart made him look upon all his brother officers as brothers indeed. One of them, shot down fighting for his country, as he lay on the deck in the agonies of death, entreated Uncle Boz, who knelt over him, to look after his two orphan boys.

" That I will, that I will, dear brother. There's One above hears me, and you'll soon met Him, and know that I speak the truth."

" Boz, you have always spoken the truth," whispered the dying lieutenant. " I trust in Him; I die happy."

The action was still raging. Another round-shot took off Uncle Boz's leg.

" I don't mind," he observed, as the surgeon

finished the job for him; "there's the pension to come, and that'll help keep poor Graham's children."

It's my belief that he did look after those children, as if he felt that God was watching everything he did for them, or said to them; and the best of fathers could not have managed them better. They both entered the navy, and were an honour to the service. They naturally called him uncle, and so their friends and other children of old shipmates came to call him so, we among others; and as we were always talking of what Uncle Boz had said and done, he became generally known by that name. His name wasn't Boz, though. His real name was Boswell. He was no relation, however, to Dr. Johnson's famous biographer, and he was a very different sort of person, I have an idea. I never saw him angry except once, when some one asked him the question.

"No, sir; I have the privilege, and I take it to be a great one, of being in no way connected with the dirty little lickspittle—there!" he replied, as if with a feeling of relief at having thus delivered himself.

Miss Deborah Boswell was shorter and more feminine than her brother, seeing that icy gales, and salt water, and hot suns had not played havoc with her countenance, but she was fully as round and jolly.

Uncle Boz was, as may have been surmised, a lieutenant in the navy. He got no promotion for losing his leg, and though he went to sea for some time after that, a lieutenant he remained, and what was extraordinary, a perfectly contented and happy one. Not a grumble at his ill fortune did I ever hear. Not a word of abuse hurled at the bigwigs at the head of affairs. And Tom Bambo,—Tom

Bambo had followed Uncle Boz for many long years over the salt ocean. Tom had been picked up (the only survivor of some hundreds) from a sunken slave ship off the coast of Africa. Uncle Boz had on that occasion hauled him with his own hands into the boat. He was grateful then. Falling overboard afterwards during a heavy gale, in the same locality, where sharks abounded, when all hope of being saved had abandoned him, Uncle Boz from the topsail of the ship saw him struggling.

"I cannot let that poor negro perish," he cried. "Pass me that grating." Grating in hand, he plunged overboard, swam to Bambo with it, and a boat being lowered, both were picked up. Bambo well understood the risk the brave lieutenant had run for his sake.

"Ah, Massa Boz, me lub you as my own soul," he exclaimed, coming up to him with tears in his eyes.

Uncle Boz had taught him that he had a soul.

Such were Uncle Boz, Aunt Deborah, Tom Bambo, and the house they lived in. I again repeat, I have spent the happiest days of my life with them. Holidays they really were. He seldom had less than five or six boys at a time with him stowed away in the before-mentioned little excrescences of the mansion. Summer or winter we liked both equally well. There was always a hearty, chirruping welcome for us, and even now I see before me those three honest, round, kind faces in the porch, Uncle Boz and Aunt Deborah in front, and Bambo in the rear, for being generally employed in the back premises, he was last on the scene, and it was physically impossible for him to pass his master and mistress.

The Christmas holidays arrived. A jolly journey we had of it; our pea-shooters were not inactive.

There were Jack, and I, and big Ned Hollis, and
David Fowler, and Tom and Harry King; Ned was
older than any of us, and had been at sea, and we
all looked up to him greatly. The friends of Uncle
Boz were mostly commanders and lieutenants,
surgeons, pursers, and marine officers. Now and
then he entered on his list a merchant he might
have met abroad, whose sons had no home to go to.
By this time the Grahams were at sea, fitted out by
Uncle Boz. Uncle Boz had had a good deal of
money come to him, and it's my belief that he could
have lived ten times better than he did, had he
spent it all upon himself, instead of thinking only
how he could do most good with it. The wheels of
the chaise which contained us youngsters rolled so
noiselessly over the snow, that not till the wicket
opened, and a secret bell which communicated with
the interior rung, did the tableau I have described
appear in the porch. There it was though, in all its
attractive freshness, by the time we had tumbled,
some of us head foremost, out of the chaise.

There was a blazing fire and a plentiful dinner,
and we were all soon as merry as crickets, telling
our adventures, Uncle Boz listening as if they were
important matters of state. It was bitterly cold
outside, or the snow would not have remained as it
did so close to the sea. We were looking forward
to skating the next day on a piece of water a mile
or so inland, and we were to build a snow man, and
a snow castle, which Uncle Boz undertook to defend
with Bambo against all assailants. Aunt Deborah
not being a combatant, was to be employed in the
heroine-like occupation of making ammunition for
both sides, in the shape of snowballs. It was
decided that we would in the first place build a
castle, and we were to commence early the next

morning; our only fear was that the snow might melt, but as there was a very satisfactory biting, black, northerly wind blowing, there was not much chance of that.

Our conversation all the evening was about saps and counter saps, of which Uncle Boz remarked that the red coats ought to know far more than he did; and this led him to talk of some of the scenes in which he had taken part, and Bambo was sent for to assist his memory, and together they enthusiastically fought their battles over again. They were like Uncle Toby and Corporal Trim, except that the ocean was their field of glory, and that the cut of the two old seamen's jibs was strongly in contrast to the figures of their brother red-coats. It was a pleasant evening, that it was. How their tongues wagged! How they flourished their legs of wood! Bambo seemed to be sitting on quicksilver, on the top of the wooden stool which he had brought in and placed near the door. His exclamations and gesticulations kept us in hearty roars of laughter, as he became interested in the account of any gallant deeds thus brought by Uncle Boz to his recollection. It is impossible, however, for me now to repeat any of their accounts. I may do so by-and-by, when I have got on a little more with my story, for story I have, and a very interesting one it ought to prove.

Breakfast over the next morning, having put all wheel-barrows, hand-barrows, and baskets we could find into requisition, we set to work to rear the stronghold to be defended. Such a castle as was the result never was seen before or since. Uncle Boz declared that he should be proud to defend it to the last gasp, Bambo echoing the sentiment. It was built on the side of the hill, with a perpendicular rock six feet high at least below it, and we all pro-

nounced the fortress equal to those of Gibraltar,
Ehrenbreitstein, San Sebastian, or any others of like
celebrity. Both defenders were armed with shields
—tops of saucepans—while, standing back to back,
they with them defended their heads, or bravely
bobbed as the snowy missiles flew towards them.
We made our attacks now on one side, now on the
other, they spinning round on their wooden legs
with astonishing rapidity, to meet them. At length
our general resolved to storm. The most difficult
side was chosen—where the cliff was steepest. A
feint was made on the opposite side, towards which
the defenders turned all their attention. We had
reached the summit. Our friends on the opposite side
pushed so vehemently against the walls, that an
impetus was given to the whole fabric. Thundering
over the cliff it came, with defenders and assailants,
and all together were buried in the ruins. Uncle Boz
soon scrambled out; but where was Bambo? At length
a brown stump was seen wagging faintly. "That's
his leg, haul away, boys," shouted Uncle Boz. We
hauled and dug with might and main, for we had
no small fear lest our black friend should be
smothered outright ; but the body followed the leg,
as we hauled, and happily there was not only life,
but activity in him, and jumping up, before we were
aware what he was about to do, he began to pelt us
so vehemently, that, amid shouts of laughter, we
were compelled to take to flight, and scamper down
the hill, Uncle Boz aiding him in following up the
victory.

That evening Uncle Boz showed us an apparatus
for sending a line on board a stranded ship, whether
invented or improved by him I am not prepared to
say, nor whether the projectile was a rocket or a
shot, or both, fired from a gun. Hollis, the eldest

of our party, who had considerable mechanical talent, seemed clearly to understand its use, I remember.

Great preparations had been made for Christmas-day. Such a turkey, such a piece of beef, and such a plum pudding! We went to church in the morning in spite of the distance, and a heavy gale blowing in our teeth coming back. Fine old English holly, with many a scarlet berry on it, adorned the church; and the instruments, violin, violoncello, flageolet, etc., etc., with the voices, were in great tune and wind; and the sermon was appropriate,—"Love, goodwill towards all men," just long enough to send us away in a happy temper, with its leading idea or principle in the heads, and may be in the hearts of some hearers. Our appetites, too, were sharpened by our walk, and the keen wind and the recollection of the appearance of our destined viands as we saw them displayed in Miss Deborah's larder. The wind was blowing strong on shore, not softened by its passage across the North Sea; the snow began to fall; thickly and more thickly it come down. "Stop," cried Uncle Boz, as we neared the cliff, "there's a gun!" We listened. The low, dull sound of a gun came across the seething, tossing ocean, but the ship from which it was fired was unseen. "She's a large ship, dismasted, possibly lost her anchors, or has no confidence in our holding ground. She is right. It is bad," he remarked; "firing to warn us to be on the look out for her. We'll do that same at all events, poor souls. Where will she drive ashore, though?" Stooping down, he listened attentively for some time, then standing up, he exclaimed, "She'll strike not far from this to the south'ard. Bambo, we must try to help them."

"Ay, ay, sir. Dat we will," cried Bambo.

"Then find out Dick Hawker, Sam Swattridge, and the rest. Tell them if they'll go I'll command them, and if they won't, that they're a set of cowardly ——. No, no, don't say that, they'll go fast enough."

While Bambo hobbled off to the neighbouring fishing village, where there was a small harbour, we accompanied Uncle Boz home. Near the harbour a fine boat was kept ready to launch, which, though not a professed lifeboat, from her having been fitted up by Uncle Boz, she possessed many of the necessary qualifications for dangerous service. As soon as we reached the house, Uncle Boz got out the apparatus I have described, and gave it in charge of Ned Hollis, with Tom King as his lieutenant, and the rest of us as crew. He directed us all to obey Hollis implicitly. Hollis had not only been at sea, but had already superior scientific attainments.

"Remember men's lives may depend on the way you manage that affair, lads. Now bear it along with you to the beach, to the spot where the ship is likely to come ashore. Deb, we'll be back for dinner I hope, and shall not have worse appetites. Perhaps we may have a guest or two," he added, as we went out.

We had not gone far before we met two of the coast-guard men, who had heard the firing. The head station, where the lieutenant resided, was at a considerable distance, and it was feared that he had gone in an opposite direction. Though the coast-guard men would be of great assistance, Hollis was still to have charge of the apparatus. Uncle Boz having speedily made his arrangements, hurried off to the village, while we continued our course along the beach. Behind us was a lofty sand-hill, and Hollis ordered King and me to climb up to try and discover the ship. It was bitter work, even on the beach, much worse for the poor fellows wet through and through at sea. At first, on reaching the top of the sand-hill, we could see nothing, but soon the snow fell less densely, and through it we discovered the dim outline of a large ship, now almost buried in the trough of the sea, now lifted to the foaming summit of a wave as she drove onward towards the beach. Her masts were gone, though her bowsprit remained. The tide was carrying her somewhat along the beach, so that it seemed as if she would drift not far from the harbour itself. While we were watching, the snow ceased falling, and our interest was now turned towards the boat with Uncle Boz and Bambo in her. She had just reached the mouth of the harbour. It was perilous work. Huge seas were rolling in. A lull was waited for. Out dashed the boat. It seemed as if it were impossible she could live amid those troubled waters. How we held our breath as we watched her progress. Now it seemed as if she were overwhelmed by the curling, foaming seas; then again she emerged and struggled on, buoyantly floating on their summits. To save the ship was beyond human power, but the wish of Uncle Boz was evidently to try and pilot her in between two rocks, where her crew might perhaps reach the shore. Lives are more generally lost when a ship drives on an open beach than when among rocks. In one instance the people may cling to the rocks, but the undertow from the beach sweeps them out as often as they struggle towards it, till their strength fails, and they sink beneath the waves. With a glass King had brought, we could see the people on the deck of the hapless craft. King handed it to me. "What do you see now?" he asked.

"Women as well as men, two or three at least,"
I exclaimed, almost breathless. "Poor creatures!
Oh, King, suppose there were children among
them!"

The ship rolled fearfully, while the seas meeting
with the resistance of her already water-logged hull
broke over it in showers of foam, which must have
frozen as they fell on her deck. Her crew were
huddled together, some forward and some with the
passengers aft. For her size there appeared to be
very few seamen. We told Hollis.

"When the masts went, many of them likely
enough went also," was his answer.

Hitherto they had not observed the boat. We
saw Uncle Boz waving to them. There was a movement among the men. They saw him; an attempt
was made to hoist a sail on the stump of the foremast. It was blown away in an instant.

"No anchor would hold; yet it is their only
chance," said Hollis. The coast-guard men agreed.

The attempt was made. We saw the crew cutting the stoppers. It was a moment of breathless
anxiety. "Yes, it holds," was shouted. The ship
brought up head to wind. The boat was making
way towards her.

"It will never hold," cried Hollis.

Now was the opportunity for the boat to get
alongside. Should the cable part, three minutes
would see the ship amid the cruel breakers. The
boat seemed almost stationary; the people on deck
stretched out their hands to her imploringly. Our
eyes ached with gazing on her. We thought not of
the biting wind, the piercing cold.

"She is driving," cried Hollis. "But—but—see!
see! Uncle Boz is alongside. Heaven protect
him!"

There was a rush to the side. Several persons were lowered into the boat. We saw others descending by ropes : whether they all got in we could not tell. Some remained on deck. The boat suddenly appeared at a distance from the ship.

"The cable has parted!" cried Hollis. "No hope for them now!"

We hurried along to where we saw the ship must strike. A huge roller seemed to lift her, and with a terrific crash down she came on the sand, the foaming sea instantly dashing over her, making every timber in her tremble, and tearing off large fragments of her upper works.

"The stoutest ship ever built couldn't stand those shocks many minutes," observed one of the coastguard men.

Hollis had planted his apparatus. A shot was fired, and the line fell over the wreck as the sea took one poor fellow who had let go his hold to clutch it. In vain he lifted up his hands to grasp some part of the wreck. He was borne helplessly into the seething caldron below. Now he was carried towards us. We could see his straining eyeballs, and his arms stretched out. In vain, in vain. The hissing roller, as it receded, swept him far away ; a shriek reached our ears, and we saw him no more. Such has been many a brave seaman's lot. Another seaman was more successful, the line was secured, and now we signalled to those on board to secure a stouter line that we might haul it on shore. One was found, and we began hauling away, but our united strength could only just do it. How should we ever get a cable taut enough to allow of the people passing safely along it? Happily at that moment several fishermen arrived with stout poles, boats' masts, and oars, and began planting them in the sand.

Then taking the rope in hand, they hauled it in with ease. A hawser had been made fast to the rope. That in the same way was got in, and the end secured to the poles. A traveller had been wisely placed on the hawser. The first man securing himself to it worked his way along, carrying a line with him. He was one of the mates. There were six more people on board alive, including the captain, he told us. The rest had been lowered into the boat, with the women and children. "Children out in such weather as this!" more than one of us exclaimed. But the boat; where was that? Now, for the first time, while the line which the brave mate had brought on shore was being hauled back, we had time to look out for her. I ran up the sand-hill. In vain I turned my eyes over the angry, foaming sea. Not a glimpse of the boat could I obtain. Down came the snow again. My heart sank within me. "Haul away!" I heard shouted. I ran to take my part. The big tears sprang to my eyes. I couldn't tell my companions what I feared. At last I could refrain no longer. "Oh Hollis! oh King! the boat has gone," I cried out, bursting into tears. "Uncle Boz! dear Uncle Boz and Bambo!" sobbed more than one of us.

"No fear, masters—no fear," exclaimed one of the fishermen. "The boat is in long ago, and the lieutenant and those he has saved from a watery grave are safe on shore, and on their way up to the house by this time."

How our hearts felt relieved, and if we didn't shout for joy, it was because they were too full for that. Well, I must cut my story short. Three more men came on shore safe; a fourth attempting to get along, trusting to his own strength without the traveller, was washed off, and in spite of a rush made into the water to save him, was carried back and lost. The brave captain was the last man to leave the ship, and scarcely had he reached the strand than a huge sea, like some great monster, with a terrific roar struck the wreck, and literally dashed her into a thousand fragments. I must not stop either to describe the appearance of the beach strewn with fragments of wreck, with cargo and baggage, or how the people from far and near collected to appropriate what they could, eager to secure a large booty before the proper authorities arrived to take possession of the property. Bambo, who appeared to invite all those we had rescued up to the house, satisfied us that Uncle Boz was safe. We hurried on with our companions, for we were all wet through, and bitterly cold. The house was hot enough when we got inside, for there were blazing fires in each room, Uncle Boz presiding over one, Bambo over the other, with saucepans and spoons, and a strong smell of port-wine negus pervading the atmosphere. In the dining-room, into which Miss Deborah did not venture, were five or six rolls of rugs, with rough human heads sticking out of them. In the drawing-room, the dear lady's own domain, was a large basket, serving as a cradle, in one corner, and two big chairs forming a bed in another; one occupied by an infant, the other by a little creature with fair face, and beautiful blue eyes, which would look up with bewildered gaze to watch what was going forward. Aunt Deb was deeply busied in grating nutmeg, squeezing lemons, and stirring up sugar.

"Oh, dear boys, run and change your clothes, or you'll all catch your death of cold!" she exclaimed.

Up we went, but soon discovered that she had forgotten to warn us that most of our rooms were

occupied. However, she recollected very quickly,
and hurrying, panting after us, brought us all dry
garments into Hollis' room.

The captain had followed us, and arrived as we
came back. Uncle Boz was about to make another
jorum of negus. He looked up, spoon in hand.
"Welcome on shore, 'tis no time for ceremony," he
cried out. "Always glad to receive a seaman in
distress. There, turn into my bed in the room
through there. Your men shall have rugs in the
other room there, till their clothes are dry."

Where was our Christmas dinner all this time?
That had the caboose to itself, and Bambo every
now and then stumped off to see how it was going
on, Miss Deborah also occasionally looking in for the
same purpose. By the time the dinner was cooked,
the seamen's clothes were dried, and then the table
was spread in the dining-room, and Uncle Boz,
standing up, asked a blessing on the food, and told
the shipwrecked seamen to fall to. Miss Deborah
carried off certain portions of the turkey and ham
up-stairs, and Uncle Boz, in like manner, took some
into his best guest-chamber, the one built for his
late shipmate. All I know is that every scrap had
disappeared before he found out that neither he nor
any of us had eaten a morsel. He winked to us to
say nothing about the matter, and Bambo soon after
placed on the drawing-room table some bread and
cheese, and a huge pile of gigantic mince-pies. We
demolished them, and I may honestly say that I
never more thoroughly enjoyed a Christmas dinner,
at least seeing one eaten.

I have a good deal more to say about that pair of
blue eyes, now closed by sleep in the arm-chair, and
those up-stairs to whom the little owner belonged;
but I must cry avast for the present. Well! there

is a satisfaction in toiling, and denying ourselves to do good to others, and to make them happy, and that is the reason why I have an idea that that same day I have been describing was one of the most satisfactory Christmas days I ever spent.

CHAPTER II.

MORE than a year had passed away since those Christmas holidays when the wreck happened, and my brother and I were again to become inmates of Uncle Boz's unique abode. It was midsummer; the trees were green, the air warm and balmy, the wind blew gently, and the broad blue sea sparkled brightly, and seemed joyously to welcome our return. A somewhat poetical notion; the fact being that we were so happy to get back to the dear old spot, and the dearer old people, that we could not help feeling that all the objects, inanimate as well as animate, on which our eyes rested were equally delighted to see us. Yes, I am certain of it. The yellow sand looked cleaner and yellower; the sun shone, and the wide ocean glittered more brightly; and the blue sky looked bluer, with the bold cliffs standing up into it; and the gulls' wings whiter, as they darted through the glowing atmosphere, than we had ever seen them before. At all events, there were certain animate objects who were delighted to see us, or we must have been very bad decipherers of the human countenance. There stood Uncle Boz, Aunt Deborah, and Bambo, and another personage who presented a very great contrast in personal appearance to any one of the three. Not from

being very tall, or very thin, or very grave, or very
sour-looking, or very white, or very ugly. The personage in question had none of these peculiarities.
Who said that Uncle Boz was ugly? He wasn't!
nor was Aunt Deborah, nor was Bambo. They
were all beautiful in their way; at least, I thought
so then, and do now. Well, but about this personage. There was a pair of large blue eyes—the
sky wasn't bluer, nor the sea more sparkling when
they laughed; and there was a face round them very
fair, with a delicate colour on the cheeks and lips.
I should like to see the coral which could surpass
them, polished ever so much. There was hair in
ringlets, adorning the face; not flaxen exactly,
though light with a tinge from the sun, or from
something which gave it a bright glow. This head
belonged to a little girl—very little, and fairy-
like, and beautiful. A different sort of beauty to
Bambo's or Uncle Boz's, or even to Aunt Deborah's. I don't indeed think that Aunt Deb ever
could have been like Katty Brand, even in her childhood's days, or if she had, she was very considerably
altered since then. The blue eyes opened wider
than ever with astonishment, and the lips parted, as,
jumping out of the carriage, we were kissed by Aunt
Deb, and had our hands wrung in the cordial grasp,
first of Uncle Boz, and then of jolly old Bambo.
It was evidently a matter of consideration in that
little head of Katty's how she should receive us.
We settled the point by each of us giving her some
hearty kisses, which I don't think offended her
much, though she did wipe her cheeks after the
operation, and we very soon became fast friends.

"She is a beauty," whispered Jack to Aunt Deb;
on which Aunt Deb nodded and smiled, as much as
to say, "Indeed she is."

H

We were soon discussing with Uncle Boz the programme for our summer amusements. We were to have salt-water fishing and fresh-water fishing, and shooting, and boating, and egg hunting, and shells and other curiosities were to be looked for on the sea-shore, and long walks were to be taken; and then we were to have bathing, and to learn to knot and splice, and to cut out and rig a ship; indeed, every moment of our time would be fully occupied.

Somebody wishes to know about the owner of those blue eyes. I first saw them, on the evening of the wreck, watching Aunt Deb performing certain culinary operations at the drawing-room fire. There is a sad story connected with the beautiful little owner of which I have not liked before to speak. I mentioned a lady in one room, and a gentleman in another, and a little baby in a basket. They all now lay at rest in the burying-ground of the church we went to that memorable Christmas morning.

We little thought at the time that there would be soon so many fresh occupants. The lady soon sank under the effects of her exposure on the stormy ocean that bitter winter's day. Her baby followed, and her husband did not survive many days. Katty alone of the family remained. She was too young to know the extent of her loss, or feel it long; and had Aunt Deborah been her mother's dearest friend, instead of a total stranger, she could not possibly have more tenderly cared for the little orphan. This event formed a melancholy termination to those Christmas holidays, and excited the warmest sympathy in our hearts for Katty Brand. We knew well, however, that she was in good hands while Uncle Boz and Aunt Deborah had charge of her. We were not disappointed. Hers was a happy life, and a brighter or sweeter little rosebud never was seen.

It may easily be supposed that she was a pet among us boys in the holidays, and each one of us would have gone through fire and water to serve her. Jack, who was somewhat emphatic in his assertions, declared that he would swim through hot pitch and burning sulphur, or sit on the top of an iceberg in the coldest day of an arctic winter, if so doing would give her a particle of pleasure. He was very safe in making the offer; for as she was the most sensible, amiable little creature in existence, it was not likely that she would ever thus test his regard. I must say that Miss Katty ran a very great chance of being spoiled between Uncle Boz and Aunt Deborah and Bambo, in spite of the wise saws about training children to which Uncle Boz continually gave utterance. "The little lady mustn't have her way, or mustn't do that thing," he was continually saying; but the little lady notwithstanding had her way, and did the very thing she wished. However, Aunt Deborah, with her watchful care, though loving the little creature as much as any one, managed quietly to correct the faults which would undoubtedly otherwise have sprung up in her character, and deeply grateful some one is to her for so doing. However, of that more anon. She was, of course, rather a pet than a playmate of us youngsters; but even the least sentimental among us considered her infinitely superior to any dog, even though he could have danced a hornpipe, or monkey, however full of tricks, or parrot, however talkative, which could have been provided for that purpose. As Aunt Deborah was not much addicted to rapid locomotion, nor accustomed to walk to any distance, Katty was her constant companion. Indeed, as we were out all day shooting, or fishing, or boating, with Uncle Boz or Bambo, we saw her, except on Sundays, only in the morning and evening. When by any chance Aunt Deborah was unable to go out with her, my brother Jack was always ready to take her place; and certainly no mother could have watched over the little creature with more gentle care. It happened that Aunt Deborah had caught a cold, and was compelled to keep the house; the rest of us were going out trout-fishing with Uncle Boz; but Jack made excuses for remaining behind, wishing, in fact, to offer his services to take Katty a walk, or perhaps a row in our boat, if Bambo could be spared to accompany him; if not, he proposed asking one of the fishermen from the village, should any be found sauntering about on the beach. As it happened, Bambo could not go; but Jack did not mind that, as he knew that Bill Cockle would be ready to accompany him. We left him working away at a vessel he was rigging, and waiting patiently till the afternoon, when Aunt Deborah would let Katty go out with him. We had a capital day's sport. Uncle Boz caught ten brace of trout, I killed five, and the rest not many less. We took our dinner with us, and discussed it sitting on a green bank, under the shade of a willow, with the rapid stream flashing and sparkling by over its pebbly bed at our feet. It would be a memorable day, we all agreed, as it was a most pleasant one. What trout-fisher cannot recall some such to his memory, not to be surpassed by others in subsequent years!

When we got back we found Aunt Deb in a state of agitation at the non-appearance of Katty and Jack. Bambo had gone out to look for them, and had not returned. We, of course, ran off immediately to the beach, expecting to find them there.

Neither up nor down on the beach were they to be
seen. We ran to where our boat was moored in the
little harbour; she was not there. We cast our
eyes over the sea: there were several specks in the
distance, undoubtedly boats; ours might be one of
them. There were also white sails in the horizon,
vessels sailing to or from Scottish ports. Every
fishing-boat had gone out; Uncle Boz's large boat
was hauled up, undergoing repairs. We saw Bambo
up at the village, making inquiries. Bill Cockle
had gone away early in one of the boats. The
women had been busily engaged in their houses, and
had not watched the harbour. I did not for one
moment believe that Jack would have taken Katty
into the boat, and pulled out of the harbour by himself; yet how to account for their disappearance?
Uncle Boz himself, tired as he was, very soon came
down to us. He seemed quite calm; but loving the
little girl as he did, I knew how anxious he must
have felt. Having first examined the boat, "She'll
float," he observed, and he then directed Bambo to
get her gear down from the boat-house in the village. The news spread that something was wrong,
and women and a few old men collected from all
sides to hear about it. The children also came, and
were seen talking among themselves. They had
seen something unusual. We tried to elicit what it
was. We, not without difficulty, discovered at last
that they had seen some strange people on the
beach; that they had come down in a cart or waggon, which had afterwards driven rapidly off; that
they had got into a small boat, and pulled away for
a lugger, which stood in to meet them. Uncle Boz
inquired where the coast-guard men had been at the
time. They had been summoned in different directions, so that none were near at hand.

"I see it all," he exclaimed; "the scoundrels! That is the way they take their revenge on me. They cannot have got far with this breeze; we must be after them."

It may seem surprising that Uncle Boz should have had any enemies—that he could have offended any one; but the fact that he had is only another proof that men who act uprightly cannot at all times avoid giving offence to the bad. This part of the coast was occasionally visited by smugglers from Dunkirk, as well as from the coast of Holland. Their vessels were manned by a mixture of Dutch, French, and English, and they were in league with Englishmen of various grades, who took charge of the goods they brought over. During the previous winter, a young man, struck down by sickness, and brought to repentance, sent, just as he was dying, to Uncle Boz, and revealed to him a plot, in which he was concerned, to run a large cargo, in doing which there was great risk that the lives both of coast-guard men and smugglers would be sacrificed. Uncle Boz instantly went off himself to the Inspecting-commander of the district; and so strong a force was sent down to the spot, and so sharp a look-out kept up along the coast, that the smugglers found their design impracticable, and were compelled to abandon it. Had the young smuggler survived, they would have wreaked their vengeance on him; but he was safe from them in his grave. Their rage, therefore, was turned towards Uncle Boz, as they had discovered that he had given the information, and assisted to make the arrangements which had defeated their plans. Although not wishing to act the part of a volunteer coast-guard man, Uncle Boz had always set his face against the smugglers, and spoke of their proceedings as lawless and wicked. "Black

is black, and white is white; and it is because
people will persist in calling black white that the
ignorant are left in their ignorance, and unable to
discern right from wrong," he used to observe, when
speaking on the subject. It seemed almost incredible,
however, that the smugglers, bad as they might be,
would maliciously injure a young boy and a little
child, even though they might suppose, as they probably did, that they were the children of the man
who had offended them. Still, such things had
been done before. There was no other way of
accounting for the disappearance of Jack and Katty.
Jack would never have put off in the boat by himself. Had he done so she would still be visible,
and there had been no wind to upset her. He
would certainly not have remained out so long willingly; besides, the account given by the children,
who had seen the strangers come down to the beach
and push off in a boat, seemed to settle the question.

We had still to wait for a crew. Uncle Boz sent
up to the house for his tools, and an old carpenter
in the village lent a hand, and they, with Bambo,
worked away to get the boat ready for sea. We,
meantime, hunted among the rocks along the shore
for any traces of the missing ones, not without a
feeling of fear and dread that we might discover
some; then we searched the cliffs, and every cave
and cranny we could think of. Poor Aunt Deborah
came down, when at length her fears had been
aroused, to ascertain what had become of her little
darling. I never saw her so grieved and agitated
before. I was afraid that she would blame Jack;
but not a word against him did she utter. On the
contrary, she could only say, " Poor, poor fellow!
I know that he would die sooner than let the
sweet angel be injured; and if she has gone, so has

he." Before I heard her say that I had not realised what might have happened, and I burst into tears. While we were waiting, in the hopes that some of the men for whom Uncle Boz had sent might be found, one of the specks in the distance, which we knew to be boats, was seen approaching. Slowly she drew nearer and nearer the shore. We watched her anxiously. She might bring us some information. At length she was seen to be a fishing-boat. We hurried down to the beach, as with a light breeze she came skimming in over the calm sea. The first person who jumped out of her was Bill Cockle.

" Have you seen Jack? Have you seen Katty Brand?" I eagerly cried out.

Bill pulled off his hat, scratched his head, and with a look of astonishment, turning round his head as if some one had hit him, exclaimed, " No! Why, what's happened?"

We told him. On which giving a slap on his thigh, and a hitch to his waistband, with a forcible expression, which I need not repeat, he exclaimed, " The villains! That's what we saw, then. We couldn't make it out. Well, I didn't——"

" What was it you saw? What happened? Say, say!" we all exclaimed in one breath.

Cockle's explanation was somewhat long, and sorely tried our patience. He and his mates had hauled in about half of one of their long nets, when a large lugger, they had not before seen, passed them, very nearly running them down. She stood close in, and exchanged signals with the shore. A boat in a little time was seen to come off with several people in her, and Cockle declared that he had seen a boy handed up the side of the lugger, and he was nearly certain a baby or little child. The lugger then hoisted in the boat, and made sail to the southward. As, however, there had been either a calm, or but a slight breeze ever since, from the southward, she could not have got far. This seemed to settle the question. We had now collected enough men to form a crew. We required arms and authority for boarding the lugger. Edward Grahame was with us, but though a midshipman, dressed in his uniform, with a dirk by his side, he could scarcely in his own person answer all our requirements. He was of course to go, and, to my great satisfaction, Uncle Boz gave me leave to be of the party, in consideration that it was my brother who was lost. The rest went back somewhat unwillingly to attend on Aunt Deborah. In spite of her grief, Aunt Deborah recollected that we could not live without eating, and had gone home to provide as large a store of provisions as the house could furnish. The men, meantime, got some kegs with water, and several loaves of bread and a cheese. We all ran backwards and forwards bringing the provisions Aunt Deborah had provided. We were not likely to starve, even though we might have had a chase of many days before we should overtake the lugger.

Though we had collected all the weapons to be found, we were not over well armed. "Never mind, lads," cried Uncle Boz, "we have the boat's stretchers, stout hearts, and a right cause, and if we can once get alongside the villains, there's no fear but that we'll win back our little jewel, and give them some broken heads for the trouble of heart and body they've caused us."

"Yes, dat we will," echoed Bambo, flourishing a heavy handspike over his head, with a vehemence which showed that age had not impaired his vigour. "We will treat dem as we did dem picarooning villains in de Vest Indies, ven you led de boarders, massa Boz, eh !"

"And you followed close at my side, and saved my life, Bambo," cried Uncle Boz. " Shove away boys, lift her handsomely, she'll be afloat directly."

We were running the heavy boat down the beach into the water. Just as we were about to shove off, who should appear but Lieutenant Kelson, of the coast-guard, with two of his men.

" There's not much chance that he'll ever set the Thames on fire," I heard Uncle Boz once remark of him, from which I concluded that he was not a very bright genius. However, he was now cordially welcomed. He possessed the authority we wanted. His men were well armed, and would help us in fighting, of which I had a secret hope that we should enjoy a fair amount. I did not know what fighting was in those days. I had never seen blood drawn— human beings in the pride of manhood, shot down, and mangled and torn by shot and shell and langrage fired by brethren's hands, writhing and shrieking in their death agony. Fighting may be a necessary evil, but an evil it is, and a dreadful one too. Mr. Kelson hearing what had occurred, agreed to come, and he jumping in with his men, off we shoved amid the cheers of all who remained on shore, and their good wishes for our success. The men let fall their oars. Bob Grahame and I had one between us, and Uncle Boz steered ; Kelson sitting like an admiral in his barge, and doing nothing. The little wind there had been fell completely, that was just what we wanted. If the calm continued, we should be nearly certain to come up with the lugger. Though the days were long, the sun was sinking down over the land, amid a rich orange glow which suffused the whole western sky. We were anxious before daylight had gone to catch sight of the lugger, lest we might pass her during the night. Fast as she was, however, with the light breeze which had been blowing for a short time, she might have slipped along through the water for a considerable distance. Cockle reported that she had edged off from the coast, and so having no other course to choose, we steered in the same direction, at the same time keeping a bright look-out in-shore, lest she might have afterwards kept in again, in the hopes of a chance of running some contraband. Several of the revenue cutters on the station had gone into port to refit, and the smugglers were just now indulging themselves, as do mice when the cat's away. Numerous vessels were seen in the offing, but none of them like the lugger. We pulled steadily on. It was not likely that the smuggler would have gone much to the eastward, as she was probably bound for the coast of Holland or France. We should be certain, therefore, to come up with her. Twilight lessened, and darkness was gathering round us, when the moon, a vast globe of golden hue, rose out of the water, and as she shot upwards, cast a brilliant sparkling pathway of light athwart its surface. Never was I out in a more glorious night. Had we not had serious work before us, it was one to engross all our thoughts. Even the fish seemed to enjoy it, as we could see them leaping up on either hand. Many of them must have been big fellows, by the loud splash they made. On, on we pulled. "If we don't soon come up with her, it will make our fellows very savage," observed Kelson to Uncle Boz.

"Yes, we eat 'um," cried out Bambo, who was a privileged joker.

The remark was appreciated by the other men.

"Yes Bambo, a jolly good supper we'll make of

them, the waggabonds," sung out one of the other men.

It was time, however, for real supper, so we knocked off rowing, and provisions, with grog, were served out, and not sorry I was to rest my arms. A capital supper was made, and the crew seemed to enjoy it much. Once more, with renewed strength, we took to our oars. To pull all night long, with the chance of a fight at the end of it, is not so pleasant as lying snugly in bed; but, under the circumstances, I infinitely preferred being where I was—eagerness gave strength to our arms. We could not go on much longer without falling in with her, it was thought.

"It depends whether she is full or empty," observed the lieutenant. "If the latter, she'll be making the best of her way across to the Continent; but if she's full she'll be hovering about the coast for the chance of running her cargo. She'll probably just now have her canvas lowered on deck, so that it will be a hard job to make her out."

There seemed wisdom in this remark, but as she could have run some of her cargo when she stood in in the afternoon if she had had any on board, the general opinion was that she was steering a course for Dunkirk, to which a smuggling lugger frequenting the coast was known to belong, and it was thought that she must be that same lugger. All we hoped for was that the calm would continue. We were pulling steadily on, the men chatting with each other, when Mr. Kelson sung out, "Silence! a sail a-head!" I could not help looking anxiously over my shoulder to ascertain what she was. I could just discern a dark object no great height out of the water.

"She's the lugger, I really think," observed Mr. Kelson. "I hope she may have some tubs aboard."

" I pray that she may have the dear children safe," said Uncle Boz.

" Yes, she's a lugger, there's no doubt about that," remarked the lieutenant.

Everyone was now on the alert, and I saw the men feeling that their weapons were ready for use. My heart beat considerably quicker than usual. We neared the stranger.

" Pull out of stroke, lads," said Uncle Boz. " They'll take us for some merchantman's crew."

There were several men we could see on the deck of the lugger. It was very difficult to prevent ourselves from dashing up alongside in the way our feelings would have dictated. It seemed strange, however, that they did not exhibit any alarm at our approach. Uncle Boz steered as if going to pass her, then suddenly shearing the boat alongside, we jumped on board.

" Well, what is all this about?" exclaimed a man standing aft, no one offering a show of resistance.

" That we are in His Majesty's revenue service, and that you are our prisoners," cried Lieutenant Kelson.

" That we have contraband on board, or that you have a right to detain us, must be proved," said the master calmly. " Step below, you will find my papers correct ; there is some mistake, I suspect."

The lieutenant went down into the little cabin and I followed, half hoping to find Jack and Katty ; but not a sign of them was there. Uncle Boz now came below ; when the mate saw him he exclaimed, " Ah, sir, I know you ; I was second mate of the *Rosamond*, wrecked near your house, when you saved our lives and treated us all so kindly. What has happened?" Uncle Boz told him.

" Then I'll help you if I can," said the master.

"A lugger with sweeps passed us not an hour ago, quite close. I had an idea I knew the fellow, and but little honesty is there in him. Do you pull on as before, and I will follow if there comes a breeze, and lend a hand should you want me."

There was no time for talking, and as the vessel was evidently honest, we tumbled into our boat and pulled on as lustily as before.

We soon caught sight of another vessel. "Hurrah! there she is," cried Uncle Boz. "The fellows won't balk you this time; but we must go alongside as we did the other."

The lugger had taken in her sweeps, having got well off from the land. As we drew near we began to pull carelessly as before. The people on her deck evidently did not know what to make of us. They seemed, however, satisfied, for several continued to walk up and down the deck, as they had at first been doing, hands in pockets. We quickly made them draw them out though. The boat in another instant was alongside, and we were leaping on deck. Oaths in Dutch, French, and English burst from the lips of the crew.

"We are betrayed," shouted the captain of the lugger. "But cheer up, lads. Overboard with the fellows!"

As he began to show fight, a knock on the head silenced him, and the crew on deck quickly succumbed. The lieutenant and his men jumped below, and secured several of the men in their berths. Uncle Boz and I meantime made our way into the cabin. A bright lamp hung from a beam above. On a locker was seated my brother Jack, Katty resting on one arm, while with his other hand he was feeding her with gruel from a basin held by a tall thin old Frenchman, dressed in a faded suit. of

ancient cut, and a white nightcap on his bald head.
I should have said had been feeding, for the process
was arrested by the noise on deck. They all looked
up as we entered, and Katty in her eagerness upset
the basin as she sprang forward to throw herself into
Uncle Boz's arms. She instantly ran back and
took Jack by the hand, crying out, " Dear Jack
couldn't help it. If he bigger, he wouldn't let naughty
smuggler carry me away."

They had not been ill-treated ; the old Frenchman
especially had been very kind to them.

" Ah ! yes, I have von littel grandchild lik dat at
home," he remarked.

So sudden had been our attack that we found
plenty of things on board to condemn the vessel ;
while, of course, those concerned would be tried for
the abduction of Jack and Katty. As the old Frenchman was clearly only a passenger, he was put on board
the lugger we had previously boarded. I was glad
that he escaped, on account of his kindness to sweet
Katty and Jack, though I suspect that he was an
absconding debtor. I should think, however, that his
creditors might as well have tried to skin a flint as
him. We carried the lugger in off the coast-guard
station, where more hands were put on board.
Before noon we had placed sweet Katty in Aunt
Deb's loving arms, not much the worse for her
excursion.

Jack went to sea, and Katty's cabinet was adorned
with numberless articles strange and beautiful from
all parts of the world. Jack, of course, wherever he
could get a run on shore, had to come and inspect
them. By many a gallant deed he won his commander's commission, and then Katty became his
fond, devoted wife.

In that old churchyard high above the German

Ocean are three small monuments placed by some loving friends of those who lie beneath. To no one more truly can the epitaph be applied than that which is cut on each tomb—that of the brother, of the sister, and of the faithful African—*Hic jacet in pace.*

"San Fiorenzo" and her Captain.

THERE was not a happier ship in the service, when I joined her towards the end of the year 1794, than the gallant *San Fiorenzo*, Captain Sir Harry Burrard Neale, and those were not days when ships were reckoned little paradises afloat, even by enthusiastic misses or sanguine young midshipmen. They were generally quite the other thing.

The crews of many ships found it that other thing, and the officers, of course, found it so likewise. If the men are not contented, the officers must be uncomfortable; and, at the same time, I will say, from my experience, that when a ship gained the title of a hell-afloat, it was always in consequence of the officers not knowing their duty, or not doing it. Pride, arrogance, and an utter disregard for the feelings of those beneath them in rank, was too prevalent among the officers of the service, and was the secret of the calamitous events which occasionally happened about that time.

My noble commander was not such an one as

those of whom I have spoken. There were some
like him, but not many his equals. I may truly say
of him "that he belonged to the race of admirals of
which the navy of Old England has a right to be
proud ; that he was a perfect seaman, and a perfect
gentleman." "He was one of the most humane,
brave, and zealous commanders that ever trod a
deck, to whom every man under him looked up as a
father." I was with him for many, very many
years—from my boyish days to manhood,—and I
may safely say that I never saw him in a passion,
or even out of temper, though I have seen him
indignant ; and never more so than when merit—
the merit of the junior officers of the service—has
been overlooked or disregarded. I never heard him
utter an oath, and I believe firmly that he never
allowed one to escape his lips. I will say of him
what I dare say of few men, that, in the whole
course of his life, he was never guilty of an act
unworthy of the character of a Christian and a
gentleman. I was with him when his career was
run—when, living in private on his own estate, the
brave old sailor, who had ever kept himself unspotted
from the world, spent his days in "visiting the
fatherless and widows in their affliction"—walking
from cottage to cottage, with his basket of provisions or medicines, or books, where the first were
not required.

Genuine were the tears shed on his grave, and
hearty was the response as the following band gave
forth the air of "The Fine Old English Gentleman,
all of the Olden Time !"

And now, on the borders of his estate, visible afar
over the Solent Sea,* there stands a monument, raised

* The "Solent Sea" is the name of the channel between the
Isle of Wight and the mainland.

by his sovereign and by those who knew and loved
him well, all eager to add their testimony to his
worth.   But yet he lives in the heart of many a
seaman, and will live while one remains who served
under his command.   But, avast! whither am I
driving?   My feelings have carried me away.

After what I have said, it is not surprising that
the *San Fiorenzo* should have been a happy ship.
Her captain made her so.   From the highest to the
lowest, all trusted him; all knew that he had their
interest at heart—all loved him.   The *San Fiorenzo*
might have been a happy ship under an inferior
commander—that is possible; but I doubt very
much whether her crew would have done what they
did do under any officer not possessed of those high
qualities for which Sir Harry was so eminently distinguished.   The *San Fiorenzo* was highly honoured,
for she was the favourite ship, or rather, Sir Harry
was the favourite captain of His Majesty George the
Third, who, let people say what they will of him,
was truly the sailors' friend, and wished to be his
subjects' friend, as far as he had the power.   Sir
Harry was a favourite, not because he was a flatterer,
but because the King knew him to be an honest man.

George the Third, as is well known, was very fond
of spending the summer months at Weymouth,
whence he could easily put to sea in his yacht, or on
board a man-of-war, placed at his disposal.   He
seemed never to tire of sailing, especially with Sir
Harry.

Whist was the constant game in the royal cabins.
Sir Harry, who did everything as well as he could,
though far from a good player, often beat the King,
who was an indifferent one.   Lord A——, a prac-
tised courtier, was, on the contrary, a remarkably
good one, and generally beat Sir Harry.   When,

however, Lord A—— played with the King, His Majesty always came off victorious. The King used to pretend to be exceedingly puzzled.

"It's very odd—very odd. I beat Lord A——, Lord A—— beats Sir Harry, and Sir Harry beats me. How can it be—how can it be?"

The King was always anxious to stand out to sea, so as to lose sight of land. This, however, was too dangerous an amusement to allow him. Sir Harry's plan was to put the ship's head off-shore, and to make all sail. This satisfied the King, who was then easily persuaded to go below to luncheon, dinner, or tea, or to indulge in his favourite game. Sail was soon again quietly shortened, and the ship headed in for the shore. Sometimes the King seemed rather surprised that we should have made the land again so soon; but whether or not he suspected a trick, I cannot say. His only remark was, "All right, Sir Harry; you are always right."

It was impossible for a monarch to be more condescending and affable than was the good old King to all on board. He used to go among the men, and talk to them in the most familiar way, inquiring about their adventures and family histories, and evidently showing a sympathy with their feelings and ideas. Did they love the old King? Ay, there was not a man of them who would not gladly have died for him. It was the same with the midshipmen and officers. He used to delight in calling up us youngsters, and would chat with us as familiarly as would any private gentleman. He showed his real disposition, when able thus to cast aside the cares of state, and to give way to the kindly feelings of his heart. I say again, in that respect the King and his captain were worthy of each other. The following anecdote will prove it:—

We had gone to Portsmouth, leaving the King at Weymouth, and were returning through the Needles, when, as we got off Poole harbour, a small boat, with three people in her, was seen a little on the starboard bow. One man was rowing, the other two persons were beckoning, evidently towards the ship. As we drew near, we saw, through our glasses, that the two people were an old man and woman, and, as we appeared to be passing them, their gestures became more and more vehement. Many captains would have laughed, or taken no notice of the old people. Not so Sir Harry—he had a feeling for everyone. Ordering the ship to be hove to, he allowed the boat to come alongside.

"Oh, captain, is our ain bairn Davie on board?" shouted the old people, in chorus.

Sir Harry, with the benignant smile his countenance so often wore, directed that they might be assisted up the side.

"Who is it you want, good people?" he asked, as soon as their feet were safely planted on the deck, where they stood, gazing round with astonished countenances.

"Our ain son, Davie—David Campbell, sir," was again the reply.

"Is there any man of that name on board?" inquired Sir Harry. "Let him be called aft."

A stout lad soon made his appearance, and was immediately pressed in the old people's arms. This son was a truant, long absent from his home. At length, grown weary at delay, quitting their abode near Edinburgh, they had travelled south, inquiring at every port for their lost son, and only that morning had they arrived by waggon at Poole, believing that it was a port where men-of-war were to be found. A boatman, for the sake of a freight, had persuaded them to come off with him, pointing out the ship which was then coming out through the Needles.

Sir Harry was so pleased with the perseverance and affection which the old couple had exhibited, that he took them on to Weymouth, when the story was told to the King. His Majesty had them presented to him, and he and Queen Charlotte paid them all sorts of attention, and at length, after they had spent some weeks with their son, dismissed them, highly gratified, to their home in the North.

Queen Charlotte was as good a woman as ever lived, and, in her way, was as kind and affable as was the King. She had a quaint humour about her, too, which frequently exhibited itself, in spite of the somewhat painful formality of the usual court circle. As an example—Sir Harry had had a present of bottled green peas made to him the previous year, and, looking on them as a great rarity, he had kept them to be placed on the table before his royal guests. As he knew more about ploughing the ocean than ploughing the land, and affairs nautical than horticultural, it did not occur to him that fresh green peas were to obtained on shore. The bottled green peas were therefore proudly produced on the first opportunity.

"Your Majesty," said Sir Harry, as the Queen was served, "those green peas have been kept a whole year."

The Queen made no reply till she had eaten a few, and sent several flying off from the prongs of her fork. Then, nodding with a smile, she quietly said, "So I did tink."

To the end of his days, Sir Harry used to laugh over the story, adding, "Sure enough, they were very green ; but as hard as swan-shot."

But I undertook to narrate a circumstance which exhibited Sir Harry Burrard Neale's character in its true colours.   I need not enter into an account of that painful event, the Mutiny of the British Fleet. It broke out first at Spithead, on the 15th April, 1797, on board Lord Bridport's flag-ship, the *Royal George;* the crews of the other ships of the fleet following the example thus set them.   The men, there can be no doubt, had very considerable grievances of which to complain; nor can it be well explained how, in those days, they could by legal means have had them redressed.   One thing only is certain, mutiny was not the proper way of proceeding.   We were at Spithead, and not an officer in the fleet knew what was about to occur, when, on the 14th, two of our men desired to speak with the captain, and then gave him the astounding intelligence that the ships' companies of the whole fleet had bound themselves to make certain important demands, and which, if not granted, that they would refuse to put to sea.   The two men—they were quartermasters—moreover, stated that they had themselves been chosen delegates to represent the ship's company of the *San Fiorenzo*, by the rest of the fleet, but that they could assure him that all the men would prove true and loyal, and would obey their officers as far as was consistent with prudence.

Sir Harry thanked them, assuring them, in return, that he would trust them thoroughly.   He, however, scarcely believed at that time the extent to which the mischief had gone.   The next day evidence was given of the wide spread of the disaffection.   Affairs day after day grew worse and worse; and although some of the superior officers acted with great judgment and moderation, others very nearly drove matters to the greatest extremity.

Meantime, the delegates of the *San Fiorenzo* attended the meetings of the mutineers, and, though at the imminent risk of their lives, regularly brought Sir Harry information of all that occurred. He transmitted it to the Admiralty, and it was chiefly through his representations and advice that conciliatory measures were adopted by the Government. Nearly all the just demands of the seamen having been granted, they returned to their duty and it was supposed that the mutiny was at an end. Just before this, the Princess Royal had married the Duke of Wirtemberg, and the *San Fiorenzo* had been appointed to carry Her Royal Highness over to Cuxhaven. We could not, however, move without permission from the delegates. This was granted. Our upper-deck guns were stowed below, and the larger portion of the upper-deck fitted with cabins. In this condition, when arriving at Sheerness, we found to our surprise that the red flag was still flying on board the guardship, the *Sandwich*. Supposing that her crew had not been informed of what had taken place at Spithead, Sir Harry sent our delegates on board her, that they might explain the real state of affairs. The disgust of our men was very great when they were informed that fresh demands had been made by the crews of the North Sea fleet, of so frivolous a nature that it was not probable they would be granted. Our men, in spite of the character of delegates, which had been forced on them, could not help showing their indignation, and expressing themselves in no very courteous terms. This showed the mutineers that they were not over-zealous in their cause, and our people were warned that, should they prove treacherous, they and their ship would be sent to the bottom.

On returning on board, they informed Sir Harry
of all that had occurred. Our delegates, at his
suggestion, immediately communicated with those
of the *Clyde*, an old fellow-cruiser, commanded by
Captain Cunningham.   That officer, on account of
his justice, humanity, and bravery, enjoyed, as did
Sir Harry, the confidence of his ship's company.
An arrangement was therefore made between the
captains and their crews that, should the mutineers
persevere in their misconduct, they would take the
ships out from amidst the fleet, fighting our way, if
necessary, and run for protection under cover of the
forts at Sheerness.   Every preparation was made.
We waited till the last moment.   The mutineers
showed no disposition to return to their duty.   The
Clyde was the in-shore ship; she was therefore to
move first.*   We watched her with intense interest,
while we remained still as death.   Not one of our
officers appeared on deck, and but few of the men,
though numerous eager eyes were gazing through
the ports.   The *Clyde* had springs on her cables, we
knew, but as yet not a movement was perceptible.
Suddenly her seamen swarmed on the yards, the
topsails were let fall and sheeted home.   She canted
the right way.   Hurrah! all sail was made.   Away
she went; and, before one of the mutinous fleet
could go in chase, she was under the protection of
the guns on shore.   It was now our turn; but we
had not a moment to lose, as the tide was on the
turn to ebb, when we should have had it against us.
What was our vexation, therefore, when the order
was given to get under weigh, to find that the pilot,

---

* The plan was proposed and executed by the late Mr. W.
Bardo, pilot, then a mate in the navy. He returned to the
San Fiorenzo, and piloted her as he had the *Clyde*, when her own
pilot refused to take charge.

either from fear, incompetency, or treachery, had declared that he could not take charge of the ship! Sir Harry would have taken her out himself; but the delay was fatal to his purpose, and before we could have moved, boats from the other ships were seen approaching the *San Fiorenzo*. They contained the delegates from the fleet, who, as they came up the side, began, with furious looks, to abuse our men for not having fired into the *Clyde*, and prevented her escaping. High words ensued, and so enraged did our men become at being abused because they did not fire on friends and countrymen, that one of the quartermasters, John Aynsley by name, came aft to the first lieutenant, and entreated that they might be allowed "to heave the blackguards overboard."

A nod from him would have sealed the fate of the delegates. I thought then (and I am not certain that I was wrong) that we might at that moment have seized the whole of the scoundrels, and carried them off prisoners to Sheerness. It would have been too great a risk to have run them up to the yardarm, or hove them overboard, as our men wished, lest their followers might have retaliated on the officers in their power.

No man was more careful of human life than Sir Harry, and it was a plan to which he would never have consented. The delegates, therefore, carried things with a high hand, and, convinced that our crew were loyal to their king and country, they ordered us to take up a berth between the *Inflexible* and *Director*, to unbend our sails, and to send our powder on board the *Sandwich*, at the masthead of which ship the flag of the so-called Admiral Parker was then flying. That man, Richard Parker, had been shipmate with a considerable number of the crew of the *San Fiorenzo*, as acting lieutenant, but had been dismissed his ship for drunkenness, and having lost all hope of promotion, had entered before the mast.

Our people had, therefore, a great contempt for him, and said that he was no sailor, and that his conduct had ever been unlike that of an officer and a gentleman. Such a man, knowing that he acted with a rope round his neck, was of course the advocate of the most desperate measures. Everything that took place was communicated immediately to Sir Harry, who advised the men to pretend compliance, and, much to our relief, the other delegates took their departure. As soon as they were gone, Sir Harry told the ship's company that, provided they would agree to stand by him, he would take the ship into Sheerness, as before intended. The men expressed their readiness to incur every possible risk to effect that purpose. The almost unarmed condition of the ship at the time must be remembered. The men set zealously to work to prepare for the enterprise. Springs were got on our cables. All was ready. The flood had made. The object was to cast in-shore. The men were at their stations. We were heaving on the spring—it broke at the most critical moment, and we cast outward. There was no help for it. Nothing could prevent us from running right in among the two ships of the mutinous fleet which I have mentioned, and which lay with their guns double shotted, and the men at quarters, with the lanyards in their hands, ready to fire at us. Our destruction seemed certain; but not for a moment did our captain lose his presence of mind. Calm as ever, he ordered the quartermaster Aynsley to appear on deck as if in command, while the officers concealed themselves in different parts of

the ship, he standing where he could issue his orders
and watch what was taking place.   All was sheeted
home in a moment, and we stood in between the
two line-of-battle ships, the *Director* and *Inflexible*.
The ship, by this time, had got good way on her.
It appeared that we were about to take up the berth
into which we had been ordered, when Sir Harry
directed that all the sheets should suddenly be let
fly.   This took the mutineers so completely by surprise, that not a gun was then fired at us.   Sir
Harry next ordered the helm to be put "hard-a
port," which caused the ship to shoot a-head of the
Inflexible—we were once more outside our enemies.
Springing immediately on deck, he took the command, crying out, in his encouraging tone, "Well
done, my lads—well done!"

A loud murmur of applause and satisfaction was
heard fore and aft; but we had no time for a cheer.

"Now clear away the bulkheads, and mount the
guns," he added.

Every man flew with a hearty will to obey his
orders.   And need there was; for scarcely were the
words out of his mouth than the whole fleet of
thirty-two sail opened their fire on us.   The shot
flew like hail around us, and thick as hail, ploughing
up the water as they leaped along it, chasing each
other across the surface on every side of the ship.
We could have expected nothing else than to be sunk
instantly, had we had time for consideration; but,
as it was, wonderfully few struck our hull, while not
a shroud was cut away, nor was a man hurt.   The
huge *Director*, close to us, might have sent us to
the bottom with a broadside, but not a shot from
her, that we could see, came aboard us.

"They have not the heart to fire at us, the blackguards!" observed one of the men near me.

"It may be that, Bill; but, to my mind, they're struck all of a heap at seeing the brave way our captain did that," answered another. "If we'd had the guns mounted he'd have fired smack into them. We send our powder aboard that pirate Parker's ship! we unbend our sails to please such a sneaking scoundrel as he!"

"It's just this, that the misguided chaps are slaves against their will, and they haven't become bad enough yet to fire on their countrymen, and maybe old friends and shipmates," said a third.

Such were the opinions generally expressed on board. It was reported afterwards that the *Director* fired blank cartridges, and this may have been the case, but I think more probably that her people were first struck with astonishment at our manœuvre, and then, with admiration at the bravery displayed, purposely fired wide of us. As, however, we were frequently struck, some shots by traitorous hands must have been aimed at us from her, or from some of the other ships. In little more than two hours the bulkheads were cleared away from the cabin door, to the break of the quarter-deck (the whole space having, as I before said, been fitted up with cabins for the suite of Her Royal Highness). The guns on both sides were got up from the hold and mounted, and we were ready for action. As soon as the task was accomplished, the men came aft in a body, and entreated, should any ships be sent after us by the mutineers, that they might be allowed to fight to the last, and go down with our colours flying, rather than yield, and return to the fleet at the Nore.

Sir Harry readily promised not to disappoint their wishes.

We stood on, but as yet no sign was perceptible

of chase being made after us. It was possible, we thought, that no ship's company could be induced to weigh in pursuit. They well knew that we should prove a tough bargain, had any single ship come up with us. Should we prove victorious, every man might have been hung as a pirate. As to Parker, he dared not leave his fleet, as he ventured to call it.

Our master, although a good navigator, did not feel himself justified in taking charge of the ship, within the boundaries of a Branch pilot, and we were therefore on the look-out for a pilot vessel, when a lugger was discovered on the lee-bow, and we were on the point of bearing down to her, when we made out first a ship or two, then several sail, and lastly, a whole fleet, which we guessed must be the North Sea Fleet standing for the Nore. We were steering for them, to give the admiral notice of what had occurred, when the red flag was discovered flying on board them also. They had, as it appeared, left their station in a state of mutiny, having placed the admiral and all the officers under arrest. To avoid them altogether was impossible, and before long a frigate bore down to us. Should our real character be discovered, we must be captured by an overwhelming force. Still Sir Harry remained calm and self-possessed as ever. As the frigate approached, he ordered all the officers below, and giving the speaking-trumpet to Stanley, the quartermaster, told him to reply as he might direct. The frigate hailed and inquired what we were about. "Looking out to stop ships with provisions, that we may supply the fleet," was the answer. The people of the frigate, satisfied with this reply, proceeded to rejoin the fleet, while we, glad to escape further questioning, made sail in chase of the lugger. She

was a fast craft, and led us a chase of four hours
before we captured her. She proved to be the *Castor and Pollux* privateer of sixteen guns. Having
taken out the prisoners, and put a prize crew on
board, we were proceeding to Portsmouth, when the
lugger, being to windward, spoke a brig, which had
left that place the day before, and from her gained
the information that the mutiny had again broken
out at Spithead. Under these circumstances, Sir
Harry thought it prudent to anchor under Dungeness until he could communicate with the Admiralty.

This we did; but it was a time of great anxiety,
for the mutineers might consider it important to
capture us, to hold Sir Harry and his officers as
hostages, and to wreak their vengeance on our men.
We got springs on the cable, and the ship ready for
action. During the middle watch a ship was made
out bearing down towards us; she was high out of
the water, and was pronounced by many to be a
line-of-battle ship. Sir Harry was on deck in an
instant—the private signal was made—would it be
answered? Yes; but there was no security in this,
as, should the ship's company have mutinied, they
would naturally have possessed themselves of it.
The drum beat to quarters, the fighting lanterns
were up, their light streaming through our ports.
Our men earnestly repeated their request to be
allowed to sink rather than surrender to the mutineers. No sight of the sort could be finer, as the
brave fellows stood stripped to the waist, dauntless
and resolute, not about to fight with a common foe,
but one that would prove cruel and revengeful in the
extreme. The wind was extremely light, and the
stranger closed very slowly. The suspense was
awful. In a short time we might be engaged in a
deadly struggle with a vastly superior foe, and deadly

K

all determined that it should be. Nearer and nearer the stranger drew; at length our captain hailed. The answer came: "The *Huzzar!* Lord Garlais! from the West Indies." She anchored close to us, and we exchanged visits. Her people, ignorant of the mutiny, could not understand the necessity of the precaution we had taken. They were so struck, when made acquainted with what had occurred, at the bravery and determination of our ship's company, that they immediately swore they would stick by us, and that, should any ship be sent to take us back to the Nore, they would share our fate, whatever that might be. I am sure that they would have proved as good as their word, but daylight came, and no enemy appeared. We lay here for some time, that Sir Harry might ascertain what was occurring on shore. He found that most active and energetic measures were being taken to repress the mutiny, and in a few days we heard that the ship's company of the *Sandwich* had taken her into Sheerness, and allowed their late leader, Parker, to be arrested by a guard of soldiers, sent on board for that purpose by Admiral Buckner. We sailed for Plymouth, and another ship was appointed to have the honour of taking over the Princess Royal.

I must say a word or two about that mutiny. I am convinced that the proportion of disaffected men was comparatively small. The seamen had grievances, but those would have been redressed without their proceeding to the extremities into which they plunged, led by a few disappointed and desperate men like Parker. Had greater energy been shown from the first, during some of the opportunities which occurred, the whole affair might have been concluded in a more dignified manner, at a much earlier date. I will instance one occasion. Having

one day got leave from the delegates of our ship,
while we lay off Sheerness, to go on shore, I landed
at the dockyard. I found, as I passed through it,
that I was followed by the whole body of delegates,
walking two-and-two in procession, Parker and
Davis leading, arm-in-arm. Just as we got outside
the gates, the Lancashire Fencibles appeared, coming
to strengthen the garrison. As soon as the seamen
got near the soldiers, they began to abuse them in
so scurrilous a manner, that the officer in command
halted his men, and seeing the admiral and super-
intendent, close to whom I at the time was standing
opposite the gates, he came, and, complaining of the
insults offered to himself and men, asked permission
to surround and capture them. So eager did I feel,
that I involuntarily exclaimed, "Yes! yes! now's
the time!" The admiral, on hearing me, turned
sharply round, and demanded how I dared to speak
in that way? "Because there they all are, sir, and
we may have them in a bunch!" I replied, pointing
to Parker, Davis, and the rest. The admiral told
me that I did not know what I was saying; but I
did, and I have no cause to suppose that I was wrong.

When the truly loyal and heroic conduct of our
ship's company became known, it was intended to
raise a sum in every seaport town in England to
present to them. From some reason, however, the
Government put a stop to it, and the only subscrip-
tion received was from Ludlow in Shropshire, from
whence the authorities sent £500 to Sir Harry
Neale, which he distributed to the ship's company
on the quarter-deck.

Orlo and Era:

A TALE OF THE AFRICAN SLAVE TRADE.

———•◦•———

THERE exists an extensive district on the west coast of Africa, about forty miles to the north of the far-famed river Niger, known as the Yoruba country. Sixty years ago it was one of the most thickly populated and flourishing parts of equatorial Africa, the inhabitants having also attained to a considerable amount of civilization, and made fair progress in many industrial arts.

Then came those dreadful wars, carried on by the more powerful and cruel chiefs, for the purpose of making slaves to sell to the white traders, who carried them away to toil in the plantations of North and South America and Cuba, and the prosperity of the once happy people of Yoruba was brought to an end. The savage rulers of Dahomey and Lagos now became notorious for the barbarities they inflicted on the unoffending tribes in their neighbourhood. The Yoruba country was the chief scene of their hunting expeditions. Towns and villages were attacked and burned; the able-bodied men and young women and children were carried off into slavery; the aged were ruthlessly murdered,

138

fields and plantations were laid waste, and a howling wilderness was left behind. At length the scattered remnants of the population who had escaped from slavery and death assembled together in a spot among rocks, especially strong by nature, where they hoped to be able to make a stand against their persecutors. Here they built a town, to which they gave the name of Abbeokuta, or the place among the rocks. It increased rapidly in population and extent, for numerous were the unfortunates in search of a home, and rest, and peace.

Lagos, one of the chief strongholds of the slave-dealers, which the Yorubans most had to fear, has since been taken possession of by the British, and has been declared an English colony or settlement; but Dahomey, governed by its bloodthirsty monarch, with his army of six thousand Amazons and five thousand male warriors, still exists as a terrible scourge to the surrounding territories.

On the confines of the Yoruba country existed a beautiful village which had hitherto escaped the ravages of the relentless slave-hunting foe. It was situated on the banks of a rapid stream, which gave freshness to the air, and fertility to the neighbouring plantations. Palms, dates, and other trees of tropical growth, overshadowed the leaf-thatched cottages, in which truly peace and plenty might be said to reign. Although true happiness cannot exist where Christianity is not, and where the fear of the fetish and the malign influence of the spirit of evil rules supreme over the mind, the people were contented, and probably as happy as are any of the countless numbers of the still benighted children of Africa. Rumours of wars and slave-hunts reached them, but they had so long escaped the inflictions others had suffered, that they flattered themselves they should escape altogether. So little accustomed are the negro race to look to the future, contented with the pleasures of the passing moment, that as they did not actually see the danger, they allowed no anticipation of evil to mar their happiness. The hearts of the dark-skinned children of that burning clime are as susceptible of the tender sentiments of love and friendship as many of those boasting a higher degree of civilization, and a complexion of a fairer hue. No couple, indeed, could have been more warmly attached than were young Orlo and Era, who had lately become man and wife, and taken up their abode in the village. They were industrious and happy, and from morning till night their voices might be heard singing as they went about their daily work. Orlo employed himself principally in collecting the various products of the country to sell to the traders who occasionally visited the district,—palm oil, and gold dust from the neighbouring rivulet, and elephants' tusks, and skins which he took in the chase.

At length Era gave birth to a child, a little boy, which proved a great addition to their happiness, and drew still closer the bonds of their affection. Indeed no people can be fonder of their children than are the negroes of Africa.

Soon after little Sobo was born Orlo set off on a hunting expedition with several other villagers, telling Era that he must get her some fresh soft skins for their child's bed, and that he must be more industrious than ever, as he had a family to provide for.

Era entreated him not to be long away.

"Two or three days will see me back, laden with the spoils of the chase," was his answer, in a cheerful tone.

Era's heart sank within her—why, she could not

tell. With anxious eyes she watched him and his companions as, with bows, and arrows, and lances in hand, they disappeared among the trees.

Seldom had Orlo and his party been more successful. More than one lion, several antelopes, and numerous monkeys were killed. Even a huge elephant was conquered by their skill and cunning. The skins of the animals slaughtered were hidden in safe places, to be taken up on their return. Excited by their success they proceeded even farther than they intended. Night surprised them, and collecting together they formed a camp, with fires blazing in the centre to keep off the savage beasts roaming around.

Their supper having been discussed, they were merrily laughing and talking over their adventures when they were startled by some terrific shouts and cries close to them. They grasped their arms, but before a bow could be drawn a body of warriors rushed in on them with clubs and swords, knocking over or cutting down all who stood at bay or attempted resistance. Some endeavoured to escape, but they were completely surrounded. Several were killed by their savage assailants, and their bodies were left where they fell. The greater number were secured with their arms bound tightly behind them, and they found themselves captives to the troops of the King of Dahomey, towards whose capital they were marched away in triumph. They had heard enough of the fate which had befallen so many of their countrymen to know that they must never more expect to taste the sweets of liberty; but they were scarcely aware of the horrible cruelty to which the will of the tyrant King of Dahomey might compel some of them to submit. Bitter, too, was the anguish which poor Orlo suffered when he felt that he should for ever be separated from his beloved Era.

The journey was long and tedious, and the captives' feet were torn by the thorns and cut by the hard rocks over which they had to pass; but whenever they lagged behind they were urged on by the long spears of their relentless captors. Arrived at the capital, they were astonished at its extent and the number of its inhabitants, and, more than all, by the vast army they saw drawn up for the inspection of the king. They had little opportunity of seeing much, for they were soon conducted into a large low building, where they were secured by iron shackles, back to back, to a long beam, scarcely able to move.

After remaining here for several days Orlo and others were separated from their companions and carried to a building on one side of the great square of the city, where all public ceremonies were performed. Dreadful shrieks assailed their ears both by day and night. They heard they were uttered by the human victims offered up by the savage king to the spirits of his departed ancestors.

They were not long left in doubt as to what was to be their fate. They also were to be destroyed in the same manner. Some of their number on hearing this sank into a state of apathy, others loudly bemoaned their cruel lot, and others plotted how they might escape, but Orlo could think only of his beloved Era, and the anxiety and anguish his absence would have caused her.

At length Orlo and nine others were taken out and told they were to enjoy the high privilege of being sacrificed in presence of their king. They were now dressed in white garments, and tall red caps were put on their heads. Their arms and legs were then bound securely, and they were placed in a sitting posture in small canoe-shaped troughs, and thus in a long procession were carried around the square amid the cruel shouts of the savage populace. At length they reached a high platform or slope in the centre of the square, on which sat the king, under the shade of a vast umbrella, surrounded by his courtiers and chiefs. Below the platform were collected a vast mob of savages, their hideous countenances looking up with fierce delight at the terrible drama which was to be enacted. Among the crowd stood several men of gigantic stature, even more savage-looking than the rest, armed with huge knotted clubs. These they knew instinctively were their intended executioners. Not one of them attempted to plead for mercy; that they knew were vain. Their eyes glanced hopelessly round, now on the assembled throng below, now on the groups collected on the platform, not expecting to meet a look of compassion turned towards them. But yes, among one group they see a man of strange appearance. His skin is white, and by his fine dress, glittering with gold, they believe him to be a great chief. He advances towards the king, whom, with eager look, he addresses in a strange language. What he says they cannot tell, till another man of their own colour speaks, and then they know that he is pleading for their lives; not only pleading, but offering a large ransom if they be given up to him. How anxiously they listen for the reply! The king will not hear of it. The spirit of his father complains that he has been neglected; that his nation must have become degenerate; that they have ceased to conquer, since so few captives have been sent to bear him company in the world of shades. Again the strange white chief speaks, and offers higher bribes. Curious that he should take

so much trouble about some poor black captives
they think. What can be his object? What can
influence him?

He does not plead altogether in vain. The king
will give him four for the sum he offers, but no
more. He would not dare thus to displease the
shade of his father, and the white chief may choose
whom he will. The victims gaze anxiously at his
countenance. It is merciful and benign they think
—unlike any they have before seen. Which of them
will he select?

He does not hesitate; he knows what must be
passing in the hearts of those poor wretches. He
quickly lays his hand on four of them, and turns
away his head with sorrow from the rest. Orlo is
among those he has claimed. They show but little
pleasure or gratitude as they are released, and, being
stripped of their sacrificial garments, are placed
under charge of his attendants. The rest of the
miserable captives are held up, some by men, others
by the Amazonian warriors, to the gaze of the ex-
pectant multitude, who shriek and shout horribly,
and then they are cast forward into the midst of the
crowd, when the executioners set on them with their
clubs and speedily terminate their sufferings. For
several successive days is the same horrible scene
enacted, the Fetish men declaring that the spirit of
the late king is not yet satisfied.

Orlo by degrees recovered from the stupor into
which his sufferings, mental and bodily, and the
anticipation of a cruel death had thrown him. He
then found that the white chief, whose slave he considered himself, was no other than the captain of a
British man-of-war, cruising off the coast for the
suppression of the slave trade—not that he understood very clearly much about the matter, but he

had heard of the sea, and that big canoes floated on it which carried his countrymen across it to a land from which none ever came back. Still, as this captain had certainly saved his life, he felt an affection for him, and hoped that he should be allowed to remain his slave, and not be sold to a stranger. As to asking to be liberated to be sent back to Era, he did not for a moment suppose that such a request would be granted, and he therefore did not make it. At last the coast was reached, and a ship appeared, and a boat came and took them on board. The captain had seen something in Orlo's countenance which especially pleased him, so he asked whether he would like to remain with him ; and Orlo, very much surprised that the option should be given him, said, " Yes, certainly."

So Orlo was entered on the ship's books, and soon learned not only to attend on the captain, but to be a sailor. His affection for his patron and preserver was remarkable. Whatever Captain Fisher wished he attempted to perform to the best of his ability, while he was attentive and faithful in the extreme. He soon acquired enough English to make himself understood, while he could comprehend everything that was said to him.

The *Sea Sprite* was a very fast sailing corvette, and had already, by her speed and the sagacity with which her cruising-ground was selected, made more captures than any other craft of the squadron. Her success continued after Orlo had become one of her crew. He always got leave to go on board the prizes when they were taken possession of, and his services were soon found of value as interpreter. His object was naturally to inquire about news from his own part of the country. He was not likely to obtain any satisfactory information. Some time passed—another capture was made. He returned on board the corvette very depressed in spirits, and was often seen in tears. Captain Fisher asked him the cause of his sorrows. He had learned that at length his own village had been surprised during the night by the slave-hunters of the King of Dahomey, that not one of the inhabitants had escaped, and that all had been carried off into captivity. They had been sold to different dealers, and had been transported to the baracoons on different parts of the coast, ready for embarkation. Where Era had been carried he could not ascertain; only one thing was certain—she and her child had been seen in the hands of the Dahomian soldiers, on their way to the capital. His beloved Era was then a slave; and he by this time full well knew what slavery meant. He had seen several slave ships captured, and the horrors, the barbarities, and indignities to which the captives on board were exposed. He pictured to himself the terrible journey from the interior, the lash of the brutal driver descending on her shoulders as she tottered on with her infant in her arms, her knees bending from weakness, her feet torn with thorns and hard rocks—she who had been so tenderly cared for—whom he loved so dearly;—the thought was more than he could bear. He looked over the side of the ship, and gazed at the blue waters, and said to himself, "I shall find rest beneath them; in the world of spirits I shall meet my own Era, and be happy."

One of the officers of the ship, a Christian man, had watched him. He had before observed his melancholy manner, so different to what he had at first exhibited. Lieutenant L—— called him, and asked him the cause of his sorrow.

Orlo narrated his simple history.

"And no one has thought all this time of imparting any knowledge of Gospel truth to this poor African," said the lieutenant to himself; and a blush rose on his own cheeks. "No time shall be lost, though," he added; and he unfolded in language suited to his comprehension, and in all its simplicity, the grand scheme of redemption whereby sinning man can be accepted by a holy and just God as freed from sin, through the great sacrifice offered once on the Cross.

Orlo listened eagerly and attentively. All ideas of suicide had left his mind. He longed to know more of this wonderful, this glorious news.

"Then, Orlo, would you not wish to please so merciful and kind a Master, who has done so much for you?" asked the lieutenant.

"Yes, massa, dat I would," answered the African.

"One way in which you can do so, is to bear patiently and humbly, as He did, the afflictions the loving God thinks fit to send. He does it in mercy, depend on that. God's ways are not our ways; but the all-powerful God who made the world must of necessity know better what is right and good than we poor frail dying creatures, whom He formed from the dust of the earth, and who, but for His will, would instantly return to dust again."

"Me see, me see," answered the negro, in a tone as joyful as if he had found a pearl of great price; and so he had, for he had found Gospel truth.

"God knows better than we," was his constant remark after this when he heard others complaining of the misfortunes and ills of life.

The ship had now been nearly her full time in commission, and her captain was in daily expectation of receiving orders to return home. Poor Orlo's heart sank within him. He must either quit his

kind master and his still kinder lieutenant, or, by
leaving the coast, abandon all hopes of ever again
seeing his beloved Era. To be sure, he knew that
she might long ere this have been carried off to the
Brazils or Cuba; and faint indeed was the expectation that they ever should meet in this world.
Then, again, another feeling arose: "I am now a
Christian and she is still a heathen. How can God
receive her in heaven?" But after a time he
thought—"Ah, but I can pray that she may become
a Christian. God's ways are not our ways. He
will hear my prayers—that I know. He can bring
about by some of His ways what I cannot accom-
plish." And Orlo prayed as he had never prayed
before. Captain Fisher treated Orlo with unusual
kindness, and, under the circumstances, he could
not have been happier on board any ship in the
navy.

Captain Fisher was not a man to relax in his
efforts, as long as he remained on the station, to
suppress the abominable traffic in human beings by
all the means in his power. The *Sea Sprite* continued cruising, accordingly, along the coast, looking
in at the different stations, till one morning, at daybreak, a suspicious schooner was seen at anchor, close
in with the shore. The increasing light revealed
the corvette to those on board. The schooner instantly slipped her cable and stood along the coast,
while the *Sea Sprite* made all sail in chase. Of the
character of the vessel there could be no doubt, or
she would not have attempted to run from the man-
of-war. The *Sea Sprite* stood as close in as the
depth of water would allow; farther in she dare not
go. There was still a possibility of the chase escaping.
Orlo, as usual, was the most eager on board. He
delighted in seeing his countrymen freed from

slavery, and he never abandoned the hope of meeting
with Era. "I pray I meet her. I know God hear
prayer," said Orlo.

The wind fell. "Out boats," was the order.
Captain Fisher went himself. The chase was a large
schooner. A boat was seen to put off from her and
pull towards the surf : whether or not she could get
through it seemed a question. The English seamen
bent to their oars ; they were resolved to reach the
chase before she could again get the breeze. They
dashed alongside, and soon sprang over her bulwarks. No resistance was made. Poor Orlo, glancing round, discovered, to his disappointment, that
she had no slaves on board. The master, it was
found, had landed with the specie for the purchase of
slaves. One of the slave crew—a mate, he looked
like—appeared to have a peculiar thickness under
his knees ; Orlo detected it, and pointed it out to the
captain. The master-at-arms was ordered to examine him. Most unwillingly the fellow tucked
up his trousers—grinning horribly at Orlo all the
time—when he was found to have on a pair of
garters, out of each of which rolled thirty doub-
loons.

The schooner's head being put off-shore, the boats
took her in tow, till, a breeze springing up, sail was
made on her for Sierra Leone. The next morning
commenced with a thick mist and rain. Orlo, from
his quickness of vision, was now constantly employed as one of the look-outs. He was on the
watch to go aloft directly it gave signs of clearing.
His impatience, however, did not allow him to remain till the mist dispersed. Away aloft he went,
observing, "It must fine soon ; den I see
sip." He had not been many minutes at the
masthead when he shouted, "Sip in-shore !" He

had discovered her royals above the mist. Sail was instantly made in chase. Some time elapsed before the *Sea Sprite* was discovered. Suddenly the mist cleared, and there appeared close in-shore a large American slave ship. There was no doubt about her, with her great beam and wide spread of canvas.

Hoisting American colours, the stranger made all sail to escape. He was standing off the land ; but as on that course he would have had to pass unpleasantly near the corvette, he tacked in-shore, and then bore away along the surf, hoping thus, with his large sails, to draw ahead and escape. The light wind appeared to favour him, but Captain Fisher determined that it should not. Ordering the boats away, he took one with a strongly-armed crew, and pulled to windward to cut off the chase, while two others went to leeward, so that his chance of escaping was small indeed. The slave captain seemed to think so likewise. He dared not meet in fight the true-hearted British seaman. Regardless of the risk he and his own crew would run, of the destruction he was about to bring on hundreds of his fellow-creatures, the savage slave captain put up his helm, and ran the ship under all sail towards the shore.

"What is the fellow about?" exclaimed Captain Fisher. "If that ship is full, as she seems to be, she has not less than four or five hundred human beings on board, and he'll run the risk of drowning every one of them."

It was too evident, however, that this was the design of the slaver's captain. His heart was seared. Long accustomed to human suffering in every possible form, he set no more value on the lives of his cargo than if they had been so many sheep, except so far as they could be exchanged for all-potent dollars. On flew the beautiful fabric—for beautiful she was, in spite of her nefarious employment—to destruction. With all her sails set, through the roaring surf she dashed, then rose on the summit of a sea, and down she came, striking heavily, her ropes flying wildly and her sails flapping furiously in the breeze. What mattered it to the slaver's crew that they left their hapless passengers to perish! Their boats were lowered, and, with such valuables as they could secure, and some of the slaves which, for their greater value, they wished to save, they made their escape to shore, leaving the ship, with the American colours flying, to her fate.

Captain Fisher and the other boats now closed with the wreck, while the corvette also was standing in. When close as she could venture to come, she anchored, and the master came off from her in a whale-boat and joined the other boats. Terrible was the sight which now met the eyes of the English seamen. Orlo beheld it, too, with horror and anguish. As the ship rolled fearfully from side to side, the terrified negroes forced their way up on deck, and in their wild despair, not knowing what to do, many leaped into the raging breakers which swept by alongside, and, helplessly whirling round and round, were soon hidden beneath the waves. One after the other the poor wretches rushed up on deck; many, following the impulse of the first, leaped overboard to meet a like speedy death; others, clinging to the wreck, were washed overboard; some of the stronger still clung on; but many yet remained below.

"This is sad work," exclaimed Captain Fisher. "We must save these poor people at all hazards."

A cheer was the reply, and, the men giving way, the boats dashed at great hazard through the surf to leeward of the wreck; but here it seemed almost impossible to board her from the heavy lurches she was making, sending the blocks and spars and rigging flying over their heads, and threatening to swamp the boats should they get alongside. Still Captain Fisher and his gallant followers persevered. He was the first on board, and Orlo leaped on the deck after him. The scene appeared even more horrible than at a distance. The negroes, as they could get clear of their manacles, climbed up from the slave deck, and ran to and fro, shrieking and crying out like people deprived of reason. Some ran on till they sprang overboard; others turned again, and continued running backwards and forwards, till the seamen were compelled to catch them and throw them below till the boats could be got ready for their rescue. The captain ordered Orlo to try and pacify them. He answered, that their extreme terror arose from the idea which the slaver's crew had given them, that the object of the English in taking possession of the vessel was to cut all their throats. Orlo did his best to quiet their fears when he learned the cause, assuring them the reason the British seaman had come on board was to do them good, and to try and save their lives. It was some time, however, before they would credit his assertions. The ship's barge had now been brought in and anchored just outside the rollers, while the cutter was backed in under the slaver's counter. Three of the slaves at a time were then allowed to come up, and were lowered into the boat, from which the whale-boat took them through the surf to the barge, and that when full ultimately carried them to the corvette. The process was of necessity slow, the toil was excessive, and the danger very great; but the British seamen did not shrink from it. Orlo had from the first, while acting as interpreter, been scanning the countenances of all he met, making inquiries of those who could understand his language (for all could not do so) if they could give him any information about his beloved Era. Again and again he went below, but the darkness prevented him from distinguishing any one, and the shrieks, groans, and cries from making his voice heard, or from hearing what any one might have said.

Night closed on the hitherto unremitting labours of the gallant crew. They had thus saved two hundred poor wretches, but upwards of two hundred remained on board when darkness made it impossible to remove them. Still, could they be left to perish, which they probably would if left alone? The slaver's crew might return, and either attempt to land them, to keep them in captivity, or burn the ship, to prevent them from falling into the hands of the British. The risk of remaining was very great, but several officers volunteered. Orlo's friend, Lieutenant ——, claimed the privilege, and Orlo begged that he might remain with him. The last performance of the boats was to bring off some rice which had been found in the captured schooner, and cooked, thoughtfully, by the captain's orders, in his coppers, in readiness for the liberated negroes. Plenty of men were ready to remain with Lieutenant ——. Without this supply of food, few, probably, of the slaves on board would have survived the night; even as it was, many of those who were rescued died on their passage to the corvette, or on her decks. Lieutenant —— and his brave companions had truly a night of trial. The wind increased, the surf roared louder and louder as it broke around them, the ship rolled and struck more and more violently, till it seemed impossible that she could hold together, while all this time the unhappy captives below were shrieking and crying out most piteously for help. Poor creatures! they knew not how to pray, or to whom to pray. They thought and believed, and not without reason, that a Fetish, or spirit of evil, had got possession of them, and was wreaking his malice on their heads. Orlo gladly, by the lieutenant's orders, went frequently below to try and comfort them, and to assure them that by the return of daylight fresh efforts would be made for their rescue. Still great indeed were their sufferings. Many, both men, women, and children, died during that fearful night, from wet, cold, fear, and hunger, as they sat, still closely packed on the slave deck. Orlo's kind heart made him suffer almost as much as they were doing—the more so that he felt how little could be done to relieve them.

At length the morning dawned, when it was found that the ship had driven considerably farther in towards the beach. As daylight broke, people were seen collecting on the shore; their numbers increased; they were gesticulating violently. Did they come to render assistance to their perishing fellow-countrymen? No; led on by the miscreant whites who had formed the crew of the slave ship, and deceived by their falsehoods, they had come to attempt the recapture of the ship. The corvette had, of necessity, stood off-shore for the night. Lieutenant ——, hoisting a signal of distress, prepared to defend the prize to the last. He examined the shore anxiously. The slaver's crew and their black allies were bringing boats or canoes to launch, for the purpose of attacking the ship. Should the wretches succeed, he knew that his life and that of all his companions would be sacrificed.

At length the corvette was seen working up under all sail. She approached; her anchor was dropped, and her boats, being lowered, pulled in towards the wreck. As they got near, the people on shore, balked in their first project, opened a hot fire of musketry on them. The boats had not come un-armed. The larger ones were immediately anchored, and, each having a gun of some weight, opened a hot fire on the beach. This was more than the slave dealers had bargained for. They were ready enough to kill others, but had no fancy to be killed themselves. Several times the blacks took to flight, but were urged back again by the white men, till, some of the shot taking effect on them, the beach was at last cleared.

The wreck was now again boarded. Lieutenant —— and his men were found almost worn out; the hold was full of water, and the ship was giving signs of breaking up. No time was to be lost. The larger boats anchored, as before, outside the rollers, and, by means of the smaller ones, communication by ropes being established, the negroes were, a few at a time, hauled through the surf. Many were more dead than alive, and several died before they reached the corvette. Some were brought up by their companions dead, and many were the heart-rending scenes where fathers and mothers found that they had lost their children, husbands their wives, or children their parents. Orlo had held out bravely all the night, but his strength, towards the morning, gave way, and Lieutenant ——, seeing his condition, directed that he should be carried back to the corvette, which he reached in an almost unconscious state.

This living cargo was composed of all ages. There were strong men and youths, little boys, women, young girls, and children, and several mothers with infants at their breasts. How fondly and tenderly the poor creatures pressed them there, and endeavoured to shelter them from the salt spray and cold! Fully two hundred were carried on board the corvette during the morning, and it was found that the immortal spirits of nearly fifty of those who had been left on board during the night had passed away. The last poor wretch being rescued, the wreck was set on fire, both fore and aft; the flames burst quickly forth, surrounding the masts, from which still floated that flag which, professing to be the flag of freedom, has so often protected that traffic which has carried thousands upon thousands of the human race into hopeless and abject slavery. The seamen instinctively gave a cheer as they saw it disappear among the devouring flames.

The labours of Captain Fisher and his brave crew were not over. They had to provide food and shelter for fully four hundred of the rescued negroes. Rice, as before, was boiled, and cocoa was given them, and those who most required care were clothed and carried to the galley fire to warm. Among the last rescued was a young woman with a little boy, on whom all her care was lavished. Though herself almost perished, before she would touch food she fed him, and when some clothing was given her she wrapped it round him. She had been found in the fore part of the ship in an almost fainting condition, where she had remained unnoticed, apparently in a state of stupor, with her little boy pressed to her heart. Orlo had been placed under the doctor's care. It was not till the next morning that he was allowed to come on deck, where his services were at once called into requisition as interpreter. Though unacquainted with the language of many of the tribes to which the captives belonged, he was generally able to make himself understood. A sail had been spread over part of the deck, beneath which the women and young children were collected. The doctor, when about to visit it, called Orlo to accompany him, as interpreter. Among them, sitting on the deck, and leaning against a gun carriage, with her arm thrown round the neck of a little boy, was a young woman, though wan and ill, still possessing that peculiar beauty occasionally seen among several of the tribes of Africa. Orlo fixed his eyes on her; his knees trembled; he rushed forward; she sprang up, uttering a wild shriek of joy, and his arms were thrown around her. He had found his long lost Era and their child. "Ah! God hear prayer; I know now!" he exclaimed joyfully. "Wife soon be Christian, and child. God berry, berry good!"

Happily, the next morning the corvette fell in with another man-of-war, between which and the schooner the rescued slaves being distributed, all three made sail for Sierra Leone. The blacks were there landed, and ground given them on which to settle. Orlo begged that he and Era and their child might also be there set on shore. He did not go empty-handed, for, besides pay and prize-money, generously advanced him by his captain, gifts were showered on him both by his officers and messmates, and he became one of the most flourishing settlers in that happy colony. At length, however, wishing once more to see his own people, and to assist in spreading the truth of the Gospel, which he had so sincerely embraced, among them, he removed to Abbeokuta, where, with his wife now a Christian woman, and surrounded by a young Christian family, he is now settled, daily setting forth, by his consistent walk,

the beauties and graces of the Christian faith.
Whenever any of his friends are in difficulties, he
always says, "Ah! God hear prayer! You pray;
never fear!"

My First Command, and How it Ended.

THE OLD ADMIRAL'S YARN.

——◆◆——

I HAD been at sea about five years, and had seen some pretty hard service, when I was appointed to a dashing frigate, the *Tiger*, on the West India station. Our captain had never been accustomed to let the grass grow on his ship's bottom, and he took good care to keep that of the *Tiger* pretty clean. Those were stirring times. England was engaged in a fierce war, both by sea and by land, with the larger proportion of the civilized nations in the world, and it was more easy to find an enemy than a friend wherever we sailed. I cannot say that we had any complaint to make with that state of things, as we came off generally the victors, and made lots of prize money. The more of the latter we got the more we wanted, and we spent it as lavishly as if there would be no end of it. We had taken several prizes, when we received notice that a large French privateer was in those seas, committing a good deal of havoc among our merchantmen. It is said that everything is fair in love and war—in war,

159

it may be the case ; in love, nothing is fair that is not straightforward and honourable. Our captain considered that stratagem in war was, at all events, allowable, and he used to disguise the frigate in so wonderful a way, that even we ourselves, at a little distance, should not have known her. By this means many an unwary craft fell into our clutches. One day we lay becalmed, with our seemingly black and worn sails hanging against the masts, our ports concealed by canvas, painted to represent the weather-beaten sides of a big merchantman, our yards untrimmed, and all our rigging slack. At length a breeze was seen coming towards us, bringing up a large ship. When the stranger was within a couple of miles the wind fell. We were soon convinced that our trap was well baited, for we saw the stranger lower three boats, which came rapidly towards us. We, in the meantime, lowered three others, well armed and ready at a moment's notice to pull off in chase, when the enemy should discover his mistake. Not, however, till the Frenchmen were close up to us, did they find out that we were not what we appeared. We saw by their gestures of astonishment that they suspected all was not right. Before, however, they had time to pull round, our boats were after them. I was in one of them. We were alongside in two minutes—they attempted to defend themselves ; they had better have been quiet ; a few were knocked overboard and hauled in by our fellows, and all three boats were taken. We found that we had got the captain and second and third officers of the stranger among our prisoners, and that she was the privateer of which we were in search. The Frenchmen frantically tore their hair, and swore terribly at us for the trick we had played them. "Ah ! you perfides Anglais, had we been on board our ship, you would not have taken us so easily," exclaimed the French captain. "Then, sir, you are welcome to go back and fight it out!" answered our captain. "Ah, morbleu non!" cried the Frenchman, with a shrug of his shoulders, "I know what sort of fellows you are in this frigate, and I would rather stay where I am with a whole skin than return to be riddled by your shot. If my ship escapes, though, do not blame me." "Certainly not; but I have no intention that she shall escape!" said our captain, with a bow, directly afterwards ordering all the boats ahead to tow us towards the enemy. They pulled on till we got her well within range of our guns, when the painted canvas being cleared away, we opened fire. In five minutes she hauled down her colours. We found on board the crew of a large English West Indiaman, captured that morning, and supposed not to be far off, though not in sight. Depend on it we whistled with right good will for a breeze. It came at length, and disguising ourselves as before, and having the French ensign over the English, we and our big prize made sail in chase. Greatly to our delight, the merchantman was seen standing boldly towards us, attracted by the firing. It was amusing to watch the countenances of the French prisoners—they would have done their best to warn her off had they dared, but they could only make grimaces at each other, and hurl low muttered curses on our heads, while their richly-laden prize was recovered by us. She was a West Indiaman—the *Diana*. I cannot say much for the beauty of the goddess of the night, for she was a huge wall-sided ship, capable of stowing away a vast quantity of sugar and molasses, articles much in request at the time in Europe. The French prize crew were being removed when the captain sent for me. My heart

fluttered unusually.   " Mr. Brine, you have behaved
very well, very well indeed, since you joined this
ship, and I have much confidence in you," he began.
I bowed at the compliment—I had an idea that it
was deserved, though I did not say so—I had done
two or three things to be proud of, and I knew that
I stood well in the captain's opinion, although I
was not yet a passed midshipman ; " I accordingly
place you in command of the *Diana*, more willingly
than I should any other midshipman.   You are to
take her to Bristol or Plymouth, and remember that
she is of no small value to us."   I thanked the captain
for his good opinion of me, but begged to have a
mate capable of navigating the ship, should I fall
sick or lose my life ; and I named Tony Fenwick,
another midshipman, my junior, and a great chum
of mine.   I had an old follower, Paul Bott, who had
been to sea with my father.   His name was short,
but he was a tall man.   I asked if he also might
come.   The captain granted both my requests, and
allowed me to pick out six other men for my crew.
I felt wonderfully proud as I walked the deck of my
first command, and certainly no two happier or better
satisfied midshipmen could be found than Tony Fenwick and I, as we navigated the sugar-laden *Diana*
across the Atlantic.   We only wished that we could
meet a letter of marque of our own size, which might
attempt to interfere with us.   What thought we of
tempests or foes, the possibility of wreck or recapture?
We both of us hoped soon to obtain our promotion,
for those were the days when a post-captain of nine-
teen commanded one of the finest frigates in the
navy, and had dared and done deeds as gallant as any
which naval history can record, and requiring knowledge, judgment, and discretion, as well as bravery.
Old heads were often worn on young shoulders,

though there were plenty of harum-scarum fellows, as now, who did no good to themselves and much harm to others, whenever they chanced to be placed in command. We had a fine passage across the Atlantic—Cape Clear was sighted, and we expected, in a few days at most, to carry the *Diana* safe into port. Fenwick had the first watch on deck one morning—daylight had just broke when the look-out at the mast-head shouted, "A sail on the weather-bow—a large ship!" I heard Fenwick's reply, and jumped on deck, for I always slept in my clothes ready for work. The stranger, we concluded, was probably an English cruiser. The *Diana* was kept accordingly on her course; still, not free from suspicion, we narrowly watched the stranger's movements. I was looking in another direction, when I heard Tony utter a loud exclamation, not complimentary to the French, and looking round, when it was now too late to escape from her power, what was my annoyance to see the hated tricolour flying from the stranger's peak! Still neither Tony nor I had any thought of yielding up our charge without a struggle. "She's a big one to tackle, and we shall have a squeak for it at best!" observed Tony, eyeing the Frenchman with no loving glance. All sail was made, but nothing but a miracle could have saved us. The men showed their opinion of what was to happen by slipping down one by one below, and putting on their best clothes, as sailors always do when they expect to fall into any enemy's hands. I have known some to do so when they expect to be wrecked, with but little prospect of saving their lives. Now they had good reason for what they did, for the Frenchman, should they take our ship, were sure not to leave us more than we had on our backs, even if so much. All we could do to escape, we did, but in

vain.　Before long, we found ourselves under the guns
of a French seventy-four, the *Droits-de-l'Homme*, one
of the squadron, with troops on board, intended for the
invasion of Ireland.　With sad hearts, Tony Fenwick,
Paul Bott, and most of our crew found ourselves
conveyed on board our captor, which soon afterwards
made sail for France.　It was the winter season;
the nights were long, the weather tempestuous.
When near the coast, two sail were seen—large ships,
supposed to be British; we devoutly hoped that they
might prove so.　The *Droits-de-l'Homme* made sail
to escape them.　Shortly afterwards two other ships
were seen steering so as to cut her off from the
land.　They were undoubtedly enemies.　Though
surrounded, as they supposed, by foes, the Frenchmen made every attempt to escape, but fortune was
against them.　"We caught a Tartar t'other day—
the Mounseers have caught half-a-dozen!" observed
Tony, as we watched what was going on through
one of the main-deck ports.　A heavy squall, as he
spoke, carried away the fore and main-top masts.　It
was no easy matter for us to refrain from cheering
at the accident, but the probability of getting a clout
on our heads, and being sent below for our patriotism,
kept us silent.　"There's no fear now, that before
many hours are over we shall be under our own flag
again," whispered Tony to me.　"The same mishap
which has occurred to the Frenchman may befall our
friends," I answered.　"There are but two frigates
in sight, but I hope that they are more than a match
for a French seventy-four."

The Frenchmen were so busy with clearing away
the wreck of the masts to be ready for their foes,
that no one thought of us and the other English
prisoners they had on board.　The gale increased;
the sea ran high; the English frigates were seen to

be reefing topsails. "Why, they are not going to
desert us, I hope!" exclaimed Tony. "No, no, they
are getting under snugger canvas for more easy
handling, depend on that," I answered, laughing;
"they are after us again—hurrah!" Before long the
largest frigate approached, and suddenly hauling up,
fired her broadside, which would have proved most
destructive, had not the *Droits-de-l'Homme* hauled
up likewise, the troops which were posted on the
upper-deck and poop replying with a heavy discharge
of musketry. Fortunately, perhaps, for us, though
we did not consider it so at the time, one of the
French officers thought of sending us to join the
other prisoners in the cable tier, out of harm's way.
Most unwillingly we descended, though we should
have run a great chance of having had our heads
knocked off without the honour and glory. On
getting below we found ourselves placed under
guard, in almost total darkness. The big ship rolled
and tumbled in a way which made it appear as if
the waves alone would wrench her asunder; the
great guns roared with greater frequency, the
musketry rattled, the shot from the active frigates
came crashing on board and tearing through the
stout planks; there was the tramp of men bearing
their wounded comrades below; their shrieks and
groans, as the surgeons attempted in vain to operate
on their shattered limbs; and the rush of water
which came through the ports, with the fearful
rolling of the ship. All these various sounds gave
us an idea, and not a pleasant one, of the work going
on above our heads. Now and then, too, louder
reports and more terrific crashes told of guns
bursting, and masts gone by the board. Hour after
hour passed by, and still the fearful uproar continued.
We prisoners would all of us rather have been on

deck, notwithstanding the more than possibility of having our heads knocked off, than shut up in the dark, bilge-water smelling, stifling hold. "I say, these Frenchmen fight bravely, but I wish that they would give in; it would be wiser in them, and they must before long," observed Fenwick, as he sat on a cask by my side, kicking his heels against the staves.

"All in good time," I answered. "But consider that this ship carries more guns than the two frigates put together, and of heavier metal; and aboard here there are more than twice as many men as will be found between them. There will be a tough fight before we get our liberty, but we shall get it, never fear." While we were speaking there was a cessation of firing. "Can she have struck?" was asked by many of our fellow-prisoners. We waited in breathless suspense. No intimation was given to us of what had occurred. "The frigates cannot have given up the fight, of that I am certain," I exclaimed. "Maybe they have just hauled off to repair damages, and will be at it again," suggested Paul.

He was right. Like the voice of a giant awaking out of sleep the big ship's guns began again to roar forth, quickly followed by a duller sound, showing that her enemies were replying with as much energy as before. For long the battle raged furiously. How we unfortunates, like rats in a hole below, longed to be on deck, that we might see what was going forward! Again there was a cessation of firing. What could have happened? Had the Frenchman struck? That either of the English frigates had done so of course none of us would believe. It was a time of awful suspense to us all. One thing was certain, that though the battle might have ceased the war of the elements was raging more

furiously than ever. From the way the ship rolled
it was evident that she was dismasted. Various
sounds, the cause of which seamen alone could
understand, were heard. "I suspects, sir, as how
we're in shoal water; they've let go an anchor," said
Paul, calmly, though he knew full well the peril of
our position. "But it doesn't hold, d'ye see, sir."
Signal guns were heard. A few minutes passed, to
most of us the time appeared far longer. A dull,
ominous roaring sound reached even to our ears
down in the depths of the ship. "We are among
the breakers!" I sung out, jumping from my seat;
and scarcely were the words out of my mouth when
a cry was heard from above, and words of compassion reached our ears. "Pauvres Anglais! pauvres
Anglais! Montez bien vites; nous sommes tous
perdus!" The sentinel rushed from his post and
we prisoners sprang on deck. Fenwick and I, with
Paul and a few others, stopped, however, to help the
more weak and helpless, for among them were
women and children, unable to take care of themselves. The early dawn, as we reached the deck,
revealed a scene of horror rarely equalled: breakers
on every side, the masts gone, the decks slippery
with human gore, and the ship driving to destruction. At a little distance lay one of the English
frigates, the surf breaking over her, her fate sealed.
The other was observed standing off from the Pen-
mark Rocks, which threatened her with instant
destruction. "Can she be saved?" asked Fenwick,
for, in spite of our own danger, we had been intently
watching her. "If her sticks stand and she is well
handled; if not, Heaven have mercy on the souls of
all on board, for their condition will be worse than
ours!" I said, in a sad tone. "The people in the
other frigate, already on shore, are badly enough off,

M

but the sea as yet does not appear to break heavily over her." "As it will, howsom'dever, over us, before the world's a minute older," cried Paul; "I've been cast ashore more than once with your honoured father, Mr. Brine, and the advice he gave us was, 'Lads, hold on to the wreck till the time comes for getting ashore.' He wished to say, 'Don't let the sea take you off the wreck if you can help it, but just hold on till you see that you have a fair chance of setting foot on land in safety.'"

This advice was not thrown away. In another instant a terrific shock was felt; the wild seas dashed furiously over the huge wreck; shrieks arose from every part of the ship; horror and dismay were depicted on the countenances of all around us. As the foaming waters came rushing over the decks many were swept helplessly away.

We and our men kept together, holding fast by the upper bulwarks. We could make out clearly a village on shore, and crowds of people, who lined the beach but were unable to render us any assistance. There were no lifeboats in those days, no apparatus for carrying ropes to a stranded ship; boats were indeed launched by the hardy fishermen, but were quickly dashed to pieces against the rocks. Rafts were built, but those who ventured on them were swept off by the furious seas. Others tried, by swimming, to convey a rope from the ship to the shore, but in vain. Thus the day closed, and a night of horrors commenced, during which numbers were washed away. Still my companions and I kept our posts. All this time not a particle of food could be obtained, as the hold was under water. Paul had observed a small boat uninjured. He told me of it; I undertook to carry a line safely by her to the shore. Fenwick and Paul agreed to accom-

pany me, and we had no lack of other volunteers
among our men. At low water we three, with seven
others, stood ready to launch her. We allowed a
heavy sea to roll by, "Now in with her, boys, and
give way," I shouted. Through the boiling cauldron
we pulled. None, indeed, but stout-hearted British
seamen could have made way in such troubled waters.
Sea upon sea came rolling on after us. On the
summit of one we reached the beach. Before another sea could follow we had leaped out and
dragged our boat high up above the power of the
waters. We set to work, and had the satisfaction
of saving the lives of several of the French crew;
but, unhappily, the rope parted, and in vain we
endeavoured to secure another.

A second night passed—a third came, and few
were saved. We remained on the beach to afford
all the aid in our power to those still on the wreck.
What occurred on board was not known to us till
afterwards. The Frenchmen endeavoured to launch
one of their largest boats, but discipline was at an
end. In vain the officers ordered the men to keep
back—it was right that the sick and wounded should
first be removed. No one obeyed; a hundred and
fifty men crowded into her. They shoved off, a sea
rushed on, they were hid from view; the shattered
boat and their lifeless corpses alone reached the
shore. Eight hundred human beings, it is supposed,
had by this time perished. Those few who now
reached the shore, aided chiefly, I have a right to
boast, by my party, reported the dreadful condition
of the remainder. Numbers were dying of hunger;
the decks were covered with corpses; expedients
too horrible to be believed for sustaining life had
been proposed. A fourth day came, and with it a
more serene sky. The sea went down. "A sail! a

sail!" A man-of-war brig and an armed cutter appeared. Their boats quickly approached, but the sea still broke so violently over the wreck that they were unable to get alongside. The famishing survivors, therefore, constructed some rafts, to be towed off by the boats, but many of those who ventured on them were swept away by the surf. About a hundred and fifty were, however, conveyed on board the brig that evening, leaving still nearly four hundred human beings on the wreck to endure a sixth night of horrors. The sufferings of many were more than human endurance could sustain, and next morning, when the men-of-war's boats returned, half of the hapless beings were found dead. We, meantime, when our services could be of no further avail, found ourselves, being in an enemy's country, marched off as prisoners; but I am bound to say that we were treated with the greatest kindness by the French. The spot where the wreck occurred was, we found, the Bay of Audierne, and the town near it that of Plouzenec. Here we met part of the officers and crew of the British thirty-six-gun frigate, *Amazon*, which had been wrecked with us. Her whole ship's company (six men only excepted, who had stolen the cutter and were drowned) had, by means of rafts, landed in safety by nine A.M. of the morning the frigate went on shore. This might have been partly owing to the position of the ship, but more particularly to the admirable discipline maintained on board. We rejoiced to find that the other frigate, which was the *Indefatigable*, of forty-four guns, Captain Sir Edward Pellew, had escaped the danger which threatened her. Fenwick and I were sighing over the prospect of our expected captivity, and the destruction of all our hopes of promotion, when the captain of the French ship, who had been among the last to leave the wreck, sent for us, and, complimenting us on our behaviour, assured us that as we had been fellow-sufferers with him and his people, we and our men might rely on being liberated without delay. To our great joy we and our companions were shortly afterwards placed on board a cartel and sent to England without ransom or exchange, an act of generosity on the part of the French worthy of note.

Our First Prize.

———◆———

AWAY on her course, before a strong north-easterly breeze, flew her Majesty's brig *Gad-fly*. Every stitch of canvas she could carry was set, each sail was well trimmed, each brace hauled taut, and it might have been supposed that we were eager to reach some port where friends and pleasure awaited us. But it was far otherwise. We were quitting England and our home, that spot which contains all a seaman holds most dear, and were bound for a land of pestilence and death, the little delectable coast of Africa, to be employed for the next three years in chasing, capturing, or destroying, to the best of our power and ability, all vessels engaged in the traffic of human flesh. We touched at the Azores, and reached Sierra Leone, the chief port on that station, without meeting with any adventure worth relating. We remained there a week to wood and water, to perform which operations we shipped a dozen stout Kroomen. These people come from a province south of Sierra Leone, and are employed on board all vessels on that coast to perform such occupations as would too much expose Europeans to the heat of the sun   They are an energetic, brave,

172

lively set of fellows, and very trustworthy; indeed, I do not know how we should have got on
without them. They work very hard, and when
they have saved money enough to buy themselves
one or more wives, according to their tastes, they
return to their own country to live in ease and dig-
nity. As they generally assume either the names of
the officers with whom they have served, or of some
reigning prince or hero of antiquity, it is extraordinary what a number of retired commanders and
lieutenants, not to speak of higher dignitaries, are to
be found in Krooland. Sierra Leone has been so
often described that I will not attempt to draw a
picture of its romantic though deceitful beauties.
Its blue sky and calm waters, its verdant groves and
majestic mountains, its graceful villas and flowering
shrubs, put one in mind of a lovely woman who em-
ploys her charms to beguile and destroy those who
confide in her.

On turning to my log, I find that on the ——,
at dawn, we unmoored ship, and under all plain sail
ran out of the river of Sierra Leone. As soon as
we were clear of the land we shaped a course for the
mouth of the Sherbro River, a locality notorious for
its numerous slave depots. On our way thither we
chased several sail, but some of them got off altogether, and others proved to be either British
cruisers, foreign men-of-war, or honest traders; so
that not a capture of any sort or kind did we make.
It was for no want of vigilance, however, on our
part; early and late, at noon and at night, I was at
the masthead on the look-out for a sail. I knew
that if I did not set a good example of watchful-
ness, others would be careless; for I held the re-
sponsible post, with all the honour and glory attached
to it, of first lieutenant of the *Gadfly*.

"Mr. Rawson," said the captain one day to me, in a good-natured tone, as I was walking the quarter-deck with him, "you will wear yourself out by your never-ceasing anxiety in looking out for slavers. There may be some, but my opinion is that they are a great deal too sharp-sighted to let us catch them in the brig. We may chance to get alongside one now and then in the boats and up the rivers, but out here it's in vain to look for them."

He was new to the coast, and the climate had already impaired his usual energy.

"Never fear, sir," I answered; "we may have a chance as well as others; and at all events it shall not be said that we did not get hold of any slavers for want of looking for them."

The next day we made the land about the mouth of the Sherbro River, and had to beat up against as oppressive a wind as I ever recollect experiencing. One is apt to fancy that the sky and water in that climate must always be blue. Now, and on many other occasions, instead of there being any cerulean tints in any direction, the sky was of a dirty copper tinge, or rather such as is seen spread out like a canopy over London on a calm damp day in November; while the sea, which rolled along in vast and sluggish undulations, looked as if it was formed of sheets of lead of the same hue. Looking astern, one almost expected to see the wake we ploughed up remaining indelible as on a hard substance. Over the land hung a mist of the same brownish-yellow hue, hiding everything but the faint outline of the coast.

"This is what I call a right-down regular Harmattan," said the master, who, like me, had been before in that delectable clime. The rest of the officers were new to it. "It will put the purser's whiskers in curl if he gives them a turn round with a marline-spike. Don't you smell the earthy flavour of the sands of Africa ?"

" In truth I think I do," said Jenkins, the second lieutenant, one of a group who were collected on the weather side of the quarter-deck. " I can distinguish the lions' and boa-constrictors' breath in it, too, if I'm not mistaken. Not much of Araby's spicy gales here, at all events."

" Blue skies, and verdant groves, and spicy gales sound very pretty in poetry, but very little of them do we get in reality," said the master. " And when there is a blue sky there's such a dreadfully hot sun peeps out of it, that one feels as if all the marrow in one's bones was being dried up. But this won't last long. We shall have a change soon."

" Glad you think so," observed Jenkins ; " I'm tired of this already."

" I didn't say the change would be for the better," answered the master. " We may have a black squall come roaring up from off the land, and take our topsails out of the bolt-ropes, or our topmasts over the side, before we know where we are, if you don't keep a bright look-out for it ; and we shall have the rainy season beginning in earnest directly, and then look out for wet jackets."

" A pleasant prospect you give us, Smith," said I. " I wish I could draw a better, but my experience won't let me differ from you."

The fog and the heat continued, and the wind, which put one in mind of the blast of a furnace, was equally steady, so that we slowly beat up till we got close in-shore. It was dark when we made our approach to the mouth of the Sherbro, and when we were off it we furled everything, and let the vessel go where she might, in the hopes that should there be a slaver inside ready to sail she might take the opportunity of running out while the land-wind lasted, and, not seeing us, might fall into our clutches. Every light was doused on board, and the bells were even not allowed to be struck. There we lay, like a log on the water, or, as Jenkins said, like a boa-constrictor ready to spring on its prey. Besides the regular look-outs, we had plenty of volunteer eyes peering into the darkness, in hopes of distinguishing an unsuspecting slaver. We of course kept the lead at the bottom, to mark the direction we were driving; but we did not move much, as the send of the sea on shore was counteracted by the wind blowing off it. Everybody made sure of having a prize before morning. Jenkins said he was certain of having one, and the master was very sanguine. The first watch passed away, and nothing appeared, but neither of them would go below.

" I think we must have driven too much to the southward," said Jenkins to the master, growing impatient. " The written orders for the night are to hold our position. Don't you think we had better make sail back again?"

" What! and show our whereabouts to the slaver, if there is one?" answered the master. " Besides, we haven't driven the sixteenth of a mile, except offshore; and there isn't much odds about that. Hark! did not you hear some cries coming from in-shore of us?"

We listened, but if sounds there were they were not repeated; and as Jenkins had the middle watch, I turned in, desiring to be called if anything occurred. I was on deck again just as the light of day was struggling into existence through the heavy canopy which hung over us; and as the sun, which must have been rising in the heavens, got higher, so

the mass of vapour over the land increased in
density and depth. At first it hung just above the
mangrove bushes, and we could see the tops of a
few lofty palm-trees on shore, and some distant
mountains popping their heads above it; but by
degrees they and the whole scene before us were
immersed in it.

The people's breakfast was just over when the
captain came on deck.

"No success, Mr. Rawson, last night," said he.
"We'll try my plan now. I'm convinced that there
must be slavers up that river; so we'll send the cutter and pinnace up to look after them. Desire Mr.
Jenkins to be prepared to take the command of
them, and let Mr. Johnston go also."

"Ay, ay, sir," I answered. "Shall I get the boats
ready, sir?"

"Yes, you may, at once," was the answer.

And the boats' crews were soon busily engaged
in making the necessary arrangements for their departure. With three cheers from the ship, away
they pulled towards the mouth of the Sherbro. We
watched them anxiously; for although the wind was
off-shore, the swell which rolled in threw up a heavy
surf on the bar, which at times makes the entrance
to that river very dangerous. There was, however,
every probability of Jenkins finding a smooth
place to get across, and if not, he was ordered to
return.

The crews gave way with a will, and the boats
flew across the dark, slow, heaving undulations, now
on the summit of one of the leaden rises, and now
lost to view from the deck. At last they reached
the irregular line of white foam, which danced up
glittering and distinct against the dark mass of land
and fog beyond. Into it they seemed to plunge, and

we saw no more of them, for the wall of breakers and the height of the swell entirely shut out all view beyond. With hearty wishes for the safety of our shipmates, we hoisted the topsails and ran off the land.

When we had run some eight or ten miles by the log, it came on a dead calm, and there we lay, rolling and tumbling about, as the master said, like a crab in a saucepan, without being able to help ourselves. At length it cleared up a little in the northwest, and a line of whitish sky was seen under the copper. The line increased in size and blueness, till our topsails were filled with a fine strong breeze from that quarter. The brig was then kept away, in order to run down to the southernmost extremity of our station.

I had just gone aloft to have a look round, when my eye fell on a sail broad on our starboard bow, which, from the size of her royals, just appearing above the horizon, I judged to be a large square-rigged vessel. I descended to the cabin to inform the captain, and to ask leave to make sail in chase.

" What, another of your phantom slavers, Rawson ?" he answered, laughing. " Make sail, by all means ; but I'm afraid we shall not be much the wiser."

Hauling up a little, I soon had every stitch of canvas on the brig which she could carry, with starboard fore-topmast studding-sails. We drew rapidly on the chase, and in half-an-hour could see nearly down to her topsails. The breeze freshened, and we went through the water in earnest.

" A thumping brig ; there's no doubt about it," said the master. " Observe the rakish cut of her sails ; one can almost smell the niggers on board her."

"She's carrying on, too, as if she was in a hurry to get away from us," I remarked.

"So she is," said the captain, coming on deck. "But it strikes me that those slave-dealers generally send faster craft to sea than she appears to be. It's only some of your wise governments who don't care about the slavers being caught who send out slow-coaches, which are fit for nothing but carrying timber."

"Then why should she be in such a hurry?" I observed.

"A sail right ahead!" sang out the man at the masthead.

"Because she's in chase of something else," remarked the captain, laughing. "Hand me the glass. I thought so. What do you make out of that ensign which has just blown out at her peak?"

I took a look through the telescope.

"A Yankee brig, sir," I exclaimed, in a tone of vexation. "I should not wonder but what she is an American man-of-war, after all."

Well, though it must be owned that the Yankees can build fine and fast ships when they wish to do so, and want them to go along, I must say that the chase sailed as badly as any ship-of-war I ever met. We came up with her hand-over-hand, and we were soon sufficiently near to exchange signals, when we made out that she was the United States brig-of-war the *Grampus*, in chase of a suspicious-looking craft to the southward.

Exchanging a few courteous expressions with the American captain, who stood on the weather side of the poop eyeing us with a look of envy, we passed rapidly by him.

"If you make yon stranger a prize, I think we ought to go shares," he said, laughing. "We sighted her first."

" You shall have the whole of her if you overhaul her first," answered our captain.

" Then I calculate we may as well give in, for your legs are a tarnation deal longer than ours, it seems."

The sun, which now shone forth for a brief space, glittered on the bright copper of the brig as she lifted to the send of the sea, and the foam flew over her bows and washed fore and aft along her dingy sides as she tore through the water; but it would not do, the little *Gadfly* laughed her to scorn, and, as we headed her, seemed impudently to kick up her heels at her in contempt at her slow ways. We were not long in coming up with the chase, nor in making out by the cut of her canvas, her short yards, and heavy-looking hull, that she was no slaver. As soon as we fired a gun, and hoisted our ensign and pennant, she hove to, and on sending a boat on board we found that she was the *Mary Jane*, of Bristol, a steady-going old African trader. She had been carrying sail, both because she was on her right course, and because she could not tell but what the *Grampus* might be a slaver or pirate, anxious to overhaul her.

The master, who was a very civil old fellow, came on board, and gave us some valuable suggestions. He had witnessed some of the horrors of the middle passage, and was a strong advocate for the abolition of the slave-trade.

" Africa will never improve while it exists, and it will exist as long as people find it profitable, and the governments of the world either encourage it or only take half measures to abolish it. I am sorry to own, too, that people nearer home gain too much by it to withstand the temptation of assisting those engaged in it, and I know for certain that many

English merchants have account-currents with slave dealers, and send their vessels out here full of goods expressly for them."

I afterwards found that what he said was perfectly true. After taking some luncheon with us, he tumbled into his boat and stood on his course, while we hauled our wind to return to the northward.

"We have not made our first prize yet, Rawson," said the captain, as I took dinner with him in his cabin that day.

"No, sir; but I hope we soon shall," I replied. "Better luck next time!"

As chance would have it, just after sunset we again fell in with the *Grampus*, and passed close to her.

"You didn't find many woolly heads on board that 'ere craft, I calculate?" said a voice from the main rigging, followed by a loud laugh from several persons.

"No," I answered, indignantly, thinking of the conversation with the master of the *Mary Jane*. "But there's a time coming when your people will bitterly regret that woolly heads or slavery exists in your country, and will wish that you long ago had done your best to abolish it. Good night, gentlemen!"

There was no answer, and we rapidly flew by each other.

For two or three days we cruised about as unsuccessful as before, the weather continuing fine; but the sky giving indubitable signs of the approach of the stormy and rainy season, we beat back along shore to pick up our boats. The wind had been veering about for some time, and at length seemed to have made up its mind to enjoy a stiffish blow

out of the south-west. This, of course, would have
kicked up a considerable surf on the bar, and as
Jenkins had orders, as soon as he saw signs of such
being the case, to come out and look out for us, we
were in hourly expectation of falling in with the
boats.   We had, however, seen nothing of them,
though we kept a very sharp look-out, and had
almost got up to the mouth of the river, when, in
the afternoon watch, I bethought me that by way of
a change I would go aloft, and try if a fresh pair of
eyes would see farther than those of the man stationed there.   I had been up about five minutes,
when my eye fell on the white canvas of a largish
vessel standing along shore under easy sail.   She
had a most suspicious look; indeed, I felt convinced
that she, at all events, was a slaver.   I was on deck
in an instant, and, hurrying into the captain's cabin
with a look of triumph, though I tried to be perfectly calm and unconcerned, I uttered the words,
"A sail on the lee beam!"

"Very well, Mr. Rawson.   What does she look
like?" said the captain.

"She's a large topsail schooner, sir, and she's
without doubt a slaver," I answered quite calmly,
as a matter of course.

"What, another of your slavers?" he answered.
"I'm afraid they'll all turn out Flying Dutch-
men."

"Not this time, sir, I'm certain," I replied.   "Shall
we make sail in chase?"

"Oh, certainly—certainly!" he replied.   "I'll be
on deck immediately myself."

I flew on deck, and, without waiting for him, sang
out, in a cheery voice, to the boatswain, "Turn the
hands up!   Make sail!"   The pipe sounded along
the decks with a shriller sound than usual, I thought,

and the news that a suspicious sail was in sight having already travelled below, the men were all ready, and flew aloft before the last sound of the order was given. The gear of the courses was over-hauled whilst the topgallant-sails and royals were being loosed, and in a few seconds all plain sail was made on the brig. The stranger, who had not apparently before seen us, was not long in following our example. He set his foresail, topgallant sail, and royal, gaff-topsail and flying-jib, in addition to the canvas he had been before carrying, and, putting down his helm, stood off-shore on a bowline, with the intention of crossing our bows. The reason of his doing this was, that to the northward a long and dangerous reef ran off from the shore, so that he had no other means of escape. We had him, indeed, partly embayed, and yet, if he was able to carry on, it was clear that he might still manage to get out ahead of us. The *Gadfly* sailed well, and carried her canvas admirably, but so did the stranger; and, by the way every sail on board her was set, it was evident he was in earnest in doing his best to weather on us.

" What do you think of that fellow now, sir?" I said, as the captain came on deck. "There's no mistaking what she is."

" Why, Rawson, I think you are right this time, at all events," was the answer. "Stand by the royals, though. We must not carry the masts over the side; and she will go along as fast without them."

I saw it was time, indeed, to take in our lighter canvas, for, as we were obliged to haul more up, the masts were bending like whips, and the green seas came washing in bodily to leeward, while the spray flew in sheets over our weather bulwarks. The day

N

wore on, and evening was fast approaching, with
every prospect of a dirty night; the wind was
increasing, and dark masses of clouds came rolling
up from the south-west, and flying over in the
opposite quarter, though as they came on faster than
they disappeared, the sky overhead soon got pretty
full of them.   The stranger, meantime, was carrying
on in gallant style—not an inch of anything did he
slack.   He seemed to think that it was neck or
nothing with him.   It must be understood that
while his course was about west, and that nothing
off that could he venture to go, we were able to keep
rather more away.   There was no chance, however,
of our getting him under our guns before dark,
when he, of course, would do his best to double on
us.   It was an exciting time, and even the most
apathetic on board would not go below.   We were
longing to get near enough to give her a shot or
two with any probability of hitting her.   All this
time the sea was getting up, and as she was evidently
a sharp, shallow vessel, this much impeded her progress.   Instead of, as when we first saw her, gliding
gently through the waves, or putting them grace-
fully aside with her bows, she now rose and fell as
they passed under her, and hammered away at them
as she strove to make her onward progress.

We caught one bright gleam of the sun on her
copper as she lifted on the top of a wave, just as the
glowing orb of day sank into the water, and in a few
minutes darkness would cover the face of the deep.
Now was to come the tug of war, or rather, the trial
of our patience.   The moon had not yet risen,
although it soon would, but, in the meantime, she
might tack and stand away to the southward, or she
might pass ahead of us.

"Try her with a shot, Mr. Rawson," said the

captain. " If we could hull her, the fellow would heave-to."

" I would prefer knocking away some of her wings, and thus secure her, rather than trust to such slippery gentry," I thought, as I elevated one of the lee guns and fired.

The shot went over her or between her masts, for no damage was done. It showed, however, that she was within range.

" Have another slap at her," said the captain. " But I do not think there's much chance of hitting her with the sea we have on."

This time the gunner took aim, but with no better success. Another and another shot was fired with the same want of result, and nothing seemed in any way to daunt the chase. Darkness had now come on in earnest, and we could just distinguish the schooner's sails through the gloom. A number of sharp eyes were kept on her, though they at times almost lost sight of her, and the dark clouds which hung overhead, to increase our difficulties, every now and then sent down deluges of rain, which still more impeded our prospect. After some time the captain, who had been below, returned on deck.

" Whereabouts is the chase, Mr. Rawson?" he asked.

" Right away under the lee cat-head," I answered, " She was there a moment ago."

I looked again. She was nowhere to be seen. I flew to the binnacle; we had not in any way altered our course.

" Provoking enough," observed the captain, coolly. " But I thought it would be so."

I had nothing to say in return, but I did not despair of seeing her again.

"She must have tacked," said the captain, "and hopes to get away to the southward of us before the morning."

"I think not, sir," I answered. "I suspect she'll hold her course; for, when last seen, she was drawing near us, and she hopes to pass ahead of us in the dark; but if we can but get a gleam of moonlight to show us her whereabouts, we may yet clip her wings for her before she gets away from us."

Almost as I was speaking, the moon rose above the waters undimmed by a cloud, its pale light revealing the schooner just where I expected her to be. A cheer burst from the lips of many of the anxious watchers.

"Now or never is the time to knock some of her spars away!" I thought. "Shall we give her another shot, sir?" I asked of the captain.

"Yes; you may give her a broadside, Mr. Rawson, and slap it into the fellow's hull. He deserves no mercy at our hands. But stay; we might run the chance of killing some of the unfortunate blacks who may be below."

Going round to the guns, I elevated them as much as possible, and told the captains to try and hit her masts. The order was given to fire as each gun could be brought to bear. No easy task, let me observe, for so much did the brig heel over, that the men in the waist were up to their knees nearly all the time in water. It was a night to try the mettle of fellows, and none could behave better than did ours. The wind howled and whistled as it rushed through the rigging, the waves roared and splashed as we dashed through them, and threw their white crests over us, the masts seemed to bend, and the hull to utter unusual groans of complaint as we tasked her powers to the utmost. Darkness was around us, an enemy at hand, and a dangerous shore under our lee; but all hands laughed and joked with the most perfect unconcern. Again the moon was obscured, and on we tore through the foaming waters. There was no use in firing, for no aim could then be taken. Once more the clouds cleared away, and the moonbeams shone on the hull and sails of the schooner with all her canvas set, just about to cross our fore foot.

"Now's your time, my men!" I sang out, as I sprung forward, luffing up at the same time, so as to get our broadside to bear on her.

The foremost gun was the first fired, followed by the others in succession. Nothing daunted, the fellow was holding on, his jib-halyards alone having been carried away, and the jib was slashing about under his bows.

"By Jupiter! he'll weather on us now, if we don't take care and slip away in the wind's eye," I exclaimed.

The captain thought so too; and again ordering me to fire right at her hull, a yaw was given, and gun after gun as they were brought to bear was poured into the slaver. The effects of the shot made her fly up into the wind. Several of her braces and halyards were cut away, and, she now nearly a wreck, we in a few minutes were close aboard her. "Hands, shorten sail." In three seconds Her Majesty's brig was under topsails, hove-to alongside her prize.

"Mr. Rawson," said the captain, addressing me, "there will be some difficulty in boarding that vessel, and I wish that you would go in the gig and take possession of her. She is our first prize, remember, and it would not do to let her slip through our fingers."

" Ay, ay, sir. Gig's crew away, then !" I sung
out, as I stepped to the binnacle to take the bearings
of the schooner from us. Luckily I did so, for we
could only then just distinguish her, and a dark mass
of clouds driving across the moon shut her out
completely from our sight. " Bear a hand there,
and lower away the gig !" I sung out, for I was
anxious to shove off before the brig entirely lost her
way through the water.

It was not particularly pleasant work in the heavy
sea there was running having to grope about in the
dark for a craft manned probably by desperadoes,
who would be too happy to cut our throats if they
had the opportunity. I had a brace of pistols, and
a few cutlasses had been thrown into the boat. Thus
prepared we cast off, and the men bent bravely to
their oars as the boat topped the heavy seas over
which we had to pass. The brig showed a light for
us to steer by, but the schooner was in no way so
civil. On we pulled, however, in the hope of hitting
her, but though we had gone over fully the distance
I calculated she must have been from us, yet nothing
of her could we see. I was almost in despair, and
as while looking for her I could not attend carefully
to the boat's steering we shipped two or three
heavy seas, which almost swamped her, and we had
to bale them out as fast as we could. For some
time the men lay on their oars, just keeping the
boat's head to the seas while we looked round for
the chase.

" She has gone ! The rascal took the opportunity
of the last shower to sneak off," I thought. " Pleasant. But patience; c'est la fortune de la
guerre."

Disconsolate enough I was steering back for the
faint glimmer of light which I believed proceeded

from the lantern on board the *Gadfly*, when I
fancied I heard the loud flapping of a sail near us.
I looked earnestly into the darkness.

"There she is, sir," sung out the coxswain.

"You're right. Give way, my boys," I cried;
and in a few minutes we were alongside the
schooner.

Not a rope was thrown to us, nor was any assistance offered, so we had to scramble on board as best
we could. It was fortunate that we met with no
resistance, from which we afterwards found we had
had a narrow escape, when all our lives would have
been sacrificed. As we leaped down on board over
the bulwarks we found only one man on deck, on
the after-part of which he was walking by himself,
evidently in a furious rage, by the manner in which
he cursed and gesticulated. As the light of the
lantern fell on his countenance I thought I had
never seen one with a more diabolical expression.
He was a little man, slightly built, with dark
weatherbeaten, and sharp features, excessively ugly.
His eyes were small, but black as jet, and I fancied
that I could see them twinkling even in the dark.
The crew had all been sent below, but we soon
roused them up, twenty in number; fierce, cut-
throat-looking villains most of them were. The
between-decks we found crowded with slaves; and
we found, when we came to count them, that there
were three hundred men, women, and children,
so closely packed that they could not lie down
even to rest. They had suffered dreadfully during
the chase, with the fright and heat, and from
having the hatches battened down. Our first
business was to shorten sail, which we made the
Spaniards and Portuguese who formed the crew
go aloft to do; and we then edged the schooner

down to where the brig was, and lay-to close to her.

The master of the slaver, when at length he became convinced that there was no help for what had occurred, grew more calm, and he then told me that everything he had in the world was embarked on board that craft, that he had set his canvas and made every sheet and tack fast, when, sending all his people below, the hatches being battened down, he himself had taken the helm, determined to weather us or to run his vessel under water.

"I should have escaped, too," he continued, "if your cursed shot had not carried away my topsails while all the hands were below. A quarter of an hour more and you might have looked for me in vain."

I did not tell him how nearly we were missing him after all; indeed I had enough to do to watch him and his crew, and to see that they did not play us any trick. All the men I confined in the fore peak, after securing all the arms I could find, while I allowed him to turn into his own berth, where he slept, or pretended to sleep. I never passed a more anxious night, what with the stench and the groans of the wretched slaves, and the risk of a crew of desperadoes rising on us. We kept, however, as close to the *Gadfly* as we could, and hailed every time the bell was struck, to say all was right. Towards morning the wind moderated and the sea went down, and at daylight a prize crew came on board to set the schooner to rights. This we were not long in doing, as her damages were slight, and such as, had the slaver's people been more determined, they might without difficulty have repaired. There was by that time merely a light breeze, and as soon as we got the canvas on the schooner we found that we could sail round and round the brig, so that it was fortunate we had managed to wing her before the sea went down, or we should have had no chance with her.

While the slave captain was still asleep, and the rest of his crew were below, one of the fellows shoved his head up the fore hatchway, and asked to speak with me. I told him to come aft, and I recognised him as a Portuguese whom I had taken once before in the West Indies. With an affrighted look he glanced towards the round-house on deck, where the captain was sleeping, and motioned me to come as far from it as possible.

" I have run every risk, senhor, to come and warn you of danger, in the hope that you will be lenient to us," he began. " That man in there, senhor, is the very devil. Don't you recollect him? You took him in the *Andorinha*, off the Havannah. He was really her master, though he pretended to be the mate."

It had struck me from the first that I had seen the fellow's face before, but I could not recollect where.

" Yes, I remember him," I replied. " But what of that ? "

" Why, senhor, you know what a desperate fellow he was then, and he has not altered. Even last night, when we rounded to to prevent your sinking us, he called us all aft, and asking us if we would stick by him, proposed heaving some shot into your gig as you came alongside, knocking you and your people on the head, and while your vessel was looking about to pick up the sinking boat, in the dark to try and slip away from you. He was in a furious rage when we would not consent. Some were afraid of the plan miscarrying, and of being caught notwithstanding, and hung for murder. Others were

unwilling to kill you, as you never ill-treat your
prisoners, of which number pray rank me, and while
he was still urging his project you jumped on board.
You had a narrow escape though, senhor, for he was
nearly pistolling you as you appeared, to set us the
example."

So I felt, especially when I saw the diabolical-
looking little villain soon after appear on deck. I
promised the informer that I would not forget him,
and would be on my guard, though I did not give
him any credit for disinterested motives in mention-
ing what had occurred. I had no difficulty by daylight in recognising my friend the captain, nor shall
I again forget his ugly mug in a hurry. He also
saw that he was known, and had the impudence to
claim me as an old acquaintance.

Everything being put to rights on board the
schooner, I handed her over to a mate and the
crew, who were to take her to Sierra Leone. Before
leaving her, however, I had all the slaves up on
deck, a third at a time, and had them washed and
cleaned, as also the hold, as well as circumstances
would allow. A great number of the poor wretches
died before they reached their port ; not on account
of bad weather, or the length of the voyage, but
from their having been a long time confined in the
barracoons previously to their being embarked. The
little captain and most of his crew, however, we sent
on board the *Gadfly*, as it would not have been
prudent to trust him in the schooner.

With a flowing sheet our first prize stood away
for Sierra Leone, and three hearty cheers accompanied her on her course.

"We've not made a bad night's work of it,
master," said I, as I sat down to breakfast with
him.

" No," he answered, " if the prize ever reaches her port."

" Why should you think she will not ?" I asked.

" It's better not to be too sanguine. There's many a slip between the cup and the lip," was the reply.

" Too true an adage," I felt. " I'm sure I've found it so in my course through life."

We, meantime, stood in shore to look for our boats. The night closed in without our meeting with them, till at length we became seriously alarmed for their safety. The next day, when just off the mouth of the Sherbro, two black objects were descried from the masthead. We made towards them, and with no little satisfaction welcomed our shipmates on board. They had had hard work of it, with damp fogs or rain nearly half the time, and without having enjoyed any other shelter than such as the boats and a sail could afford. Poor Jenkins was ill with fever, as were several of the people, and they were for some time on the doctor's list. We now shaped a course for Sierra Leone, to assist in the condemnation of our prize. We found her arrived there safe enough, and having been taken with slaves on board, there was no doubt of her capture being legal. We were not sorry to get rid of the little slave captain and his crew. He kept up his character to the last, and I never met a man so energetic and daring in doing evil. Before we left we discovered that he was trying to induce some other slave captains and their crews to join with him in cutting out a condemned slaver which lay in the harbour; but it appeared that they considered the risk of the undertaking too great to attempt it. He formed afterwards several other similar projects, and was finally shipped off to the Havannah as too dangerous a character to remain in the colony.

We afterwards captured a number of slavers, but none of them afforded us so much interest and gratification as the taking of our first prize.

Cast Away on a Sand-bank:

OR, MY EXPERIENCES OF LIFE ON THE OCEAN.

IDSHIPMAN wanted for a first-class India trader! "Oh! mother, that will just do for me!" I exclaimed. "Do let me go; I shall be back in no time, and have all sorts of yarns to tell you." I pressed and pressed. My mother saw that I should do little good by remaining longer at school, or thought so at all events, and I gained my point. Within a month I found myself on board the good ship *Betsey Blair*, of six hundred tons, Captain Joseph Johns, master, gliding over the Atlantic at the rate of nine knots an hour, bound out to Singapore. We had two mates, a surgeon, two midshipmen besides myself, one of whom was making his first voyage, and three apprentices who had never before been to sea, with a crew, including the boatswain, of five-and-twenty hands. I did not find things quite as pleasant as I had expected, from reading "Tom Cringle's Log" and Captain Marryat's novels, and other romantic tales of the sea.

Captain Johns was every inch a sailor. He told us midshipmen that he intended we should become sailors, and he began by sending us aloft the first calm day to black down the rigging and grease the masts. I began to go aloft with my span new uniform on. "No! no!" he said, calling me down, "the second mate will serve you out a shirt and trousers fit for that work." The mates laughed and the men laughed also. I got the shirt and trousers, and spent a couple of hours aloft, making good use of tar-brush and grease-pot, till my clothes were as black as the rigging and as greasy as the masts. It was my first real lesson in the duty of a seaman. I am now much obliged to our worthy master. I mention it to show that the realities of a midshipman's life on board a merchantman, if the captain does his duty, are not quite what young gentlemen anticipate.

We had a quick passage to Singapore. There discharging our cargo, which, from that important mart of the East, was distributed in small craft in all directions among the numberless islands of those seas, we got ready for our return home, having to call at Melbourne on our way. Having taken in our cargo, we polished up, and hearing that several passengers were coming on board, we midshipmen put on our best uniforms to receive them, flattering ourselves that, as the paint-brushes and polishing leathers had been kept going, we and the ship cut a very respectable appearance. Captain Johns was proud of his ship, and prouder still of keeping his crew in perfect order. We had several passengers, a Mr. and Mrs. Haliday and three children, a Mrs. Burnett, Mrs. Magnus, and a Mr. Turner, a merchant. The ladies were going home, I believe, on account of health. My chief friend on board was the surgeon of the ship, Mr. Gilbert. He was a young man, but very intelligent and scientific, and took a pleasure in imparting the information he possessed. There seemed thus every prospect of our

having a pleasant voyage home. Mr. Crawford
was the first mate. I was in his watch. Our second
mate was a Mr. Morgan. With colours flying, our
smart little ship stood out of the harbour of Singapore. The weather was fine and the sea smooth.

"Do you think we shall have this sort of weather
all the way home," asked Mr. Haliday, who was
a timid man, and anxious about his wife and
family.

"Well, sir, I have made three or four passages,
when we carried the fine weather the whole way out
and home, but if we do not, we must do our best
and trust to God, Mr. Haliday, that is my maxim,
and I have always found it hold good. I have been
at sea ever since I was a boy, and in more hurri-
canes and gales of wind than I can well count up,
and yet I never was shipwrecked, and here I am
alive and well," answered Captain Johns, to whom
the question had been put.

"But, captain, there is a saying, 'the pitcher
which goes often to the well gets broken at last.'"

"That, I rather think, means to refer to those
who tempt God, and a man who has to run into
danger in the way of duty is not to my mind doing
that. We must trust God whatever happens, Mr.
Haliday. Even if the stout little ship were to be
cast away, He would find a means for our escape if
He thought fit."

I overheard this conversation, and it made a
strong impression on me. For some time the fine
weather continued, when it came on very thick, with
baffling winds. For three days or more we had
been unable to take an observation. The chief
mate had the morning watch. Soon after I got on
deck I heard him sing out, "Keep a sharp look-out
there forward!" Then stepping aft he said to the

man at the helm, " Keep the ship north-by-west."
The wind, I should say, at this time was west-by-
south, and we were going nearly nine knots through
the water. The events of that morning were vividly
impressed upon my memory.

" Mr. Jennings," said the first mate to me, " what
is that black look in the water a-head !"

I ran forward. The look-out man declared that
it was the reflection of a heavy black cloud hanging
just over the ship.

" It is no such thing!" exclaimed the mate,
sharply looking over the gangway. " Hard up with
the helm ! All hands on deck ! Wear ship !"

I, with the watch on deck, flew to the braces.
The ship wore round, but almost before we could
touch the ropes a terrific crash was heard, and she
struck heavily aft. The following sea drove her
broadside on to the reef, part of which we now saw
clearly rising out of the water not a cable's length
from us. The first crash sent the captain and other
officers rushing on deck, while cries and shrieks
arose from the poor passengers in the cabin. The
next sea which struck her, after she had touched,
came flying over us, and there seemed scarcely a
possibility of our saving our lives. " Lads !"
shouted the captain, " obey my orders, and I will
do my best for you. See to cutting away the masts.
Clear the rigging as the masts are cut away. Mr.
Jennings, clear the pinnace for launching." Another midshipman was sent down to entreat the
passengers to remain quiet below till the boats were
ready, assuring them that they would run great risk
of losing their lives if they came on deck. Although
the masts were quickly cut away, the ship continued
to lurch heavily upon the reef, and it seemed that
she must quickly go to pieces. She now lay com-

pletely on her beam ends, so that it was difficult to stand on her deck. I had made the pinnace ready for launching, but she was a heavy boat, and though all hands exerted themselves to the utmost, we could not manage it, our good captain getting his leg jammed in the attempt. We hauled him up to the weather bulwarks, where he held on, still giving his orders. Our next attempt was to launch the jolly-boat. To do this we had to hoist her up to the davits on the upper quarter. When placing oars, and a couple of good hands in her, we watched our opportunity, and, after a sea had broken over us, quickly bailing her out, allowed her to glide into the water. Captain Johns ordered the men to pull to the rock which we had at first seen, and which lay a short distance inside the reef. We had a small well-built lifeboat. To preserve her from injury was of the greatest importance. We got her up in the same way to the upper davits and launched her in safety. As soon as this was done the ladies and children were brought up from the cabin, which was already half full of water, and, being placed in her, she pulled away for the jolly-boat. The ladies' husbands watched them anxiously. It was impossible to say at what moment the ship would break up. So terrific were the blows she was receiving that it seemed scarcely possible she could hold together many minutes; indeed, already portions of her had been torn away, and were seen floating to leeward.

In the next trip the men passengers and the young seamen were taken to the jolly-boat.

"Do you, Jennings, and you, Mr. Gilbert, go in her," said the captain.

"No, sir, thank you, I will stay by you," I answered.

o

"I order you both into the boat. I am not to be disobeyed," he exclaimed.

Of course we could not refuse. Already the jolly-boat, when we got into her, was very full, and there seemed some risk of her being swamped. Just then one of the seamen struck his boat-hook down along-side. "Why, the water is quite shallow here!" he exclaimed. "Overboard lads! The ladies shall run no risk on our account;" and six or eight men instantly jumped into the water, holding on to the boat, it being tolerably smooth under the lee of the rock where she lay.

By the last trip the master came off, bringing some charts and nautical instruments, which he had secured. "What about food?" some one asked. A small quantity, it appeared, had been secured, but not a drop of fresh water had been brought off. The master now ordered some of the men to get into the lifeboat, and we were pretty evenly divided among the two.

"How far off are we from the Australian coast?" asked Mr. Haliday.

"Four hundred miles at the nearest," was the answer. "It is true, my friends," said the master, "but half-a-mile off there is a sand-bank. We will make for that, and there pray that God will give us the means of escape." The grey dawn broke soon after we reached the bank, where we landed in safety. "Now, my friends," said the master, as we stood grouped around him, "let us lift up our hearts in thankfulness to that merciful God who has thus far preserved us." Hearty and sincere was, I feel assured, the prayer that rose from that barren sand-bank. We thanked God for preserving us, and we prayed that He might yet watch over us, and carry us in safety to land.

The bank was scarcely more than a hundred and fifty yards long, and about a third of the width. Still we had reason to be thankful. Not a life had been lost, in spite of the fearful risk we had run. Had a gale been blowing, however, not one of us could have escaped. As the sun rose our clothes quickly dried, but its rays soon became fearfully hot, and beat down upon our unprotected heads. The master was suffering all this time from the injury he had received, and was obliged to lie down. He, however, first directed the two mates to return with the boats to the wreck, to bring off whatever they could find likely to be of use, and anxiously we watched them as they pulled away. Our lives depended upon the success of their expedition. Meantime, the hot sun increased, and we all began to suffer from thirst. It was sad to see the poor little children crying for water when there was none to give them. Some of us, with pieces of board, began to dig in the sand, hoping to find water, but after making several deep holes we came each time to the coral rock. That, however, was moist and free from salt. Though the amount of fluid we could obtain was trifling, it afforded us some slight relief to lick the bare rock, and helped to cool our tongues. At length the boats returned. Eagerly we all hurried down to welcome them, and haul them up on the beach. A shout of joy arose when we found that the jolly-boat had a cask of water on board, besides some provisions—a cheese, some potted meat, and some biscuit. How thankfully we poured the sweet liquid down our throats. Captain Johns, however, would allow only half-a-gill to each of us, all sharing alike. These things might prolong our lives for a short time, but yet our hopes of escaping were small indeed. The wreck still hung together, but the wind appeared to be again getting up ; indeed, there was so much sea, that the captain was afraid of sending back the boats. Anxiously that night passed away, but our courage was kept up by the captain's cheerful and manly voice.

"Trust in God, friends," he continued to say, "that is the best advice I can give you. As I have said before, I will do my best, and I hope all you will do your best, and let us never despair." Next morning, in spite of the heavy sea running, the mates pushed off in the boats in the hopes of obtaining further supplies from the wreck. Dangerous as was the undertaking, the condition of our party on the sand-bank was not less perilous, for should the boats be lost, our fate, in all human probability, would be sealed. We watched them anxiously. Now they appeared on the crest of a sea, now they were hidden by the foaming breakers. At length they were altogether lost to sight from the sand-bank. We stood, our hands on each others' shoulders, our necks stretched out, eagerly watching for their return. Now a dark object was seen. We thought it was one of the boats. No, it was a piece of the wreck. Another and another piece appeared. Some drove on to the beach, and we hurried down to secure them. At length I saw the lifeboat drawing near. Alas! was the other lost? "See! see! she is astern of her!" cried some one. On they both came, and we hurried down to welcome them. Both of them came laden. In the jolly-boat were some sails, and several casks of provisions, and in the lifeboat, among other things, a small keg of lime-juice. The surgeon spied it out, and literally shouted for joy. "It may be the saving of our lives," he exclaimed ; "and will at all events keep scurvy at bay." That night we were able to erect a tent for the poor women and children, as also for some of the men passengers, and two or three of the seamen and boys who were suffering from exposure. Still my friend the surgeon looked grave.

"Jennings," he said to me, as we were taking a turn together, "there is one thing I dread more than all others—the want of water. What we have will go a very, very short way, and then——! My lad, do you know what it is to die of thirst—the throat becoming drier and drier, the tongue swelling, and getting as hard as shoe-leather, and blacker and blacker, the sight growing dim, the voice failing?"

"A fearful picture!" I said. "What is to be done?"

"Why, we must go off at all risks, and see if we cannot get materials from the wreck to form a still. The ship struck at high water, I observed, and possibly what we want, even though washed out of her, may be obtained at low water. Will you go off with me to make the search?"

I, of course, agreed, and the second mate steered the lifeboat. A fresh crew was quickly found, and we put off from the bank.

"Another night may see the wreck broken up, and we may lose everything," observed the surgeon. We pulled on. The wreck had by this time driven up so far on the reef that at dead low water part of the coral rock was exposed, and we could wade up to her. We hunted about till we came upon some copper piping. "This is valuable," exclaimed the surgeon. We next found a boiler, and afterwards a large cistern, still inside the vessel. We got it out, though not without difficulty, and on board the boat. Several tools, an iron ladle and some solder were also found; indeed, we regretted that the jolly-boat had not come off, that many more things might have been landed. All we could hope was that the weather would continue moderate, and that other articles might be saved on the following day. We returned in safety with our prize. As soon as we landed, the surgeon summoned the blacksmith and his mate to his assistance, and a fire being lighted, immediately set to work to erect a still. A shout of joy was raised when the first fresh water was seen to issue from it. We lay down that night with one of our chief causes of anxiety removed. "We may thank God for this," said the master, summoning all the people round him. "Now I have a proposal to make. It is clear we cannot remain on this reef for ever. I wish to know whether those who are fit to assist in the work will undertake the building of a boat, in which we may reach the mainland." A considerable number held up their hands to signify their readiness to assist in what he proposed. "Then, my friends," he said, "I will divide you into three parties—one to assist Mr. Gilbert in distilling the water, another to visit the wreck and obtain all the materials which can be saved, while the third will be employed in building the boat." All agreed to this proposal, and early next morning, as soon as daylight broke, we were on our feet ready to commence work. I was employed with the second mate in going off to the wreck, while the first mate and the master assisted the carpenter's crew in building the boat. We were fortunate in obtaining all sorts of articles, amongst others, useful tools and a supply of clothing. With the articles we found, the surgeon improved his machinery for distilling the water, and at length he produced nearly thirty gallons a-day. Our pro-

visions, however, were getting short, and at length
we were reduced to half-a-pound of flour a-day,
which we made up into puddings with salt water—
very heavy dough, but it stopped our hunger and
kept us alive. It took us just a month from the
day the boat's keel was laid till she was launched.
It was a day not to be forgotten. The ladies and
children stood round cheering lustily. We called
her the *Hope*. She sat well on the water, but
leaked considerably. We had therefore to haul her
up again, and stop the leaks. When again launched
she was found to be thoroughly watertight. It took
us two days to get her rigged and stowed. All the
casks we had been able to save were filled with
water, Mr. Gilbert working day and night to obtain
a supply. At length, after a residence of five weeks
on the sand-bank, which would assuredly have
proved our grave, had it not been for the invention
of our surgeon, we bade the sand-bank farewell, and
stood towards Moreton Bay, on the Australian coast.
The wind was fair and moderate. About thirty of
us were on board the *Hope*, while six preferred
trusting their fortunes to the lifeboat. The wind
shifting, when we were, according to our calcula-
tions, about twenty leagues off the land, drove us to
the mouth of the Brisbane river. A somewhat
heavy sea was running, but the *Hope* behaved
beautifully, and our captain knew the entrance.
What an idea it gave us of perfect rest, when, after
being tossed about for so many days, we glided up
the tranquil river! The settlers came down as we
reached the shore, and warmly welcomed us.
"Thanks, friends, thanks!" said our good master,
"but before I thank you I desire to thank One by
whose means we have been preserved," and kneeling
down, the fine old man poured out his heart in

prayer. I am thankful to say that one and all of us followed his example, and if we did not pray with as much fervour and earnestness as he did, I believe that the prayer and the gratitude we expressed came from our hearts.

Owen's Revenge.

A TALE OF THE SEA.

CHAPTER I.

I WAS then scarcely ten years old. My father possessed a fine estate, and we lived in the greatest luxury. I had ridden out by myself on my pony, and had reached a somewhat secluded part of the park, where the bridle-path passed among grassy knolls, and tall trees, flinging their branches across a narrow dell, formed a thick canopy overhead, and gave a somewhat gloomy aspect to the sequestered spot. It was one I seldom visited, and I was wondering whether sprites or fairies, good or bad, of whom I had heard the country people speak, really came there to gambol and play their pranks, when a figure started up from behind a bush with a menacing gesture, and before I could make my pony gallop on to escape him, I found the rein seized by a stout man with bushy whiskers, a sunburnt countenance, and, as I then thought, very unpleasant features. He appeared to me much older than he probably really was, comparing, as I naturally did, his face

207

with those on which I was most accustomed to look. Though his features were rough, he was tolerably well dressed, and did not look like a common ruffian who designed to rob me. For more than a minute he held my rein in the attitude of forcing back my pony, and glared fiercely at me.

"I have come to look at you, that I may know you again when we meet," he exclaimed at length; and, to my surprise, the tone of his voice was that of a gentleman. "You have deprived me of my inheritance—you have come between me and fortune and happiness and the only things worth living for in this world, and I am determined to have my revenge. While we remain together on earth, I will pursue you—whatever your course in life may be, I will find you out; I will balk you in your dearest wishes—I will prove your bane in whatever you undertake—I will destroy your happiness—I will stand like a lion in your path, and bar your progress. I will not injure you in life or limb—I might kill you, but I will not do that—as you have injured me by legal means, so will I keep within the law in taking my revenge, but it will be a full one notwithstanding. Now go, youngster, and my bitter curses go with you! You may tell your fond father and mother what you have heard; their love cannot protect you—their anger cannot overtake me. Before they could decide what to do I shall be far away beyond their reach; and tell them that, though they may not for many a long day hear of me, that I bide my time. Now go—go —or I may be tempted to do more than I intended, and remember that I hate you!"

He flung the pony's head from him, making the animal rear and almost fall back over me, but I stuck on, and, digging my spurs into his flanks, dashed on along the path, leaving the man gazing fiercely at me with his fist clenched and his arm extended in the direction I had taken. When I again took one more alarmed look round, he had disappeared. My first impression was that the man was mad, but still his curses and his threats and fierce looks frightened me, and I must own that I felt somewhat inclined to cry. I did not, though, but galloped on as hard as I could till I reached the house. Giving my pony to a groom, I ran up into my room without speaking, and, locking myself in, burst into a fit of tears. Two hours afterwards my mother, wondering at my non-appearance in the drawing-room, came to my door, and when I opened it and exhibited my scared countenance, she inquired if anything dreadful had happened. "Oh no—nothing," I answered. "Only an odd man appeared in the woods, and said something strange—but it's all right now." This was the only account I ever gave of the adventure. It was surmised that I had met a gipsy, who probably hoped to extort money from me. My father made inquiries in every direction, and gave notice that he should prosecute any rogues and vagabonds found trespassing on his property.

I, however, could not help often thinking over the adventure, and wondering what the man could have meant when he said that I had come between him and fortune. I determined to try and get my mother to solve the mystery, so one day I asked her, casually, if my father had inherited his estate, or how it was that he became possessed of it. She seemed surprised at the question, but told me, with some hesitation, it seemed to me, that he had gained the property a short time before, after a long-contested lawsuit. Somebody coming in prevented me from asking further questions, and my mother never again alluded to the subject.

CHAPTER II.

THREE years passed by. I had been seized with an ardent desire to go to sea, and as my parents had never been in the habit of thwarting my wishes, they could not refuse me this somewhat unreasonable one in a young gentleman heir to some fifteen thousand a-year. What they might have done had I been an only son I do not know, but as I had several brothers and sisters, they considered, I conclude, that should I be expended in fighting my country's battles, my place as heir might readily be supplied by my next brother, who highly applauded my determination. To do him justice, however, I am very certain that he had no selfish motives in so doing; indeed, his great wish was to be allowed to go also, and share my fortunes.

The matter settled, while my father wrote to our county member to beg that he would look out for a good ship for me, I wrote to my tailor, directing him to make me a uniform without delay, and to arrange my outfit. Young gentlemen with large expectations are as fond of fine clothes as are sometimes poor ones; and on the day my uniform arrived, and during three months or so afterwards, I took every opportunity of wearing it in public. Young as I was, I was made a good deal of in the neighbourhood, and it thus became pretty widely known that I was about to go to sea; or, as I told people, with no small amount of vanity, to become an officer in the navy.

I believe that very few young gentlemen ever
went to sea with a better kit than I had when I at
length was directed to join the *Ianthe* frigate, of
forty guns, commanded by Captain Hansome. I
found that I was not thought nearly so much of on
board as I had been in our county, at those houses
where five or six flaxen-haired young ladies formed
part of the family. I remember that Jack wrote me
word, however, that they had begun to make fully
as much of him on one occasion when it was supposed that war would break out, and on another
when it was reported that the frigate had been sent
to the West Indies ; but that might have been only
his fancy.

My father was unwell, so the steward took me to
Portsmouth, and he, not liking the look of the somewhat foam-covered Solent Sea, sent me off under
the charge of a waterman in a shore boat to the
ship, which lay at Spithead. We had a dead beat,
and I was very sick before we got half-way across.
The first lieutenant was on deck as I crawled up the
side.

"You have not been to sea before," he observed,
glancing at my woe-begone countenance, and then at
the numberless articles handed up after me. "A
pity your friends hadn't any one to tell them that a
frigate has no lumber-room for the stowage of
empty boxes. Boy ! send Mr. Owen here."

The lieutenant did not wait for an answer, and I
stood expecting some other remark to be made to
me, but he did not deign to address me again.
While looking about and wondering at the strange
appearance of the frigate's deck, of which I had no
previous conception, I saw a broad-shouldered man,
with large whiskers and a sunburnt countenance, in
the uniform of a master's mate, appear from below,

and approach. He touched his cap to the lieutenant, without looking at me, and asked for what he wanted him.

"To take charge of this youngster, Mr. Owen," answered the lieutenant. "You must dispose of his traps as you best can. The superfluous ones will, I doubt not, be soon expended. Introduce him to the mess, and see that he gets into no mischief."

"Ay, ay, sir. I have had many a youngster to look after in my time (some are now post-captains), and I know how to treat them," he answered, glancing at me with as much indifference as if I were a lady's poodle committed to his charge.

There was a sympathy between the lieutenant and the mate—the first might have been an admiral as far as age was concerned, the second a post-captain. Without speaking, he led me into the midshipman's berth. There were a good many people seated round the table, of all ages—assistant-surgeons, and clerks, and master's-assistants, besides midshipmen and master's mates, as passed midshipmen were called.

"Let me introduce to your favourable notice, gentlemen, Mr. Harry Nugent," he said, leading me in by the hand with much ceremony, but speaking in a tone which sounded somewhat sarcastic. It struck me as odd at the time that he should have known my name, as the lieutenant had not told him. "I must go and look after his traps," he added, as the rest of the party made room for me.

They treated me kindly enough, offering me dinner, which had just been placed on the table, but the food looked very coarse, and I was too sick to touch anything. They soon drew from me all the information I had to give about myself, and when they learned that I was an elder son, with large expecta-

tions, and was to have what seemed an unlimited
supply of money, some of the older ones treated me
with far more respect than at first.

"I wonder what could have induced you to come
to sea, to be kicked and cuffed by your superiors,
till you are big enough to kick and cuff others in
return," observed an oldster, John Pearson I found
was his name. "If I had had a tenth of your tin,
I'd have stayed on shore to the end of my days.
The sea is only fit for poor beggars like you and me,
Owen. Isn't that the case?"

A curious expression passed over Owen's countenance, and a frown settled on his brow, as, having
disposed of my property and just retaken his seat,
he answered:

"I suppose Nugent comes to sea to show us what
a pleasant life it may prove to a man of fortune,
eh!"

"No!" I answered, with simplicity. "I came to
sea because I have read of Howe and Jervis and
Nelson and Collingwood, and because I expected to
find it a field of fame and glory, as they did."

There was a general laugh, in which the youngsters
joined the loudest.

"A sucking Collingwood!" cried one.

"A field of water, which the ship has to plough,"
said another, who set up for a wit.

There was no end to their remarks.

"Never mind, Nugent," remarked Owen. "We'll
soon get you out of those antiquated notions."

He was as good as his word, and I soon learned
to look at a life at sea in a very different light to
what I had done when I determined to follow it.
Still, pride made me resolve to stick to it, and when
I wrote home, to speak as if I were thoroughly
satisfied with my choice.

Two days after I joined, the frigate sailed for the Mediterranean. Owen did his best to gain my confidence, and so far succeeded, that, being placed in his watch, I was his constant companion. I was at first shocked at his opinions and open acknowledgment of his very lax morals, and though in the latter respect he might not have been much worse in reality than others in the mess, I observed that by degrees some of them, especially Pearson, began rather to fight shy of him. Often I remarked an expression on his countenance which was most disagreeable, and two or three times as I looked at him the idea came across my mind that I had seen him before. Once, and only once, I thought he must be the person who had so frightened me years before in the park, but I dismissed the idea as preposterous, as that person was a great deal older than Owen, who, besides, seemed too careless, easy-going a fellow to do anything of that sort. In the Mediterranean, that most delightful of stations to a man who has plenty of money in his pocket, we visited a number of places. Whenever Owen went on shore he took me with him, and did not scruple to make use of my purse, in order, as he said, that he might initiate me into the mysteries of life.

Those who are acquainted with what a midshipman's life on shore often is, may easily conceive the description of scenes into which he introduced me. With the wariness of the serpent, however, he took care not too early to shock my moral sense, and therefore only gave me glimpses of the scenes to which I have alluded. We were at Naples for some months. As my father had begged the captain, whenever duty would permit, to give me every opportunity of seeing all that was to be seen in the places we visited, I constantly got leave to go on shore, and being under charge of so old and staid a Mentor as Owen, I was allowed to remain away from the ship for several days together. Night after night we went to the opera; then to some billiard or gambling-rooms; and finally repaired to some place to sup, when Owen took care to order the richest viands and the best wines at my expense. He drank hard, though he did not get drunk exactly, and he encouraged me to drink, telling me that it was a manly thing, and that after a little time I should be able to drink as much as he could with impunity. One day I returned on board feeling and looking, I doubt not, very ill. While Owen was on deck, Pearson, who was always very kind to me, took me aside, and asked me, in the gentlest and most friendly way, how I spent my time on shore. I told him exactly how I had been employed.

"Take my advice, youngster, and follow a better leader than Owen seems to be, or rather act as your own sense of right and duty would prompt you," he said, in a kind tone. "I most heartily wish you well, and admire the spirit which prompted you to come to sea, when you might have lived luxuriously on shore. You have everything before you which can make life pleasant, but if you follow the course into which it is very clear Owen intends to lead you, your life itself will be shortened, and you will be incapacitated from enjoying the advantages you possess."

I felt the truth of what Pearson had said, and told him that I would follow his advice. The next day I was engaged to go on shore with Owen. I did not choose to refuse to go, but resolved to be cautious how I complied with any of his proposals. He had told the captain that we were to ride out to visit some spot of interest in the neighbourhood, and

I had fully intended going. When we got on shore, he declared that he had hurt his leg, and could not ride, and proposed resorting to a billiard-room. To this, as I did not know what to do with myself alone, I did not object, but after playing for some time, he declared that it was very slow work, and suggested that we should go to a gambling-house near at hand, where we might obtain liquor and refreshments of all sorts. I fortunately knew the character of the place, and remembering my promise to Pearson, positively refused to accompany him. He looked astonished at first, and then set to work to overcome my scruples. I was firm, and thank Heaven I was, for if a man breaks a newly-formed resolution to act rightly, he is very apt to go back to his old courses, and to continue in them more recklessly than before.

" If you don't want to lose your money don't play high stakes, and if you are afraid of getting drunk, I'll watch that you don't take more than is good for you," he whispered to me. "But don't sit there like a booby."

"I should be one if I followed your suggestions, for I have no taste for either gambling or drinking, and I do not want to get it," I answered, firmly. "Once for all, I will not go."

He uttered a faint laugh as he said,

"What has come over the fellow? However, lend me five sovereigns, and I'll try my luck. If I lose, I shall be in your debt; if I win, I will pay you double."

"I want no profits," I answered, giving him my purse, from which he helped himself. "I'll take a stroll along the shore of the bay, and come back for you in time for the opera."

Taking back my purse, without waiting to hear

what he said, I hurried out. On returning to the
billiard-room, after a pleasant walk, at the hour I
had named, Owen was not there, and I was told
that an English officer, who had been desperately
wounded in an affray, was lying in a house close by,
and apparently dying. I hurried to the spot, and
found, as I expected, Owen. He was unconscious,
and so I engaged some porters, and had him conveyed immediately on board, where I knew that he
would receive better treatment than elsewhere from
our surgeon. When he came to himself, and heard
that I had had him brought on board, he was very
angry at my interference, though the surgeon assured
me that by my promptitude his life had been saved.
According to his account, he had received his wound
from an assassin, who, probably mistaking him for
some one else, had rushed out and struck him with
his dagger ; but the surgeon, who was not among
his admirers, hinted that this was impossible, and
that there would have been no great loss to the
world had the wound been half-an-inch deeper. He
was a long time recovering, and as he never offered
to repay me the five pounds I had lent him, I concluded that his wound had made him forget the
matter.

Pearson lost no opportunity of strengthening me
in my resolution not to yield to any temptations
Owen might throw in my way. The latter, however,
was not easily to be turned from his purpose. Again
and again he tried to prevail on me to accompany
him on shore, laughing at my scruples, and accusing
me of parsimony and meanness. I did not give
him credit for any other motive for his wish to have
me as his companion beyond the very natural one of
a desire to enjoy the use of my purse. When he
found that he had lost his influence over me, and

that the more he attempted to regain it the more I kept aloof from him, his whole manner towards me in private changed, though in public, especially in presence of the captain and lieutenant, it was as friendly as before.

I now found myself subject to a number of petty annoyances, of which I was nearly certain that he was the author, though I could not trace them completely. My hammock was over and over again cut down by the head, to the risk of breaking my neck; my chest was rifled, and articles of value in it destroyed, and even my uniforms were so injured, that at last I could scarcely appear respectably on the quarter-deck. When my watch was over, and I came down to meals, I found that the worst of everything had been kept for me, often food that was scarcely eatable. At the mess-table, though still pretending great regard, he lost no opportunity of making sarcastic remarks, and placing me on every occasion in a wrong position. I found, too, that stories greatly to my prejudice were put about, of a character difficult if not impossible to refute. Had it not been for Pearson, my existence on board would have been intolerable, but as he never in the remotest degree benefited by my purse, his interest in me was above suspicion, and he stoutly maintained that the stories were false, and invented by some one wishing to do me an injury. Had my friends wished to disgust me with the sea, they could scarcely have adopted a better plan than engaging Owen to treat me as I had every reason to believe he was now doing. I should, in truth, have been completely disgusted, but my pride came to my aid, and prevented me from making any complaint. In other respects, I liked a sea life, and as Pearson, who was much respected, sided with me, many of the better-disposed midshipmen remained my friends. Thus passed the first three years of my naval career.

CHAPTER III.

THE frigate was ordered home to be paid off. I had found out one thing, that fortune will not secure uninterrupted happiness even to a midshipman. I had begun to suspect, also, that the romantic notions I had entertained of fame and glory were in a great degree illusory; at all events, that there was a great deal of hard, matter-of-fact, and somewhat dirty, disagreeable work to be gone through. I discussed with Pearson the advisability of my leaving the service. He asked me what I should do with myself if I did? I confessed that I did not know, and that I had no desire to go back to school, to a private tutor, or to college.

" Then stay in the service, and see the world," he answered. " I have heard of a ship fitting for the Pacific, on board which my friends can procure me a berth, and I have no doubt that you can also get appointed to her if you apply in time."

I took his suggestion, wrote immediately to my father to beg that he would make interest to have me appointed to the *Sappho* frigate, fitting at Portsmouth, and, though he was greatly surprised at my taste, he did not refuse my request. After a short stay at home—sufficiently long to recount my adventures in the Mediterranean, and to grow tired of doing nothing—I joined my new ship at Spithead the day after she came out of harbour. I found

Pearson on board, but some of the officers had not joined, nor had the ship her full complement of men.

Pearson liked the captain and officers he had seen, and expressed an opinion that we should have a very pleasant voyage.

I anticipated great pleasure in visiting Peru and Mexico, and the numerous strange islands in the Pacific of which I had read, and perhaps Australia, and China, and Japan, and longed to be away. The evening before the ship was to sail, Pearson came into the berth where I was sitting alone, and said:

" I must prepare you for what is not likely to be pleasant. Owen has joined; but follow my advice— receive him as an old shipmate, take no notice of his former conduct, and treat him frankly, and you will probably conquer his hostility. At all events, he knows by this time that I will not allow him to play you the tricks he before did with impunity."

On going on deck, I saw Owen talking to a group of mates and midshipmen. He expressed no surprise at finding Pearson and me on board, and though there was an unpleasant look in his eye, there was nothing to find fault with in his manner.

We had a quick passage round the Horn.

Owen appeared either very greatly changed, or proved that to his other arts he could practise hypocrisy. Our captain was a religious man, and, what was rare in those days, used to invite the officers in to read the Bible with him. Owen, who used to say that he had never been into a church since he came to sea, was among the most constant in his attendance, and completely won the confidence of the captain, who spoke of him as an excellent man who had not received his deserts. Owen, on the strength of this, insinuated that my religious principles were very defective, and offered to instruct me. He made a commencement, and might have succeeded in instilling principles not such as our excellent captain supposed he would, but directly the reverse, had not Pearson, to whom I repeated what he said, again interfered, and threatened to expose him if he continued to utter such sentiments. He excused himself by declaring that I had mistaken his meaning; but Pearson knew well enough that I had not; and I soon saw by his change of manner that he was devising some new scheme to do me harm.

When once, however, among the coral islands of the Pacific, we were so constantly employed in looking out for reefs and rocks, that we had little time for polemical discussions. Although the inhabitants of some of the islands had in those days already become partially civilized under missionary teaching, a large number were fierce and treacherous savages, and in our intercourse with them we were compelled to be very wary, to avoid the fate of Captain Cook, and that of the crews of many other ships which had been cut off in those seas. We had already discovered that the Pacific can be anything but tranquil at times, by two heavy gales we had already experienced, but of late we had light breezes and calms. At length our water began to run short, and it became necessary to obtain a supply without delay. A look-out was therefore kept for an island where it could be procured. Before long an island was sighted, and three boats were ordered away to explore it. Owen commanded one of them, and I was ordered to go in her. I was glad enough to get on shore, though I would rather have been with any one else.

As there appeared to be no inhabitants, we were

to land at different places, so as the more readily to
find water. We steered for a point which would
take us farther from the ship than the other boats.
All hands were in high spirits with the thought of a
lark on shore. A narrow passage was found in
the surrounding reef, and we ran the boat into a
beautiful and sheltered bay, with the trees coming
down on either side almost to the water's edge. If
water was to be found here it would be easy to fill
the casks and roll them down to the boats. In vain
we hunted about in every direction—no water was
to be found. Owen then ordered the men to dig;
but they were unsuccessful. Some time was thus
occupied, but he declared that he would not return
without finding water, and that we must divide,
some to push farther inland, and others along the
shore. Greatly to my disgust he ordered me to
remain by the boat, and I observed, as he spoke, that
evil look with which he often regarded me. He led
one party along the shore to the right, while he sent
another more inland. Only one boy was left with
me. They had been gone some little time, when the
report of a gun from the ship reached my ear. It
was the signal of recall. Another soon followed; I
hoped that the absent parties would hear the signal,
or would soon return. A third, and then the report
of several guns in quick succession reached my ear.
There was evidently danger to be apprehended. I
had little doubt, on observing the changed appearance of the sky, that a gale was expected, though in
the sheltered bay where the boat was I had not
remarked any threatening signs. All I could do
was to keep the boat afloat, so that we might shove
off directly the other parties arrived. I looked
eagerly out along the shore, but no one was to be
seen. The ship had ceased firing; indeed, from the

appearance of the sea outside, it was evident that the gale had commenced, and that she had been compelled, for her own safety, to stand off-shore. Our only resource, therefore, would be to wait till the gale should have blown itself out, and the frigate could come back to pick us up. I now became very anxious, for I thought that Owen must have observed the change in the weather, and that something must have occurred to have prevented him from returning. I was eagerly looking about in every direction, when I caught sight of some persons running among the trees towards the boat. I soon distinguished some of the boat's crew, with Owen among them. They had good reason for running fast, for behind came a crowd of savages, shouting and shrieking, and brandishing clubs and spears. Now and then our people would face about, fire their pistols, and then again retreat. As they drew near, Owen shouted to me to be ready to hand out the muskets, which lay in the bottom of the boat. The boy and I did as we were directed, but the savages, believing that their enemies were about to escape them, made a dash forward, and two of the crew lay gasping on the sand, struck down by their clubs, while the foremost scrambled into the boat to escape a similar fate. The first impulse of each man as he got on board was to seize an oar to shove off, Owen setting the example ; but as soon as the boat was afloat, the muskets were taken up, and a volley fired into the midst of the savages, who were wading in after us. It had the effect of keeping them back till we were out of their reach. Yet what a fearful predicament we were in—a storm raging outside, while we dare not approach the shore. The savages had canoes, so that we could not even wait under the lee of the land for fine weather. Owen announced his determination to stand out and run before the gale. We had a fine sea boat, capable of going through very heavy weather. Oh, the horrors of that voyage! We thought of the fate of our companions left on shore, that was undoubtedly ere this sealed. Our numbers were fearfully diminished.

Owen told us to be thankful, as we had thus more food left to support our lives. I thought that it mattered very little whether we had more or less food, for even should our boat weather the gale, it was very improbable that we should fall in with the ship again, and must be starved, at all events. On we ran through the passage in the reef. As we got clear of the land, it required all Owen's skill to steer the boat amid the fearful seas, which threatened every instant to engulf her. Four hands continued baling, without stopping; and even these could scarcely keep the boat from foundering. On, on we flew. Night came on, still the gale did not abate. Owen's countenance, as the darkness closed around us, looked grim and firm; but there was a look of horror (it was not common fear) in his eye which I can never forget. He kept his post, steering the boat through that livelong night without uttering a word. Day came back, and there he sat as before, keeping the boat on the only course which could afford us a possibility of escape. Not till then would he allow the coxswain, who had escaped, to take his place. On we went as before, all day long. "Where were we going?" we asked ourselves. No one could reply. Food was served out; few had an inclination to eat. It was fortunate, for we had but a scanty allowance, and still less to drink—a bottle of rum and a small keg of water. Another night and a day, and again a night, and one of our number sank exhausted. Owen still kept up, looking fierce and determined as ever. Day came, and land appeared right ahead—a high, rocky, and tree-covered island; but there was a barrier reef round it, over which the seas, rising with foam-covered summits, beat furiously. Our utter destruction seemed inevitable. To haul our wind and stand off was now impracticable. Owen stood up, and, casting a glance around, steered boldly on. I saw that there was a break in the wall of foam, but a very narrow one. We had little time for thought before we were among the raging breakers. A sea came roaring on. I felt the boat lifted, and the next moment was struggling with grim death in the yeasty waters.

CHAPTER IV.

As I came to the surface I caught a glimpse of the shore, and struck out for it, but it seemed far distant. I swam like a man in his sleep; in vain, my strength was failing me, a mist came over my eyes, and I could no longer see the shore, when I felt a powerful hand grasping my shoulder, and ere long was conscious that I had been hauled out of the water and placed high up on the warm sand. I opened my eyes at length, and the first object on which they rested was the vindictive countenance of Owen, as he gazed at me. I say vindictive, because that was the expression which had often puzzled me. Yet why should he nourish such feelings towards me?

"So you are alive, are you?" he remarked, when

he saw that I had regained my consciousness. "It
might have been better for you had you gone with
the rest, for we are the only survivors. However,
I had too long a score with you to lose you, if I
could bring you on shore safe."

"Then I am indebted to you for my life," I remarked.

"Yes, but the debt is not a heavy one, and you
may think me entitled to very small thanks; for let
me tell you your existence here will be no sinecure.
I intend to make you slave and toil for me as you
have never toiled before. At length I have you in
my power. Ha, ha, ha!" And he laughed wildly.
"Your wealth will avail you nothing here, your
refinement, your education, your romantic aspirations. You are now my slave, and I your master
Ha, ha, ha!"

This greeting was not calculated to aid my
recovery, but, in spite of it, my strength returned,
and I was able to get up on my feet.

"I am ready to obey you," I said calmly. "You
saved my life, and it is my duty to serve you as far
as I have the power."

"Always talking of your duty!" he exclaimed,
with a sneer. "It shall not be a light one, let me tell
you. Now, as you can walk, find some food—shell-
fish and water. I don't ask for impossibilities, but
take care you do not touch any till I have eaten."

I must obey him, so, observing some rocks, I
hurried towards them, and with my pocket-knife cut
off as many mussels and other shell-fish as I could
carry. He had had a flint and steel and a powder-
flask in his pocket, and had thus without difficulty
kindled a fire. While he dressed and ate the shell-
fish he sent me off to look for water. I went with
the fear every instant of falling into the hands of

savage natives, and it was not till I discovered the
small size of the island that I began to hope that
there might be none upon it. I hunted about for
some time, till I at length came upon a stream of
pure water bubbling out of a rock. My difficulty
was to convey it to Owen. Some cocoa-nut shells
were lying about. One less split than the rest I
filled with water, but the greater part was spilt
before I reached him. He cursed me for an idle
hound for not bringing a larger supply, and sent me
back for more. Fortunately, I observed some shells
on the shore. These I slung round my neck, and
with them brought as much water as he could
require. Not till then did he allow me to cook any
of the shell-fish I had collected. He had eaten all
he himself had dressed. He then ordered me to
collect materials for a hut, and when I expostulated,
as I had only my pocket-knife to work with, he
struck me with a stick, and said I must see to finding
a better tool. Still, as I had determined to do my
utmost to please him, I set to work to collect all the
pieces of drift timber I could find. To my satisfaction, I discovered also the boat's sail and some rope
cast on shore, and these articles, with a number of
thin sticks which I succeeded in cutting, I piled
up near where he sat, and asked him what else he
required.

"To help me build my hut," he growled out.

By fixing the thinner sticks into the sand, fastening
them at the top, and stretching the sail over
them, I formed something like an Indian wigwam,
strengthened by the heavier pieces of driftwood.
I observed that Owen moved about with difficulty,
and looked ill, but he made no remark on the
subject.

"Now go and collect dry leaves and grass for my

bed. Be off with you," he exclaimed, glaring fiercely at me.

I obeyed as before, but when I returned, time after time, laden with bundles of grass, not an expression of approval even did he utter. Thus he kept me employed for the greater part of the day, and when I proposed collecting some grass for my own bed, he told me that I could not occupy his hut but must form one of boughs for myself. Such is an example of the way he treated me, not for one day only, but for day after day, not one passing without my being struck and cursed. It is wonderful that I could have borne it, but I was not weary of my life, and I had resolved to show my gratitude to him for having preserved it. I was very anxious, however, to escape, and whenever I could get away from him, I used to go to the highest part of the island to look out, in the hopes of a ship appearing. With indefatigable labour, I cut out a long pole and fixed it in the ground, with a part of my shirt, as a signal, fastened to the end. When Owen found out what I had done, he ordered me to take it down, and not again to visit the hill.

"Ah! ha! youngster, you've friends you wish to return to, and wealth you long to enjoy. I have neither, and I don't intend to let you go while I can prevent it."

This was almost more than I could bear, and I could not trust myself to reply to him. I might fill a volume with my extraordinary life on that islet in the Pacific—how I slaved on for that determined, stern, evil-disposed man. Constant occupation enabled me to keep my own health. I found cocoa-nuts and numerous roots and fruits, and invented various ways of cooking them. I even made clothes of the bark of the paper mulberry-tree, so that I was able to save my own before they were quite worn out. Thus months passed away. I might have lived there from youth to old age, as far as the necessaries of life were concerned, but it was dreary work. Owen grew worse and worse, and I became convinced that his days were numbered. He did not seem to be aware of the state of the case, though rapidly growing weaker. I may honestly say that I felt deep compassion for him. I told him at last that I thought him very ill, and feared that he would not recover.

"Don't flatter yourself with that. I shall recover sufficiently to make you wish that you had never seen me," he answered, as he raised himself on his arm and glared fiercely at me.

I thought that he uttered but an empty threat which he had no power to execute. Still he lived on, and I tended him as if he had been a friend or brother. I had made my hut at some little distance from his. I had one night gone to sleep, leaving him not worse than he had been for some time past, when I suddenly awoke with a start, and hearing a noise looked out. What was my horror to see Owen stalking stealthily along with a huge piece of heavy driftwood uplifted in his hands, as if it were a club. I darted out on the other side of the hut as down came the log with a crash above where my head had just been laid, and a fearful shriek rang through the night air. I expected to see Owen following me, but he lay, as I looked back, across the ruins of my hut. I slowly approached—he did not move—the timber had fallen from his grasp. I touched his hand. He was dead.

I must bring my tale to a close. I was convinced that the wretched man was mad, though, from what afterwards came to my knowledge, there was more reason than I had supposed why his madness should have taken the form of hatred towards me. I cannot describe how I managed to pass the many dreary days I was destined to spend in solitude on that island, or how I was at length rescued by a South-Sea whaler, and ultimately fell in with my own ship, on board which I was heartily welcomed, having long been given up as lost. Owen's death excited universal horror. Pearson told me that he had been directed by the captain to examine his papers, among which he found parts of a journal, in which he described his bitter disappointment on discovering that the estate which he thought would be his had gone to another, and how, considering himself wronged, he had resolved to wreak his vengeance on the head of the person who had obtained what he conceived ought to have been his; how he had gone to see me, and finding that I had resolved to enter the navy, how he had formed the diabolical plan which he had attempted to carry out, but in every step of which he had been so mercifully frustrated.

I immediately wrote home to say that I was alive and well, with an account of my adventures, and expressed a hope that my letter would arrive in time to prevent Jack from being spoilt by the flatteries and indulgences he might receive as an elder son, advising that, if he appeared the worse for them, to effect a radical cure he should be forthwith packed off to sea.

Paul Petherwick the Pilot.

A TALE OF THE CORNISH COAST.

CHAPTER I.

THE *Sea-Gull* Pilot-boat, hailing from Penzance, and owned and commanded by old Paul Petherwick, lay hove-to, one winter's day many years back, in the chops of the Channel. The dark-green seas rose up like walls capped with snow on either side of the little craft; now she floated on the foaming, hissing summit of one of them, again to sink down into the deep watery trench from which she had risen. Thus, as rising and falling, her white staysail glancing brightly, she looked not unlike the sea-bird whose name she bore.

Old Paul was the only person on deck, and he had lashed himself to the bulwarks. His white hair, escaping from under his "sou'-wester," streamed in the wind, and ever and anon he turned his head aside to avoid the showers of spray which flew over him, covering his flushing coat with wet. Again he would look out in search of any homeward-bound vessel which might need his services. His heart was heavy, for the previous night a fearful sea had struck the cutter, and washed his mate, Peter Bud-

dock, and another man overboard. The latter had
seized a rope, but it had slipped from his grasp;
and poor Buddock was carried far away, his shriek
of despair as he sank beneath the waves being his
last utterance which reached the ears of his shipmates.

Another of Paul's crew, an old hand, had been
injured by a blow from a block, and the rest were
young men, willing and active enough, but not able
to take entire charge of the cutter. Still, old Paul
was a determined man, and as long as there was a
chance of meeting a vessel to pilot up Channel, and
as long as the cutter could keep the sea, he would
not give in.

Hour after hour passed by. Suddenly the crew,
sitting round the stove in the little after-cabin,
heard a loud report, followed by a deep groan. The
trysail gaff had parted, and, falling, had struck the
old pilot to the deck. They carried him below, and
placed him in his berth. Not a moment was to be
lost if their own lives were to be saved. The helm
was put up, and the little craft, paying off under
her head-sail, before the rough sea, which came roaring onwards, had reached her, was running up Channel towards the Cornish coast. Old Paul continued
to groan, seeming unconscious, and evidently suffering great pain. One or other of his young crew
every now and then went below to ask him the right
course to steer, for not even the outline of the coast
could be seen. It was getting very dark, and thick
flakes of snow were beginning to fall. The old pilot
probably did not comprehend them; not a word
could he utter. They endeavoured, therefore, to rig
a spar on which to set the trysail; but no sooner
did they hoist it than it was carried away, and at
length they gave up the attempt in despair. They

could not, therefore, heave the cutter to, and were obliged to run on. One of them went below, and endeavoured by every means he could think of to bring the old man to consciousness. The darkness increased as the night advanced, and the snow came down thicker and thicker. On flew the cutter.

"We must be nearing the land," said Jacob Pinner, the best seaman of the crew. "I wish that the old man would rouse up. I don't like the look of things, mates, that I don't."

Scarcely had he spoken when a deep, sullen roar, easily distinguished by a seaman amid the howling of the tempest, struck on the ears of the crew. "Breakers! breakers ahead!" they shouted.

"Port the helm—hard a-port!" cried a deep voice. It was that of the old pilot. The sound of the breakers had reached his ears even below, and roused him up. The order came too late. At that moment there was a loud crash; the cutter struck, and her rudder was carried away. The following sea lifted her and carried her on, while other seas came roaring up, and hissed and foamed round her. Though they covered her with sheets of spray, her crew were still able to cling to the rigging and preserve their lives. Providentially, most of the hours of the night were already spent, for they could not long have endured the cold and wet to which they were exposed. When daylight broke they found that they were near the end of a reef, about a mile from the shore. The gale had greatly abated. The tide was low. Inside of the reef there was smooth water. If they could launch their boat, which had remained on deck uninjured, they might save themselves before the return of the tide, when the cutter would be sure to go to pieces. Though the little boat narrowly escaped being stove in, the attempt was successful. The shore was reached. It was close to Paul Petherwick's house, some miles to the eastward of the port to which the cutter belonged.

Close to the spot where Paul and his crew landed, on the shore of a romantic bay, stood the residence of Sir Baldwin Treherne, known as the Manor House. Sir Baldwin was lord of the manor—a kind, warm-hearted, generous man. He had himself been at sea in his youth, but on coming into his estate had given up the profession. He had learned when at sea, probably from experiencing some of the hardships sailors have to endure, to sympathise with them, and to feel for their sufferings. He had seen through his telescope, while dressing in the morning, the wreck on the reef, and had immediately set off to find out what assistance could be rendered to the crew. He met the old pilot and his people not far from the shore, and insisted on their coming at once to the Manor House to be warmed and fed. Paul Petherwick would indeed have been unable to have reached his own home, as his strength and spirits were already exhausted. As the day advanced the wind again increased, and when the tide rose the *Sea-Gull*, battered by the waves, was seen quickly to disappear.

Great was old Paul's grief as he watched the destruction of the vessel. "God's will be done," he said, bowing his head. "My poor wife and children, what will become of them? With her goes all the means I have of supporting them, and part of her cost is still unpaid."

The kind baronet overheard him. "Paul, we have known each other a good many long years," he said, putting his hand on his shoulder. "I should like to make you a Christmas-box. Let you and me go off to Plymouth to-morrow, and see if we cannot fall in

with as fine a cutter as the *Sea-Gull.* It won't do
to be letting our ships knock about the chops of the
Channel this winter weather without you to show
them the way up ; so I'll find you a craft, and may
she have better luck than the poor *Sea-Gull !*"

"Oh, Sir Baldwin, you are very good ; so good, I
shall never be able to repay you," exclaimed Paul
Petherwick, respectfully pressing the kind baronet's
hand.

"I am paid beforehand with all the blessings I
enjoy," answered Sir Baldwin. "They came to me
without my having toiled for them, far less deserved
them ; I am bound to make the best use of them in
my power, so say no more about the matter."

A new cutter was found and purchased, and
named the *Lady Isabel,* after Sir Baldwin's wife ;
and for many a day, in summer and winter, Paul
Petherwick sailed her in pursuit of his calling.

CHAPTER III.

THERE was not a finer lad in the country round
than Sir Baldwin's third son, his blue-eyed, light-
haired, merry, laughing boy Harry. When he
came home from school for the summer holidays,
Harry declared his fixed intention of going to sea.
Sir Baldwin, after several conversations with his
son, felt convinced that it was his settled wish to
enter the navy, and forthwith set about obtaining a
berth for him as a midshipman on board a man-of-
war. There was but little difficulty in doing this ;
for, after a short peace, England was again at war

with France and Spain and other countries, and
ships were being fitted out as fast as they could be
got ready. Harry was in high glee. The dream of
his life was to be realised. He had not talked about
the matter. People often, when they are very
earnest in wishing for a thing, do not talk about it.
Sir Baldwin took him to Plymouth; his outfit was
soon procured, and he was entered on board the
Phœnix, a dashing 36-gun frigate, destined for the
West India station; a part of the world where
there was every chance of her having plenty of
fighting. Captain Butler, her brave commander,
lost no time in getting his crew into an efficient
state by exercising them constantly at their guns,
and in shortening and making sail. Harry Treherne
thus rapidly acquired a knowledge of the profession
he had chosen. He had determined to be a good
sailor; he gave his mind to the work, and considered
no details beneath his notice; consequently, everybody was ready to give him instruction; he gained
the confidence of the officers and the respect of the
men.

"A sail on the lee bow!" shouted the look-out
man at the masthead.

The cry made the captain and officers on deck
turn their glasses in the direction indicated. The
helm was put up, and at length, through the haze
of a warm summer morning, the stranger was discovered, with her mizen topsail aback and her main
topsail shivering, evidently awaiting the arrival of
the *Phœnix*. She was clearly an enemy's frigate,
heavily armed. The *Phœnix* had been disguised to
look as much as possible like a corvette, a much
smaller class of vessel, and it was more than possible
that the Frenchmen might find that they had caught
a Tartar.

"We shall have some glorious fighting," cried little Tommy Butts, the smallest midshipman on board. "We shall thrash 'em in quarter less no time. I hope that we shall have to board; that's the way I should like to take the enemy."

"Why, your cutlass would run away with you, Tommy," said a big mate, who delighted to sneer at Tommy. "It is a shame to send such children as you to sea."

"His spirit may run away with him," observed Harry. "Never mind what old Hulks says; Nelson was a little chap, and he did a few things to be proud of."

Many a joke and laugh were indulged in as the men, stripped to the waist, stood at their guns, while the frigate approached her powerful antagonist. At length, as she got within range, the Frenchman opened his fire, the shot flying through the sails and wounding severely the masts, yards, and rigging. Not a gun, however, was discharged on board the *Phœnix* in return till it could take deadly effect. The *Didon*, the French frigate, however, from fast sailing and clever manœuvring, always managed to keep in such a position that the guns of the *Phœnix* could not bear on her. At length the English losing patience, ran right down on the *Didon* to windward, and thus the two antagonists were brought broadside to broadside.

This was the longed-for moment, and the British crew made up for the previous delay by working their guns with a rapidity which soon strewed the decks of the enemy with the dead and wounded, damaged her hull, and cut up her rigging.

Again the French ship got clear; but, as she had lost several of her sails, the *Phœnix* was more of a match for her. Once more the antagonists closed, this time in a deadly embrace, the bow of the *Didon* running into the quarter of the *Phœnix*.

"We have you now," cried the gallant captain, lashing, with the help of some of his men, the bowsprit of the enemy to his own mizen mast.

While he was so employed, Harry Treherne and Tommy Butts saw a Frenchman taking deliberate aim at him. Tommy had got hold of the musket of a marine who had fallen wounded.

"See, Harry, what a little chap can do!" he exclaimed ; at the same moment firing at the Frenchman, who fell, his musket going off and sending the bullet flying just above the captain's head.

Captain Butler saw the act, and nodded his thanks, for he had no time to speak. The next proceeding was to bring a heavy gun to fire through a port which had been formed by enlarging one of the cabin windows. Several seamen fell, picked off by the French marines, till the gun was in its place. When, however, it once opened fire, its effects were terrible indeed, full twenty of the Frenchmen being struck down at the first discharge.

Meantime the English marines kept up so hot a fire on the *Didon's* forecastle, that the seamen could not venture on it to fire the gun which had been placed there. At length, however, the antagonists separated, both presenting a woeful appearance.

Instead of the clouds of canvas swelling proudly to the breeze with which they had entered into action, rope-ends and riddled sails hung drooping down from every mast and yard. The fight was not over ; the crew of the *Phœnix* busily employed themselves in repairing damages, and, having knotted and spliced the rigging, and trimmed sails, she stood towards the *Didon*.

With the first fresh puff of wind the foremast of

her opponent went over the side, and at the moment she was about to open her fire the brave captain of the *Didon* hauled down her colours, finding that he could neither escape nor fight with any prospect of success. Loud cheers burst from the British crew. This was Harry's first fight. It was indeed a hard-fought one. Twelve men had been killed and twenty-eight wounded of the crew; while the *Didon* had lost no less than twenty-seven officers and men killed, and forty-four wounded, out of a crew of 330, while the *Phœnix* went into action with only 245 men. She and her prize arrived safely at Plymouth. She only remained long enough to refit, and once more was at sea, and on her way back to the West Indies.

Harry's next exploit was of a different character. Passing near the Isle of Pines, two schooners and a brig were discovered far up a bight, protected by a battery. There was little doubt that they were privateers, and likely to do damage to British shipping.

"We must cut those vessels out," observed the captain.

The frigate stood off the land as if she was going away, but at night once more stood back. As soon as she was well in with the land she hove to, and three boats were manned and lowered. Harry was appointed to go in one of them. They were to pull up the harbour and attack the three vessels, and, if necessary, one boat's crew was to land and storm the fort. With muffled oars they pulled up the har-bour. They could just make out the vessels as they lay floating in silence on the calm water, a light wind blowing off shore. The boats got close up to the brig before they were discovered. The enemy then, who had rushed to their guns, which were run out, opened a hot fire from them, with muskets and pistols; but the boats being close the shots passed over the heads of their crews. With loud cheers the British sprang up the sides of the brig. The crew bravely stood to their arms, but were speedily overpowered by the impetuosity of the boarders, and were cut down or driven below, some in their terror leaping overboard.

While Harry Treherne and his crew remained on board, the other two boats proceeded to the attack of the schooners. He, meantime, having secured the prisoners below, sent some of his hands aloft to loose sails while the cable was cut, and in a few minutes the captured brig was standing out of the harbour. The roar of the guns, the clashing of steel, and the rattle of musketry had aroused the garrison of the fort, which opened fire on the brig. The shots fell around her, and several went through her sails, but no one was hurt. As he passed near the schooners he listened anxiously for the signal which was to announce their capture. First one loud cheer and then another told him that the work was done, and they were soon perceived following under all sail, little heeding the fire from the fort. Harry Treherne, with all the officers and men engaged, was warmly commended for the spirited way in which the exploit had been performed. It was not the only deed of naval daring in which he took an active part.

At length the frigate was ordered to Bermuda on her way home. Within a short distance of that island a suspicious vessel was seen from the masthead. Sail was made in chase. The stranger on discovering the frigate did her utmost to escape, steering to the eastward, the wind being from the west. A stern chase is a long chase. The night was clear and the stranger was kept in sight.

When morning dawned the frigate had scarcely gained on her. This made the captain still more eager to overtake her. All that day the chase continued—the frigate gaining, however, somewhat on the stranger, a large fore-and-aft schooner. At length, at sundown, it fell calm, and fears were entertained that, should a mist rise, the schooner might escape during the night. The captain therefore, sent three of the boats to capture her. They had been discovered some time before they got alongside. Boarding nettings were up, small-arm men were stationed at the bow and stern, and as they drew near the guns opened a hot fire with grape and canister. Still the British seamen, not to be daunted, dashed on, and, climbing up the sides and cutting their way through the nettings, in another minute the schooner's deck was won. She proved to be a Spanish privateer, a very fine new vessel. A light breeze at daybreak enabled the frigate to come up with her. The prisoners were transferred to the frigate, and the command of the prize given to old Hulks, the mate, who had been Tommy Butt's tyrant; and Harry Treherne was sent as his second in command, with orders to proceed to Plymouth.

Old Hulks had several failings: whenever spirits came in his way he could not refrain from them. Harry had, therefore, the chief charge of the schooner. It was the winter season, and as they approached the chops of the Channel the weather became very bad. Old Hulks, however, declared that he must be home by Christmas, and ordered Harry to crack on all the sail the schooner could carry night and day. Harry had taken his observations as long as the sun could be seen, but for some days the sky had been obscured by clouds.

He believed that they were not far from the Land's End, and well over to the British coast. Old Hulks insisted that they were too far to the southward, and ordered the schooner to be headed more to the northward. Night was approaching. It was Christmas Eve. The wind was strong, and a heavy snowstorm prevented the possibility of their sighting the land.

"Never mind, Harry; we shall see it in the morning,—about Plymouth, I take it, and I shall be at home in plenty of time for our Christmas dinner, and you shall dine with me, as you won't be able to get to your own place."

"I wish that I could think so. We are nearer the English coast than you suppose," said Harry.

"Well, heave the schooner to at midnight," answered old Hulks. "I shall go below—call me then; it's fearfully cold."

Harry was compelled to obey the orders of his superior. He, however, kept as good a look-out as he possibly could, wishing anxiously for midnight. The hour was approaching. The wind blew stronger and stronger, and the snow came down, covering the deck, and making it impossible to see beyond the bowsprit end. Suddenly there was a loud crash — the vessel groaned from stem to stern, the foremast went by the board. Loud cries arose: "We are on the rocks!—we are on the rocks! Heaven protect us!"—was echoed from mouth to mouth.

CHAPTER III.

A LARGE merry Christmas party was assembled under Sir Baldwin Treherne's hospitable roof. All sorts of games had been carried on till a late hour, and everybody was in high spirits.

" Oh, if dear Harry was here it would be perfect," exclaimed one of his sisters, the gentle Mary, who had been his chief playmate in his childhood.

" Oh, Harry is all right, enjoying the warm weather in the West Indies, instead of being frozen as we are here."

" Lucky dog !" said one of his brothers.

They all went to bed at last.   More than one prayer in the house was offered up that night for young Harry's safety.

Christmas morning came.   The sky was overcast, the snow was falling thickly.   Sir Baldwin had promised to visit during the day a poor family ; the mother lay dying.

" I cannot begin this blessed day better than by a work of love," he said to himself, as he looked out on the snow-covered landscape.   " If I put it off till the afternoon she may no longer be here."

He never allowed the weather to prevent him from going out.   With a thick greatcoat on, a stout stick in one hand, he set forth through the snow on his errand of mercy, long before the rest of the family had left their rooms.   He was just going into the cottage when he met Paul Petherwick, with his pilot-coat, sea-boots, and a spy-glass under his arm, accompanied by several of his crew, carrying oars and coils of rope and other ship's gear.

" What, Paul, are you going to sea such a morning as this— Christmas morning, too ?" asked the baronet, in a tone of surprise.

" Yes, Sir Baldwin, that I am ; for you see, sir, I was one Christmas-day, as you will remember, tossing about on you stormy sea till my craft was driven on shore, and I and my crew well-nigh lost.   I should have been thankful if any brother pilot had been out on that morning to have towed the *Sea-Gull* into port. For what I know, there are some poor fellows out of their reckoning; and if I can fall in with them, and pilot them up Channel, I shall be doing as I should like to be done by."

"You are right, my friend. Heaven protect and prosper you," said the baronet. "You'll come up in the evening to hear the carol-singers. There'll be a cup of mead ready for you, and for your people, too, if they will come."

"Thank ye, Sir Baldwin; we'll come," said several voices, and the pilot's crew hurried down to their boat.

The pilot vessel made several tacks along shore before stretching out to sea. She had made her last tack, and was standing off the land when, near the very reef on which the *Sea-Gull* was lost, Paul thought he saw the mast of a vessel. He called for his spy-glass. The boy brought it to him. Just then the snow cleared off somewhat.

"There are some poor fellows clinging to it, too," he exclaimed. "Ease off the jib-sheet! Down with the helm! we must beat up to them."

"Poor fellows! poor fellows! I hope that they will hold on till we reach them," he exclaimed several times, as he himself went to the helm, that he might make the vessel do her best, for tide and wind were against her. Just then a large ship hove in sight, with a signal for a pilot. "She can wait; these poor fellows cannot," he said, as he looked towards her. "She would have paid us heavy pilotage, too."

As the *Lady Isabel* drew near the wreck, one of the people on the mast was seen waving a hat feebly. The others appeared to be lashed to it, but unable to move. The cutter was hove-to and the boat lowered.

There was a broken sea running, and it was a work of difficulty and danger. Six men were clinging to the mast, most of them more dead than alive from the wet and cold.

"Take our young officer off first, pilot," said one of the men; "he's furthest gone."

Two of the most active of the pilot's crew climbed the mast, and brought down the almost lifeless form of a young midshipman. Only two other men could be carried in the small pilot boat at a time.

"Why, if it isn't Master Harry Treherne!" exclaimed old Paul Petherwick, as he received the lad in his arms, and deposited him in the bottom of the boat. "Pull, my sons, pull! the sooner we get him between the warm blankets the better."

Harry Treherne, for it was indeed he, was quickly conveyed on board the *Lady Isabel*, and placed in the old pilot's bed, where, with the aid of a glass of grog (the sailor's specific in all maladies—in this instance the best that could be applied), he soon regained his consciousness. His first inquiries were for the rest of his crew. Five had been saved, but the rest, with old Hulks, had been lost. The cutter was now rapidly nearing the small harbour close to the manor-house.

Sir Baldwin saw her coming, and having observed her manœuvres near the wreck, was sure that she was bringing some shipwrecked seamen on shore.

"We have got some one here who will be glad to see you, Sir Baldwin," said Paul, as he and his men lifted a sailor wrapped up in blankets out of the boat.

"Father, dear father, I am all right! don't be alarmed. Only rather weak from having been out in the cold all night," cried a voice which Sir Baldwin recognised as that of his son Harry.

"Paul, you have repaid me, and more than repaid me," exclaimed the baronet, after the first greetings with Harry were over. "I knew that you would. Do what is right and kind on all occasions, and good will come out of it somehow or other, though we do not always exactly see how it is to be. That is what I have always said, and what has happened is a strong proof that what I have said is true."

The shipwrecked seamen were received into the manor-house, and carefully tended. Harry was almost himself again by the evening, and all agreed that that Christmas Day, if not as merry, was as happy as any that the family had spent. They had many great blessings to be thankful for, and among them, not the least to the parents' hearts, was that their sailor-boy, after all the perils he had gone through, had once more been restored to them in safety.

THE END.